FACEBOOK

Daya Kudari

Cedar books

Published by:

Cedar books

An Imprint of

Pustak Mahal®, Delhi

J-3/16, Daryaganj, New Delhi-110002

☎ 23276539, 23272783, 23272784 • *Fax:* 011-23260518

E-mail: info@pustakmahal.com • *Website:* www.pustakmahal.com

Sales Centre

- 10-B, Netaji Subhash Marg, Daryaganj, New Delhi-110002
  ☎ 23268292, 23268293, 23279900 • *Fax:* 011-23280567
  E-mail: rapidexdelhi@indiatimes.com

- **Hind Pustak Bhawan**
  6686, Khari Baoli, Delhi-110006
  ☎ 23944314, 23911979

Branch Offices

Bengaluru: ☎ 22234025 • *Telefax:* 22240209
E-mail: pustak@airtelmail.in • pustak@sancharnet.in
Mumbai: ☎ 22010941
E-mail: rapidex@bom5.vsnl.net.in
Patna: ☎ 3294193 • *Telefax:* 0612-2302719
E-mail: rapidexptn@rediffmail.com
Hyderabad: *Telefax:* 040-24737290
E-mail: pustakmahalhyd@yahoo.co.in

ISBN 978-81-223-1103-7

Edition 2010

Printed at : Param Offsetters, Okhla, New Delhi-110020

This book is dedicated to my parents, Shri Shreeshail Kudari and Smt Nirmala Kudari. They made sure that I respect people more than things.

The book is also dedicated to my brothers, Sagar and Sachin, my maternal uncle Shri Raj Shinge and aunt Smt Manik Shinge, both of whom are connoisseurs in fine arts.

Contents

Acknowledgements

"Life teaches you everything, even if you don't want to learn."

In the same breath, I have learned so much from life and people whom I met at work, through Facebook and elsewhere that I feel dwarfed as compared to them in terms of talent and capacity.

I am indebted to my teachers, especially Mrs Lily Patel, Mrs Nisha Jacob, Mrs Celina Seymour, Mr Minoo Karkaria, Mr Vinay Haribhakta, Mr Aniruddh Gadhikar, Mr Wilson Tribhuvan, Mr Vinay Chidri, and many others. I will remain indebted for the rest of my life to their guidance and teachings, which sculpted me as a person.

"A friend's house is just some steps away." It goes the same for me, as I feel curtailed without them. Also, had it not been for my friends, this book would have remained a distant Sagittarian dream.

Lastly, I would like to thank 'All India Radio' for supporting me throughout my journey.

I will sign off with the catch line of my story, 'Life takes everything from you to give you everything'.

Author's Note

Hostel life sprinkled with cricket and ragging makes college times exhilarating, but after college, the friends get busy with their lives.

In spite of meeting almost every weekend at their favourite hangout in Mumbai, it's Facebook which manages to bind Aman, Ballu and Chetan. Aman and Chetan are working in the same firm, where Aman is desperate to move to the next level despite the office politics.

Cricket and chatting ruin Chetan's marriage but he still remains mesmerised by his wife. Ballu's failing career in music is aggravated by his failure at the MTV Roadies' auditions.

Then one fine day, D, their missing friend meets them through Facebook. After a round of partying, D suggests a game where each one of them has to share a dream and the other three have to make it come true. Everything is fine until one of the friends disappears....

– Daya Kudari

1

Balwinder aka Ballu

My life is an open book with a single page in it.

Life is not that philosophical like many of us believe. No one will ever understand life completely, and we shouldn't even try doing it in the first place. We are nothing more than characters assigned by the director above in this blockbuster movie running through ages. Engineering is good, engineering is bad, it may have lost its charm, but still it is an experience in itself. When asked about life, India's first engineer, Sir M Visvesvaraiya said, "Life is more or less similar to engineering." What we get is destiny and what we don't get is also destiny.

There are two types of people in this world – those who have a Facebook account and those who don't have. This story is about the more interesting type of the two, the first type, who have an identity called Facebook.

After a tiresome journey of two hours in a cab, which they took unswervingly from the nearest airport, Ballu and his parents reached Panchgani. Due to the luggage, even the big cab seemed swarmed.

Now, they were more than three hundred kilometres away from their plush Juhu row house in Mumbai.

They rushed to the college office and paid the fees even before checking the colossal college campus. The college was next to the windmills near the highway almost hidden in the greens until we come closer to the gigantic foyer. Ballu's substandard score in the engineering entrance test made sure that he didn't get an engineering seat in any of the city colleges, leave alone Mumbai. Ballu could not believe that a remote place could boast of having such a lavish, Victorian style infrastructure. Half hidden amongst the banyan trees, the mountains proved a perfect backdrop to the bright coloured hostel edifice. The colour flaunted by the construction matched the impregnable rays of sunlight... actually everything inside and outside matched the yellowish golden rays, be it the smother exhibited on the exterior walls or the paint on the walls of the hostel rooms.

The college looked compressed from the entrance, but when seen from the parking area, it seemed a university in itself. The trees were everywhere, be it the half-dug parking lot or the playground near the cafeteria. The signboard to the cafeteria had some maroon coloured spit prints exactly on the arrow mark. The only thing, which they couldn't understand, was the ingress of the police station near the college which seemed too close for comfort. Not many colleges can boast of having a police station just outside their entrance.

Police stations in India have a name, which helps to maintain the jurisdiction, and more often than not, the name of the location is given to the police station within the jurisdiction. Somehow, this police station proudly flaunted the college name displayed with illuminated neon lights, even before the evening set its tone. Ballu's father noted down the phone number displayed on the smaller signboard below the big rectangular board. As Ballu's father was busy talking to one of the constables on duty, Ballu took some photographs of the college building, each clicked with different angles. When they asked for directions towards the boys' hostel, the constable asked them to look for the mango orchard, as the hostel was next to it. They had to walk through the stretched football ground, which seemed immeasurable for the tired souls. The football ground had white coloured track marks washed by rains, yet running throughout the field. The signboard behind the goal post had the arrow intact but the words were just not decipherable. When asked for directions to the Mango Orchard, the tea vendor asked them to look for the "Boys Hostel" which was adjacent to it.

Finally, they managed to find the Mango Orchard. The orchard had no signboards or nameplate, and even the entrance was not visible. It just had a fence, which was reduced to some zigzag steel wires encircling the orchard.

The guard stationed at the fence had dozed off and didn't like the fact that Ballu patted his back to wake him up. He grumbled when asked about the boys' hostel, but seeing his parents, he gave the directions with a dreary look.

The semi-circular entrance of the hostel reminded many of the central jail. It looked almost the same, except for the letters printed on it. The "I" in the Z.I.T. was nowhere to be seen, but the gate also had a Hindi version of the name printed below it. The print was similar to the jail print, the same white print on the grey background.

Ballu saw the entrance and the lethargy in him could not impede a smile. Balwinder was his real name, and Ballu was what people fondly called him. Not many were aware of his real name, as even in some documents, it was the shorter version, which was easy on the tongue.

He hurriedly took his mobile phone out and clicked a picture of the entrance. In spite of the dust settled on it, the words were visible even from a distance. The guard coming towards them felt uneasy and enquired.

"I wanted to upload a picture of my hostel on Facebook," Ballu said, showing the previous pictures on his mobile. The guard could not understand the fuss and asked for his identity card. Ballu's father had to intervene seeing the commotion. He informed him about Ballu's admission to first year engineering course in the college and expressed his desire to see the hostel. The guard asked them to follow him to the hostel office. He took them to the small cabin down the hallway and requested them to be seated. Ballu turned around to ask for some water, but the guard was nowhere to be seen. Ballu tried to open the small window at the other side of the cabin, but it seemed jammed. Ballu finally gave up and sat on the bench, next to his mother. The walls of the cabin had spit stains scattered all over, which looked more like a demonstration of 'modern art' as the image created by the prints looked more or less symmetrical.

Ballu's father grumbled seeing the colour of Ballu's turban. He had scolded him earlier in the day as well for the same reason. Ballu was wearing a black shirt and a red turban. According to Ballu's father, everyone who wears a turban should match it with the shirt he is wearing. Ballu was never comfortable with his turban and like one of his cousins wanted to get rid of it, but never had the guts to argue with his father on this topic. Ballu's mother opened her purse and used a small handkerchief as a makeshift fan to get even with the lack of air in the small cabin. Even her golden sari could not hide the amount of gold she was wearing. Gold was everywhere, be it the two gold necklaces which looked almost similar or her thick gold bangles which were so big that it looked as if they would sprout in no time. She looked like a small tree laden with fruits of gold, which was exactly opposite to Ballu's father who was more than six feet and dressed like a typical government officer with the trademark grey coloured safari suit. Ballu's mother took some more deep breaths and came out of the cabin. She saw someone going towards the other side of the building and shouted in his direction. The man felt strange and ran away.

Ballu came out to check the signal strength of his mobile and asked his mother if her mobile showed any better signal, but that was not the case. She felt irritated and ordered Ballu to bring some water for her.

Ballu made a weird face, but had to follow the orders when he saw his father staring at him. As the admissions were still going on, the hostel wore a deserted look. Therefore, when Ballu shouted, his echoes could be clearly heard. Ballu's father started inspecting the washroom near the cabin like a scene straight from an episode of X-files. He covered his mouth with his handkerchief to avoid the odour, which wasn't there in the first place. The guard who had vanished came along with someone.

The man introduced himself as the hostel warden. The warden had a slight squint in his right eye but it was difficult to catch it. Ballu's father introduced everyone and asked if they could have a look at one of the hostel rooms. Ballu's mother interrupted and asked for some water. The warden instructed the guard to bring some water for her. "Cold water please," she insisted, taking a deep breath which showed her nitpick about the lack of proper airflow inside the hostel premises. All the rooms on the ground floor were closed which aroused their suspicion. "Will the students live on the first floor or on the ground floor? Ballu's father asked, wiping the sweat accumulated on his forehead.

"First year students will live on the ground floor and the senior students will take up the upper floors," the warden said looking at his phone and managing to conceal his squint.

"Yes, ground floors are better as there are no lifts in the hostel," Ballu's father said, checking the paint on the walls of the hostel.

"I don't understand one thing though. Why is the hostel so far from the college?" Ballu's father asked, adjusting his chair.

"Actually, even I don't know."

To avoid more questions, the warden tried to call someone using his mobile phone. Ballu's father was surprised that the warden's mobile phone had the necessary range required to make or receive calls.

The lame July sun had faded, giving out a breathtaking view through the hostel windows of the mountains and the mango orchard behind the hostel. Ballu was so happy with the natural surroundings of the hostel that he called his parents, and showed them the view through the big concrete windows, which had minuscule gaps between them. Actually, the surroundings were pitched so adequately in the college portfolio that the hostel seemed to be located in the midst of heaven. The college guide had the portfolio with the pictures of the same building in all possible positions with a list of 'dos' and 'don'ts' mentioned, followed by a brief history of the college. The worst part was that it was made compulsory and priced at two thousand rupees. Who on earth would buy a collection of same pictures in different mathematical angles for fifty dollars?

It was provided to each student who was admitted to the first year course. Actually, the greenery was the only good thing about the hostel, which was around a mile away from the college. Even the college principal did not have any answer when asked the same old question related to the location of the boys' hostel. Somehow, the girls' hostel was close to the other side of the college building.

Ballu felt a bit scared as he roamed around the empty passages.

One of the regrets of Ballu's father was that he could not make a doctor out of his son. Engineering was always his second preference, but he made sure his son got admitted, even if he had to pay for his seat.

Ballu's father called the guard and asked him to open the rooms on the ground floor and he ran towards the warden who was checking the leakage of the tap, just outside the hostel. Looking at his watch, Ballu's father yelled at the guard. The scream had Ballu and his mother rush towards the entrance. The warden came with the keys and handed over the bunch to Ballu's father who was still angry at their hapless way of handling things. "I am really sorry as I was supervising the plumbing work for the fourth floor. The serial number on the locks match with those printed upside down on the keys. Kindly select the room and call me on the phone number I gave you," the warden said as he repeated his phone number. He was so scared that he apologised again when he saw Ballu's mother. Ballu checked all the rooms and chose room number eighteen as it was exactly at the centre of the big vacant aisle. Ballu's parents tried to persuade him to take the first room as it was near the small telephone booth, but were helpless against their son's decision.

The room had newspapers scattered all over and the windows were jammed. Ballu's father checked the date on one of the newspapers below the king size iron bed and smiled. Ballu's mother was already feeling frustrated. She asked him to help her in opening the windows. Ballu opened the windows after a small struggle. Apart from the breathtaking view of the mountains and the orchard, some servant quarters were visible in spite of the big black hoardings, which were kept to block the view towards the scruffy servant quarters.

Ballu's father was not even sure if his son would be able to adjust in this remote location. His mind unknowingly compared this lower middle class place to his posh south Mumbai row house.

"Pay all the fees tomorrow, open a bank account and start attending college. I will return tonight and your mother will stay with you for two more days," Ballu's father said as his words failed to match the graciousness on his face.

They called the warden and enquired about the process of admission to the hostel. The warden asked them to be seated in the office cabin. He gave two sets of forms and excused himself for some time. Ballu's father took some time in reading the forms.

His mother who already felt perturbed, advised him to fill the form instead of reading it.

"These are not your property papers. We need to keep the luggage and have dinner before your flight," she said, using her handkerchief to wipe the sweat on her forehead. She requested Ballu to increase the speed of the ceiling fan, as it seemed to move slower than the artificial 'makeshift fan' which she was using. Ballu stood on his chair and tried changing the position of the switch ample number of times before the fan stopped abruptly. He did something and the fan started working again, but with the same speed. Ballu's father was still reading the papers and enquired if Ballu had any passport-sized photographs left. He opened his small suitcase and looked for the passport-sized photographs in every corner.

"Dad, I have eight photographs left but three of them are different," Ballu said, showing the photographs.

"Where on earth did you click photographs with a black background?"

"Mummy chose the background. I wanted a red one like other photographs," Ballu smiled and put the photographs back in his sack.

The warden came in with a jug full of water in his hand. He had changed his clothes, which caught the eyes of Ballu's mother. As expected, she asked him about the clothes. He told her that he lived in the quarters behind the hostel, so it was not a big deal to change his clothes.

"Can we put our luggage in the room as we would soon start living here?"

"We?" the warden asked flashing a confused smile.

His mother clarified that she would stay with Ballu for some days as and when he starts living in the hostel.

"Unfortunately madam, parents have to stay in the officer's quarters and have to pay an extra amount for this at the counter near the college duty room," he said as he offered his pen to Ballu's father who was still busy reading the forms.

"Only the candidate can stay in his hostel room after the necessary fees have been paid. Unfortunately, we cannot even help in keeping the baggage until and unless the fees are paid," the warden said, making sure he was clear with the rules.

Checking the time, Ballu asked if they could pay the fees at that very instant.

"It's 7.15 and the office hours get over at 4pm."

Ballu's mother enquired further if Ballu could get a separate room.

"Separate rooms are not available madam, as we want the students to gel with others. This helps in national integration, as our students come from each and every corner of this country," he said showing the Indian map which was pasted just behind them.

The half-torn map wore a pitiable, dusted look.

"Can we see the mess and other eating facilities for children in the hostel?" she said as she further bombarded her questions on the warden who looked exhausted like a bull after a day's work.

"Sure! You can go downstairs and have an early dinner in the hostel mess," he said, checking the time on the wall clock behind them.

Ballu turned around to check the time as well, in spite of being busy fiddling with his mobile. His father asked him and his mother to check the mess while he would sign some papers.

They went out and tried their level best to look for directions to the mess, but in vain. They came back and requested the warden to provide the directions again. "Go straight and take a left turn. As soon as you see the taps, take a right turn and follow the steps downstairs. The mess is located just besides the gymnasium," the warden said showing the directions using his palm and his finger rolling on it.

Ballu's mother was so confused that she requested the warden to accompany them to the mess instead of giving directions.

The warden relented and went out, followed by Ballu and his mother. Ballu's father signed the papers and came to know that except the last signature, all other signatures were to be done by the candidate himself. He ticked the spaces where Ballu had to sign.

In the mean time, Ballu's mother checked the food served and even entered the kitchen to check the level of hygiene maintained in the mess.

The workers in the kitchen felt awkward, but the warden requested them to cooperate. Covering her mouth with her handkerchief, she inspected some utensils and even asked the last names of the people working in the kitchen.

"How many times is cabbage served here?" she asked, reading the wrapper pasted on the packet of salt.

One of the workers cleaning the floor requested her to contact the mess authorities. When asked for the contact person or number, the same worker guided her to the handbill stuck near the entrance of the kitchen. She immediately saved the number in her mobile phone and even tried dialling it only to get a 'switched off' message.

Ballu had some other questions and this gave him a good opportunity to have them clarified. As soon as he saw his mother enter the small passage between the sitting arrangement in the mess and the kitchen, he stopped and diverted the topic to talk about the history of the college.

As they were returning from the mess, the electricity went off, scaring everyone. The warden managed to guide them through the stairs towards the cabin where Ballu's father was getting desperate with every passing minute. He wanted to discuss about the option of choosing their room partners.

"You can definitely choose, but we have been instructed not to keep two students from the same city in the same room."

They filled in the necessary forms and booked the room after showing their provisional admission receipt for the course.

While filling the form, Ballu's father saw the application form for the room adjacent to Ballu's. The form had a name scribbled rather dreadfully, which made it hard for Ballu's father to read. He adjusted his glasses and read it. Aman was the first name and he just couldn't read the last name.

He enquired with the warden, who agreed after checking the application form. "Kindly pay the fees as early as possible and submit the pink copy in the hostel office," the warden said as he checked the keys in the bunch kept on the desk.

"Pink copy?"

The warden explained the difference between the duplicate pink copy and original white copy by showing a sample copy from his drawer.

"You better choose a well-mannered partner or else let the warden choose for you," his father insisted, smiling at them.

"Both the people concerned should agree to live in the same room. As admissions are still going on, you people have a chance to choose. Once the admissions are completed, we will have no options but to allocate rooms to the students on first come first serve basis," he said playing with his keys.

Ballu agreed and told his parents that he will decide once he meets other students. His father then showered the final set of questions, which each set of parents are known to ask. The warden countered all the bouncers hurled at him with ease.

They had their lunch at a small restaurant near the highway leading to the college. Apart from the first two rows, the restaurant looked empty with most of the windows closed. It seemed the owner was about to close the restaurant, when Ballu and his parents stepped in. Ballu's father was stunned at his son's appetite. He ate like there was no tomorrow and even drank the mango juice which was specially ordered for his mother. "Anything else?" asked the waiter, seconded by his father.

Ballu felt embarrassed and reminded his father of his flight.

After the dinner, they booked a small hotel by the boulevard near the highway. The hotel, which looked rusty from outside, had excellent facilities with marble-floored aisles and multi ciusine all at reasonable rates as compared to plush Mumbai motels of the same calibre. Ballu was happy that his father was to return, but his face showed an altogether different picture. He wanted to show his teary eyes as if he was about to cry, but found it hard, and changed his plan to a milder and more effective option than making a gloomy face.

Ballu's father gave specific instructions to his mother.

He made sure that Ballu was busy in checking the connections of the television while his parents talked just outside their room in the lobby.

He gave her some money with his chequebook and thundered that he would ask her the details of every single penny spent. Ballu who was listening to their conversation hiding behind the door felt scared, ran towards the television, and completed the settings for the cable connection. His mother handed over the forms, which were duly signed even as Ballu tried his best to look naïve while checking the forms. Ballu gathered some courage and asked the amount given to his mother.

"I have given twenty-five thousand to your mother and you both need to collect every receipt and note down the expenditure, as I will check everything when your mother returns," his father said, giving a cunning smile looking at his watch.

He had actually given fifty thousand rupees and had wittingly told half the amount to check if they will be able to manage for three days within the amount. His mother started laughing, but stopped hurriedly as Ballu's father gave her a stern look, which reminded her of their talk, just a few minutes ago.

He bade adieu as Ballu made an ominous face again hearing the amount. He wanted to confirm the amount with his mother, but had to wait as his father was talking to the manager of the lodge.

His mother asked him to carry his father's suitcase till the ground floor, where a cab was waiting for them. They could hear the cab driver honking desperately to grab the manager's attention.

Ballu's father gave a five hundred-rupee note to the manager and requested him to keep an eye on Ballu and his mother. They even swapped their mobile phone numbers, after which Ballu's father rushed towards the cab. The cab driver took the shortest path to the airport, which still was around two hours from the college premises.

Ballu was busy surfing channels on the television in the room when his father called him on his mobile phone and confessed that he had kept fifty thousand with his mother for them. Ballu was damn happy, but sounded poignant on the phone. He murmured something in Punjabi and ran towards his mother who was checking a newspaper.

As soon as she saw Ballu, she immersed herself in the newspaper.

"Even I am surprised by your father's attitude," she said, looking straight at him.

Feeling a bit mortified, he disagreed. "How come you are reading an English newspaper?" Ballu asked and started laughing which made his mother so embarrassed that she flung the newspaper at him.

She reminded him about her matriculation and looked heartrending as she went to the other room. Ballu followed her and asked her about the money part.

His mother thought for a while and said that she had been warned by his father against discussing this matter. Ballu hugged her, which reminded her of his ways of getting things done, as a child.

"Your father has given thirty five thousand and we have to justify our expenditures. You know how strict your father is, right?" she asked, adding her own details to the list of instructions which Ballu's father had given.

"Thirty five thousand!" Ballu said as if he had prepared himself to hear a bigger amount. He was stunned hearing the amount and cursed himself for not sharing the truth earlier. Now one of his parents' ego would be bruised so he decided to brush it under the carpet.

The next day, they met some more students while paying the fees. The initial days of most of the first year students are the same; it's just the characters that are different. Ballu convinced his mother to stay with him at the lodge until more students started living in the hostel. Ballu's mother called the warden to enquire about Aman and other students. The warden informed them about Aman who had reported to the hostel the previous day, just an hour after they had left. The same evening, Ballu shifted his baggage and other things to room number nineteen. With the help of a duplicate key, the warden helped Ballu to shift the baggage. Aman had cleaned the room and everything looked so pleasant unlike the mess earlier. They waited for a long time but Aman did not turn up. Ballu was happy that some more rooms were occupied and he even made friends with some students. To kill time, he played chess with Riyaz who had taken the last room down the aisle. Also, Ballu felt Riyaz's room appeared slightly bigger. Riyaz maintained that it might be because of the emptiness of the room.

Aman was stunned to see Ballu and his mother in his room.

"We were waiting for you," Ballu's mother said smiling at him. Aman managed a smile even in this moment of bewilderment. The warden tried to explain all this even as Aman drifted towards his big grey coloured suitcase and even opened it to confirm. He even lifted his suitcase and flung it in air to check. He opened the suitcase quickly and put his hand in the yellow coloured handbag in it. Just a fraction of a second was enough for him to confirm the money in the plastic carry bag. He kept his suitcase inside the locker and tried squeezing some more of his belongings into the locker, near the window shield.

Aman looked sober in his formal attire of neat, stripped, white shirt and grey coloured trousers combined with nice black shoes. He wanted to change his clothes, but changed his mind instead. He took some clothes and excused himself, taking his keys.

"Do you want to live with him?" Ballu's mother asked. Ballu who was standing near the window seemed uninterested but nodded when his mother repeated the question.

Ballu had already met other students who seemed more of the studious genre. The 'Linkin Park' poster on the wall somehow made him comfortable in this not-so-casual surrounding. Ballu was sure that Aman might be acting restrained in front of his mother and had a weird twin perfectly submerged in him. Ballu used to address the mean and weird part of him as 'coyote' and thought that many of us have a coyote in ourselves but fail to realise this.

Aman entered the room and introduced himself as 'Guddu' which made Ballu apprehensive, but he managed a firm handshake. They talked for some more time and Ballu's mother convinced him to take Ballu as his room partner.

She was happy to know that Aman was from Delhi, which incidentally was her family's hometown. "Mumma, when you go home, please courier my guitar. I may feel homesick without it," Ballu said with a childish grin. His mother felt embarrassed to see him behave in his usual hedonistic manner. Even during their long exasperating journey, he jabbered about his demand for a new laptop. He would always come up with demands and pester his parents just before his or his sister's birthday. His birthday was just round the corner and he took pride that the whole of India celebrated his birthday. Ballu and India were born on the same day. It was raining cats and dogs when India got her independence on a Saturday and it rained even when Ballu was born on the fifteenth of August.

As his mother finished her call, Ballu sensed an opportunity and requested to have all his guitars shipped. His mother made an awkward face, which showed her disinterest.

Hearing the word "guitar" Aman could not control his excitement.

"Guitar!! That's great man. Is it an electric guitar?" he asked with a smile on his face.

The room smelled of freshness, offering a clear contrast to yesterday's moist, damp feel.

"I have a collection of guitars. Let me show you the pictures," Ballu said as he searched for his cell phone. He was just not able to find it. He checked the suitcase, his mother's handbag and even his locker, which he had unlocked for the first time.

Aman asked for his number and dialled it. Ballu followed the noise made by ring tone to find the mobile under his pillow. The display picture of his mobile had the proud picture of his guitar. Ballu helped his new friend go through the entire directory of the albums in his mobile. "Who is this?" he asked, handing over the mobile.

Ballu looked for his mother who seemed busy on her mobile and then checked the picture.

The picture was of a woman near the counter in a pink coloured sari and he had managed to take the picture while paying his fees. The picture was purposely taken through an angle, which showed the skirt and some skin partially visible.

Ballu did not want to delete such a hard-earned picture and moved it to his hidden folder.

The warden came looking for Aman, but Ballu's mother intercepted and requested him to check the taps and the water supply.

"It's raining heavily throughout India and you people cannot even arrange a twenty four hour water supply. Before paying the fees, everything was working fine and now we are discovering the flaws,"

Ballu's mother thundered as she opened the tap to demonstrate her point. The warden promised her to look into the matter and blamed it on the leakage. "Oh my god, there is no water on the ground floor. I can't even imagine what might be the situation on the fourth floor."

The warden apologised again as Ballu, Aman and some of their friends entered the scene.

Ballu was stunned to know the source of the commotion. Feeling embarrassed, he whispered something into his mother's ears, which made her stop cribbing, and she politely moved to their room. The warden gave the form to Aman and asked him to sign it followed by Ballu.

Aman asked for a pen, but somehow the warden's pen was just not working. He even opened the pen, took the refill out and blew some air in it. Ballu shouted loud enough to have his mother scream. The warden moved his nose as if smelling rotten fish and shouted, "Who has smoked amongst you guys?" Aman checked his breath and Riyaz imitated him.

"If I catch anyone smoking, I would make sure he is rusticated from the hostel," he said while going towards their rooms.

Ballu was not able to find his pen and the same was the case with Aman.

A pen is an inexpensive product which even the prosperous people don't posses, at times.

The warden blew some more air, which created some hilarious noises and in turn annoyed Ballu's mother. At last, the warden managed to write with a refill instead.

Aman signed the form and Ballu followed.

Ballu's mother opened her big orange coloured bag, took some apples from it, and offered one of them to Aman. "What about the official college dress? Is it compulsory?" Ballu asked as he took a bite. "On the first day itself we were told about the dress code. It's blue jeans and white shirt on Tuesdays and Fridays. We can wear whatever we want on the other days," Aman said keeping the apple in his pocket. Ballu was happy to know about the jeans and even checked his suitcase.

Ballu who was sitting on the right side of the room wanted the other side of the room. When asked, he mentioned about the sunlight, which came directly on one of the beds as the reason. Aman agreed and Ballu obliged.

"Have you brought any posters from Delhi or do you intend to buy from here?" he enquired, checking the posters. Aman started laughing on hearing this.

"You don't even get your daily needs fulfilled here and you are enquiring about the posters of the rock stars."

They talked for some more time and Ballu even helped his new friend to clean the room.

Later in the evening, they skipped the dinner and went out to eat.

❖❖❖

2

The Mango Orchard

If you have an open book exam, you will forget to bring your book, that's college life.

Ballu's mother stayed at the college guesthouse, but was seen more in her son's room.

They shopped for everything required, and for things, which they didn't require. His mother bought a month's stock of fruits and hoarded it in his small locker. Ballu used all his excuses to elude those initial college days.

He made sure he didn't receive his father's calls, making some bizarre excuses when his mother asked him about it.

Finally, the day arrived when Ballu's mother was to leave for Mumbai even as she met most of the students of the hostel. The cab, which would take her, was waiting near the hostel as she gave the final set of instructions to her son and his new friend.

"Ballu, I will call Aman to check every now and then. Also Aman, make sure that he attends the college regularly," she said while going.

Aman smiled while Ballu reminded his mother of the cab.

"See your friend. He has attended college from the first day and it's almost a week now and you haven't yet reported to your college," she tried to be polite while checking her cell phone, but moved out of the room to get a better signal.

Aman used to leave the room at nine in the morning and would come back only in the evening. The seniors from the second, third and final year who were to occupy the upper floors, still had not arrived, so the hostel was like unadorned fun for everyone. Ragging and seniors are co-related and the first year students managed to elude some rounds of "personalised victimisation" for the first week. Still, no one was aware of the exact reason to have a police station near the entrance. By Thursday, many more additions were done to the list of students opting for the hostel facilities instead of other expensive options, which had grown popular in the recent years.

Ballu tagged along Aman wherever he went. If he found himself alone, he would hop towards Riyaz's room on some pretext or the other. He had the excuse of sharing the keys to the only lock available with them, and in spite of repeated requests, Ballu never managed to make a duplicate key for the lock. With friends around, Aman and Ballu never felt homesick, but not checking their Facebook profile for quite some time made them anxious. Aman managed to get hold of an Internet terminal frequented by college students in the library as the local Internet service provider confirmed their unavailability of any connection at the hostel premises.

"We will go to an Internet café tomorrow," Ballu said, as he checked Aman's exercising equipment. Ballu lifted one of the weights and put it back, unable to balance himself.

"Why don't you come to our college library to access Internet?"

"What! Are you sure?" Ballu seemed confounded.

"I saw some students checking Facebook in the library, near the students counter," Aman said, typing a message on his cell phone.

They had their dinner at the hostel mess for the first time and then gathered at Riyaz's room for a friendly session of 'dogging'. That was what they called 'bitching', when done by men. Ballu still felt that their room was faintly smaller as compared to Riyaz's room.

They chatted for long, thereby getting an opportunity to know each other. After discussing almost everything on this earth, they slept late. Ballu and Aman along with Riyaz had decided to go jogging the next day. Ballu was not so eager to hear the plan, but the thought of being alone in the room made him concur as opposed to the better option of taking pleasure in the morning nap.

In spite of sleeping late, Aman managed to get up at five in the morning. Ballu ignored Aman, and made himself comfortable in his new bed. Ballu even asked Aman to turn off the lights.

Aman came back in ten minutes with Riyaz and Atul. Ballu had pulled the entire blanket to cover himself from head to toe. They gave a last try at the easier said than done task of waking their friend who was snoring with all his might. The thought of loneliness woke him up, all of a sudden. In about fifteen minutes, all of them were seen walking near the famous synthetic fields near the second turn of the highway connected to the petrol pump. Aman and Riyaz ran as fast as they could till the windmills. The windmills added to the picturesque beauty of the mountains filled with all ingredients required for a great natural portrait. When seen from this side, the boys' hostel seemed pretty far, but when they viewed the mountains from their rooms, they seemed just some metres away. As he was already late, Ballu had forgotten to carry his mobile phone and he cursed himself for that. His friends were nowhere to be seen and feeling a bit exhausted and sluggish, he settled his arse on a corner stone. He was always vulnerable when it came to getting up early in the morning.

"Ballu," someone shouted which generated a consequential echo of some sorts.

Ballu found it hard even to turn around and confirm. Aman came in and gave a friendly pat to his friend who was sweating heavily after the small adventure. The sweat marks proudly dwelled on the grey shirt he wore.

"Can't we go to the mango orchard instead? It looks amazing from the outside," Ballu suggested, as he was the only one amongst them, who went closest to the orchard. Aman mentioned that it might be a private property as it had the signboard of it being 'a private property and not a thoroughfare.' The signboard was visible even through the fence.

"It's so close to our hostel that I thought it's our college's property."

"The owner of the orchard might also think it this way for our hostel," Ballu intervened, staring at Aman.

They jogged for some time even as Ballu followed them under his own steam, but still trying to match them in velocity. He failed to do so and took some bouts of rest after every brief session of fast walking. Ballu had the keys of the room so he was sure that Aman would not leave him.

Aman and Riyaz managed to find their friend literary napping near the cornerstone of the windmills near the first turn. They did not want to wake him up, but the thought of "keys" made them break his slumber. By half past seven, Ballu was fast asleep in his room as his friends trained in the recently opened gymnasium.

Aman bathed, had his breakfast and was ready to go by nine. He tried to wake Ballu who managed to hold the blanket tight whenever Aman tried to remove it.

"Make sure you keep the keys on the window. I am leaving to check something important on the Internet," Aman said, checking himself in the mirror.

As soon as he heard the word Internet, the thoughts of checking his Facebook account ran through his mind. He did not want to show his desperation for checking his Facebook account, so he peeped from his blanket to confirm if Aman had left. Even after Aman was gone, he slept for some more time, as he could hear his friend talking in the aisle.

It was more than a week now since he had checked his Facebook account as his mobile Internet was also not being supported in the hostel premises. He had fought with the helpline, but they were adamant about the vicinity they support through the mobile Internet service.

Fifteen minutes were enough to take a bath, get ready and have his breakfast.

He had to fight for his breakfast as the mess timings did not match with the timings mentioned on the form.

"The timings have been changed some years ago, but still not updated on the hostel forms. No breakfast would be provided after nine from tomorrow," insisted a mess worker, giving Ballu his plate of breakfast. He set out for college, but rushed to the hostel again to take the USB cable along with him.

He knew the library was behind the parking area, but was confused and had to ask for directions. The bay area was full with students taking turns to access Internet.

Facebook and Google were the most popular websites when it came to colleges in this part of the world. As soon as the next lecture started, most of the students ran towards the laboratory and Ballu finally had an opportunity to access the Internet.

More than connecting people, Facebook is a platform for people to display their inner-self.

Nothing catches the exact mood of a person like Facebook does. Life is Facebook, and Facebook is life for the young generation.

Ballu looked for a computer, which could give him some privacy. He went to the computer stationed at the centre of the room and switched the monitor on.

To his surprise, the computer opened the Facebook page with someone already logged in. Someone had forgotten to log off from the website. It was a brilliant opportunity for him to have some fun. Unfortunately, it was a guy's profile but he was in no mood to leave a golden opportunity to have fun at others' expense. The profile seemed popular going by the number of testimonials written by people for him.

Only the acronym 'DJ' was mentioned in the name field which most probably might be an abbreviation for disc-jockey. He went through his albums, which indicated the colourful life that the so-called Mr DJ lived. He deleted all the pictures where he was seen with women around. The ever-fastidious Ballu was enjoying as he checked personal messages and even made fun of people's emotions by adding stupid quotes on others' pictures.

There were some sensuous pictures of Mr DJ and his girlfriend. Reading the romantic testimonial one could easily guess that this girl might be going out with Mr DJ. He replied with the most recent message in his profile.

"Would you like to rekindle the fun we had in Goa?" he typed in.

He could have done a million things when it came to utilising his destructive mind, but it was the scarcity of ideas at the right time that clogged him. Logging out of the profile, he logged in with his username and password now. He updated his latest pictures to his profile and checked his messages. The best part of Facebook is that you can check messages of your friends written on their wall to know what is happening in their lives.

He checked pictures and messages for the next half an hour in his and his friends' profiles. No one was online for a chat so he logged off after sending some messages.

He was the only one in the bay area assessing Internet services. Walking a few steps, he turned around abruptly and ran to confirm if he had logged off from his Facebook account. Feeling a bit anxious, he pulled the cable and had the computer shut down completely. Library was filled with the usual hustle and bustle of students common during the initial days with even parents seen with their children. This college was huge with wide passages with people all the way in every corner. Even on the first day, he seemed lost more than homesick. Initial days were a mixed bag of feelings as he met some of his classmates and felt an ounce of conformability added. Even Facebook did not make him feel at ease.

"Why didn't you attend the first lecture?" asked someone. Ballu smiled and tried to divert the conversation towards a less susceptible topic. "Where is Aman?" he enquired, trying to look for him amongst his new-fangled friends.

"I was going to ask you about him actually. Why doesn't he come to college?" Bhushan asked checking his hair curls.

"What?" Ballu shouted giving a flabbergasted look. Bhushan used his fingers and curled his hair towards the other side now.

"He was only seen during the introductory lecture," Ashish explained hinting his astonishment as well. Ballu was more staggered of the lot, but excused himself when he saw someone.

He left in a very haphazard way from the library to the cafeteria and later to his hostel.

He cursed the college authorities for the long, unbounded way to his hostel.

He rushed through the aisles to his room and the warden who saw him looked at his watch to confirm the time. "It's none of his business," Ballu told himself, while opening the door.

Later that night, Ballu pushed hard his suggestion to venture out for dinner. "Man, I have to check my budget as well," Riyaz murmured as he pulled out his wallet and forced out everything. He counted the cash and put it back. Ballu offered help but thought otherwise, when Aman pitched his vulnerability towards money.

Riyaz asked Ballu about his rushing out of the library episode.

Ballu smiled, on being asked in the first place. He had seen the person whose account he had messed with. The so-called Mr DJ was waving at someone not even aware of the problems he would fall prey to in some time. Ballu offered to pay for everyone on a condition. "We would go to the Mango Orchard tomorrow. If you people agree, then I would pay for you all. Also I will pay only if the bill is below a small Gandhi," he said, sitting on the bed. The word 'Small Gandhi' made them go nuts.

"Every currency note has an imprint of Gandhi on it, so a five hundred rupee note is called small Gandhi and a thousand rupee note is called a big Gandhi," Ballu said, showing a sample five hundred rupee note.

Ballu snatched the note when Aman tried to check it.

"Shut up you fool, people will kill you if you insult Gandhi," Aman said checking his wristwatch. Ballu folded the note and neatly put in his pocket kissing it.

"Sorry, I would never insult such a great man. It's just our way of saying things in Mumbai," Ballu said as he checked his beard in the mirror near him. A small round of giggles followed after Ballu apologised. Aman changed his posture and moved closer to the locker to check something. Ballu enquired on Aman's impetuous disappearance from college.

Aman was sure he would handle Ballu and his questions but smiled when he saw Riyaz staring at him as if waiting for an answer. "I was in the cafeteria."

"For the whole day?" Ballu asked and bit his tongue and threw a pillow at Aman.

"Actually I had gone to visit a friend in the government college near the bus station today." Aman showed first signs of nervousness when some other sharp bouncers were hurled at him.

"What about yesterday?" Riyaz asked giving a playful clap to Ballu as they saw their man being coaxed into their trap.

Aman tried his best to change the direction of the banter to a free for all topic about food and restaurants in their area, but Ballu insisted for an answer.

"This idiot acted so spruce in front of my mother, but I always knew that he too has a forced dual personality like everyone else."

Aman confessed that he went to see his girlfriend who studied in the government college.

"Girlfriend! Have you kissed her?" Ballu asked while blocking Aman's way.

Aman stared trying to find something in his pockets.

"Shut up, you ass," Aman thundered and threw a pillow at Ballu who managed to divert the pillow towards the floor. "See, if a man does not kiss a girl, she cannot be his girlfriend. Don't spoil someone's name by getting associated with her," Ballu continued.

Aman was angry as hell and pulled his wallet to show his girlfriend's photograph.

"It looks fake. She might be just a friend," Ballu said as he ran towards the door.

"What were you doing the whole day?" Riyaz enquired, pouring his suspicions.

Aman started laughing on hearing the question.

"I knew he was lying. Look at his face and compare that with the beautiful picture he showed," Ballu screamed as he stood at the door.

"You won't believe me."

"Don't worry, we don't believe you," Ballu said, keeping his mobile on the bed.

"I attended some of her lectures."

"What?" A combined voice spurt.

"I attended some of her lectures just to be with her."

"Do you think we are kids or something? The lecturers didn't recognise you?" Riyaz asked, checking the time on the wall clock.

"Admissions are still going on. Actually when the attendance was going on, the girl sitting next to me told her number, something like TMX 12 and I followed with TMX14. I swear I wasn't even caught," Aman said as he tried his best to persuade his covetous friends to believe him.

"For a change, try attending your own lectures. It will be more beneficial," Ballu said showing his witty side.

Aman threw the next pillow and shouted, "You shut up. I am better off than you. I have attended a lecture at least. Wait, I will call your mother and tell her."

"Also tell her that you attend lectures at different colleges by bunking your own," Ballu said, picking his mobile and pinching some more drollness.

Some playful exchange of words followed and they were ready to head to Riyaz's room for a big round of discussing the same things all over again.

Next afternoon, they were more than eager to go to the beautiful fruit laden Mango Orchard, but resisted Ballu's words. When his insistence grew then they agreed making him aware of their favour.

"Also we could visit the electronics market to check out the latest CDs and DVDs. What do you say?" Ballu said, smiling at them expecting a positive litter.

"Where should we put these DVDs to play them?"

Ballu insisted on buying a DVD player by contributing, but Aman and Riyaz vetoed the idea. They went for dinner as planned, but paid their share even when Ballu insisted on paying as per the discussion they had earlier in the day.

It was a lacklustre Saturday afternoon and no new plans could be made to fine-tune the budget. In addition, they were not too eager to listen to Ballu's plan who always managed to cut their pockets with his weird ideas. Riyaz and Aman were keen to explore the orchard in the dearth of a better plan on a Saturday afternoon, which would turn into a favourable evening in some anxious hours.

In spite of the name 'Mango Orchard', the orchard was filled with fruits of all kind. As many engineering colleges are located in remote places far away from the heart of the city, there is nothing much the pupils can do to pass time other than what is recommended by the hostel authorities. That's the reason most end up making the same plans.

In no time, they entered the orchard through the damaged fence even as the guard was seen fully engrossed in his midday sleep.

So now, there were at least twenty people in the orchard. "Ballu might have shared the plan with everyone," Aman told himself as he stared at the crowd. Ballu gave an uninterested look and tied his shoelaces. The Mango Orchard looked like a slice of heaven when compared to the half dug, half-spoilt concrete basketball court that could be seen even through the crowd of trees. The serene atmosphere along with the abundance of fruits every summer made it somewhat singular for the hostel students. The college authorities had tried all possible ways to acquire the orchard, but received the same answer in the typical arrogance of a politician.

The orchard owner and most of the people living on the west side of the hill station were against any kind of construction. Not just hotels, but they opposed even the recently constructed college which surpassed the green belt of banyan trees seen everywhere on the hill station.

Guava trees were more popular with students here. The small branch of the Guava tree was trying its level best to somehow hold Ballu. Ballu saw a full-grown guava and was tempted to try a jump but was not sure if the branch would handle his burlesque. The pain, which the pale looking branch was going through, could be gauged by the eerie noises, which could be easily heard. Ballu's brown coloured shorts along with his green coloured T-shirt almost camouflaged the guava tree, which seemed dwarfed by the big banyan trees surrounding it.

Ballu was slightly on the healthier side, but would always try his best to stay fit. Suddenly, he saw someone coming into the orchard from the other side. His weight and nervousness tumbled him over as he shouted. People started running in all directions. "You have to reduce, at least have mercy on the twigs," Riyaz shouted, showing his compassion on the full grown yet pitiable branches.

Ballu got up somehow and checked his pockets. They ran fast as they heard some weird sounds scorning from the trees. Riyaz ran towards the hut near the bushes even as Ballu tried to collect the guavas, which were scattered near the banyan trees. He heard something and ran as fast as he could towards the bushes. Aman whistled using both his ring fingers to let him know that he was hiding near the small hut. Ballu tried to whistle in return, but failed. He was never able to whistle, however hard he tried. Riyaz peeped out of the hut and shouted, generating a daunting reverberation. Ballu dusted his khaki shorts and tried to follow the rough sound of the whistle, but was still not able to gauge the source of the sound. Riyaz come out of the hut, and managed to drag Ballu inside. Riyaz took some deep breaths and put his hand to cover Ballu's mouth as he was about to speak. Aman stared as his eyes gave a 'shut up' kind of an expression. Ballu slipped behind to hear someone grumbling. A small pair of hands came from nowhere and pushed him. He was so scared that he couldn't even gather the courage to turn around and closing his eyes, stood motionless. Riyaz was happy that Ballu seemed hushed when they heard some people talking about the nuisance of the students, which was growing every year.

"Kids will be kids. Once the vacation starts, loneliness will creep in. The orchard is so big and beautiful that sometimes I feel it invites us to feel it," said the orchard owner checking the mess.

"At least they keep me fit and running," came a quick reply. The weather changed abruptly which was quite common on this side of the mountains. The skies grew darker and it looked as if it would rain anytime. Riyaz knew that they had to rush before the hostel gates were closed for the first year students. The gates were actually never closed, that was just a gimmick by the warden to warn the students. Aman peeped twice to confirm that everything was fine and whistled in excitement. Ballu adjusted his small turban and smiled at him.

He felt a sensation in his pockets. To be sure, he raised his hands to confirm that it was not any of his hands, which caused it. He thought for a while and ran outside shouting like crazy. Riyaz couldn't believe all this and remained in the small grubby hut. Now it seemed awful to see someone shouting like hell and disturbing the serene atmosphere in the orchard.

"What happened, you fool?" Riyaz came out and all the kids hiding in the hut followed. There were quite a few kids hiding in the pint-sized hut. Ballu stopped when he saw them. It was so damn embarrassing for Ballu that he threw the guavas, which he had guarded until now.

"I have some guavas with me. Do you want to have some?" Chetan asked, showing the guavas. Riyaz smiled and obliged. "I am sorry. I was talking to Dev," Chetan said as he handed his share of guavas to Dev. Ballu apologised for his so-called attention-grabbing shout and touched Dev to make sure he was not a ghost. Dev felt embarrassed, but still managed a babyish smile.

Other people who were hiding in the hut still tried their luck in the orchard as Chetan and Dev started counting their guavas. "You should have told me. I threw some guavas. It's just fun for me. I don't like guavas actually," Ballu said. Riyaz introduced himself and his friends to Dev and Chetan.

"We are in first year of engineering... what about you people?" Ballu asked offering a handshake. "I am doing electronic engineering and he is pursuing mechanical engineering," Chetan replied, pointing at Dev.

Aman was still not sure if their newfound friends were seniors or batch mates.

Ballu moved his eyes to scrutinise his new friends.

"Dev has a DVD player with all advanced features, if you want to join us you can come to his room around half past eight," Chetan exclaimed while eating something, which didn't look like a guava.

Guavas of the orchard were red inside, like the strawberries, which were a specialty here.

Dev offered some guavas to his friends who obliged and even thanked him for his benevolence. DVD players and laptops are considered luxury in hostels and students who had these luxurious items managed the minimum number of companions.

All four were enjoying guavas sitting near the banyan tree just outside the hostel premises. Out of excitement, Ballu threw a half-eaten guava in the air with all his might. Ballu took a deep breath and felt confused when everyone stared at him. The guava, which he threw never came down defying the laws of gravity. Ballu was amazed and in a fit of excitement, threw a full-grown guava in the air again. This time around, the guava came down quickly and hit Dev. Dev's white coloured shirt bore scattered red marks on it. Everyone started laughing including Dev as if appreciating the spirit of the not-so-droll incident. Ballu apologised, but still confused, he enquired, "Why didn't the first guava come down?" "Where did the first guava go?" he put his question in a different way with a weird smile on his face.

"It hit Dev and you will have to wash his shirt now," Riyaz said as he tried to rub the marks on Dev's shirt. The marks were getting speckled due to the rubbing.

"The guava which hit Dev was the first guava," Aman justified his stance. Common sense is the most equally distributed commodity as everyone thinks he has enough.

"If this is the first guava, where did the second go?" Ballu asked, looking at the banyan tree while carefully examining the big trunk.

Chetan wanted to laugh but changed his plan seeing Ballu's face, which had turned red thinking about the fact that he would have to wash clothes and that too for someone else. Washing was not only the biggest headache for hostel students but also the source of most hostel fights.

"Thank god! Dev was not wearing his college shirt," Chetan said, checking the marks on the shirt. Ballu smiled and made a creepy face.

"Why would he wear his college shirt on a Saturday and that too at this time?" Ballu asked, looking at the shirt. Even Ballu checked Dev's shirt and advised him to wash the shirt with some lemon-filled solution.

"If it doesn't go, I will gift you a new shirt on your birthday. I could have given you my shirt but it won't fit you," Ballu said, managing a smile on his face.

Chetan reminded everyone about Dev's birthday on twenty-ninth February which only comes once in four years. "As this is a leap year, Ballu will have to wait for another four years to gift me a new shirt."

Aman was amazed on hearing his date of birth and month.

"This is the first time I have actually met someone who was born on twenty-ninth of February," he confessed and shook hands congratulating him for being born on such a special day. Chetan told them that his real name was Chakranarayan, but was called Chetan by everyone. As soon as Ballu heard the name, he laughed his heart out but apologised later, when he saw Chetan's flabbergasted look.

"Ballu is also not a very sweet name. It reminds me of the papa bear from jungle book," Chetan said showing a thumps down gesticulation.

"Ballu looks like a bear, but is not that sweet and lovable like the papa bear," Aman said, making an amusing face with his tongue.

The new friends laughed under the banyan tree as if they knew each other for years. Ballu still tried hard to scrub the dirt from Dev's shirt when the thought of washing his friend's shirt came to his mind. He then tried to use his ring, but pulled out when Dev felt embarrassed and asked him to stop. "I will give it for laundry," Dev said looking at the mark.

"Mr Richie-rich, dry clean and all. How much pocket money do you get?" Riyaz asked while dusting his pants. Dev came from a rich business class family, but was not comfortable telling everyone about this.

"Eight thousand is the maximum I get in a month," Dev whispered as if he didn't want them to hear the amount. He almost stopped when he told the amount.

"Oh my god... eight thousand... I can't believe it," Ballu said as he was busy swinging the branches of the big banyan tree. Seeing him, Chetan also took a big branch and tried his luck. "Chakri, keep it slow."

Ballu started laughing and swung quickly adding a second branch.

Chetan was furious hearing the word 'chakri'. He never gave his full or real name until and unless it was required. He tried making a cheery face and started swinging as fast as he could. "You are a *chakri,* swirl like one," screeched Ballu.

There are very few people in this world who are not happy with their first name and Chetan was one of them. It was really strange considering the hundreds of communities which have thousands of members on Facebook where people flaunt their love for their names. Dev apologised for letting out the well-guarded secret and told them that Chetan was the real name and Chakranarayan was the pet name.

He made an innocent face, but failed to keep an eye contact with Chetan. Chetan ran towards the branch to try swinging again. "Chakri," Ballu shouted as he tried to take a third branch and fell down. Everyone had a good laugh even as Ballu stood up as if nothing had happened. "That's fine! Big boys fall and rise in no time," Ballu said as he turned to check the dirt on his shorts.

"Big boys or fat boys?" Chetan asked, laughing at him. Riyaz who was sitting on a small stone couldn't control his laughter and fell. Everyone had a good laugh again. Each thought that the joke was on the other and laughed their hearts out. Just fifteen minutes in the friendly meeting, and they behaved like old friends who met after a long time.

They discussed about the 'Laughter Challenge' which was a popular programme. Two things were common between them. All admired Amitabh Bachchan, and as expected were crazy for Facebook and cricket. Ballu even tried to mimic his favourite actor, but failed miserably. The laughter show was a collection of jokes mimicked by the contestants. In addition, it was one of those very few innovative programmes originating from Asia and going westwards rather than the other way round. Dev and Chetan were room partners and were allotted the room number sixty-five in the opposite wing. Dev was popular with his DVD player and his huge collection of movies and songs.

Next day, the whole group geared up go to the infamous electronic market near the government medical college. Apart from songs and movies, Ballu managed to grab a couple of porn flicks to add to his already mammoth collection.

❖❖❖

3

Cricket Dance!

Ragging is fun, until it happens to you.

The college was famous for many other reasons apart from engineering. Ragging was one of those reasons; the boy's hostel was never out of limelight. Last year even their female counterparts were in the news for some ragging incidents.

Ragging is a horrible way of making fun of others' freedom but comes across as a hard paradox in movies or books. The problem with most outstation students is that they come to know the ground realities after they are wedged in. Someone told Akash about the murder which had occurred a few years ago as an alleged fallout of a ragging incident.

"Someone was murdered in broad daylight right in front of the entrance of our college," he said, keeping his mobile in his pocket.

He wanted to haul their attention towards the incidents of ragging, but his friends reduced the incident to one of the many rumours haunting the hostel life.

“I am more petrified of being ragged than meeting a ghost,” Ballu said checking the time on his wristwatch. The scene looked straight from a novel based on student politics. Most of the first year students were sitting in Riyaz’s room when Kunal reminded them about the ragging incidents which he had heard from the mess workers. They had managed to elude ragging due to dearth of senior students at that time of the year. The students had taken every possible space available in the room. The untidy room looked crowded more due to the luggage kept there. Riyaz’s room was a favourite hangout for students of the first year and now with Dev and Chetan in the group, even the other wings had their share of representation.

Rajesh who was quiet for a long time stood up and said, “I will tell them that my father is a police inspector, thereby ensure my safety.”

Ragging has been known to compose a bond of unity amongst the victims.

“I am also safe then, as I am a professional body builder and I see world wrestling episodes every day,” Kunal made his point.

Everyone made some excuse or the other and Ballu was the only one left without any point.

“Let’s see. I heard students are ragged only in the first month and we have managed a week without it. What if we stay overnight elsewhere?” Ballu asked, thrashing his fright.

Sometime later, a brilliant idea struck him while listening to his favourite song which had the lyrics, “It’s fake, everything is fake.” Ballu hatched a plan along with his friends and they even enacted it to be sure, even as Aman checked the authenticity of the act. After some trials, they were ready for the show. Everyone knew the first night in a hostel would be horrible but such was not the case here. Somehow, tranquillity made way for anxiety, even as a week had passed. All the first year students were happy about the fact, but knew that someday things will change and that too abruptly.

The very next evening, a senior ordered Riyaz to fill in a water bottle. This was the first incident... the tip of the iceberg, which was to follow. He was sure that something would happen today. It was a new week and many of the senior students had arrived. As the seniors lived on the upper floors and the gates of ground floor were closed exactly at ten, there were no interactions among the two groups.

All the first year students gathered again at their favourite hangout and discussed plans to tackle the problems, which had been hinted by the first incident.

At around twelve in the night, Ballu heard a knock on his door. He peeped from his blanket to check if Aman was awake by any chance. "Oh my god! I can't even shout," he told himself. The knocks increased gradually and Ballu went and woke Aman.

"Go and open the door. It might be your friend calling," Ballu said, pointing towards the door. Aman pulled his blanket ignoring both Ballu and the noise. After a brief silence, it appeared as if the noise was coming from the knocks made on their adjacent room's door.

Ballu was happy and commented, "I was going to open the door but the scoundrel seems to have left."

The knocks were heard again yielding a bigger noise this time. Ballu who was still awake had more thoughts of being haunted than being ragged.

"Aman, please open the door. My legs are paining, I cannot walk," Ballu whispered, pressing his own legs.

"If you admit that you are a coward, I will open the door."

Ballu's silence made his standpoint clear. Aman opened the door and was immediately held by his collar by someone who appeared suddenly when the door was opened.

"Ask all the first year students to come to the terrace. Make sure they are dressed from head to toe, complete with shoes. No sport shoes, just black shoes," yelled a bearded person staring directly at him. Ballu managed to hold his breath until the unwanted guest was gone. Aman was sure Ballu would try his best to act naïve, so he went to Riyaz's room, which was locked. Shocked, he ran to Dev's room. To his surprise, Riyaz was sleeping in Dev's room. He managed to wake up most of the first year students and they gathered making speculations.

Ballu who was known for snoring with all his might made way for complete silence when Aman came in to check for his room partner. He had locked himself in the washroom but was not sure if he could sustain the foul odour coupled with absolute darkness there.

Unable to hold for more, he came out interrupting the silence, to be welcomed by his batch mates. A stunned look followed a revelation of words. "I had a bad stomach ache.You people carry on with your morning walk," he mumbled, acting unaware of the actual time. Aman who was angry by now yelled, "As you wish. We are going to the terrace for being ragged most probably. Your ragging will be done separately as you are under the weather."

Ballu thought for a second and replied when he was sure there was no bypass, "We all are united. I will be ready in a minute. Please wait for me."

All the students were nervous and went in a line tugging at each other. The terrace looked empty and some of them felt like being made a fool out of them, but their sudden happiness was torn by sounds of laughter.

"We are here." Someone shouted from the other side of the terrace making their presence felt in a rather superfluous way.

The terrace was airy, had trees surrounding it from all sides, and had the usual spit prints of tobacco on the walls governing the terrace. The terrace, which looked pocket-sized from the stairs appeared massive from the other side. It was like a debut visit to the terrace for most of the first year students. Most of them purposefully acted naïve as was expected from them.

Some of the senior students were smoking near the stairs connecting the top floor to the terrace and the presence of the first year students added to their excitement like an icing on the cake. Seeing them come in an austere queue, one of the senior said, "They know they will be ragged... that's awesome as they have come prepared, I feel."

Ballu was standing at the other end of the queue not facing the seniors but easily stood out because of his turban.

The first year boys were asked to give their introductions in their mother tongues.

Riyaz was called prior to the first person in the queue, as he was caught giggling.

"Come over and start. Dare to laugh, now."

Riyaz who was shivering, started his introduction even as words were just not coming from his mouth. He managed to tell his name as Riyaz Khan with his head down as if looking at his toes.

"Don't you have a father?" someone asked. Riyaz started repeating his words, still looking down even as Ballu mentally rehearsed his introduction like everyone else.

Everyone gave their introductions in their respective mother tongues, which brought uncountable and uncontrollable bursts of laughter on the faces of the seniors.

"We have students from whole of India," remarked Mustafa, trying his best not to inhale the cigarette smoke dashed at him. Mustafa was a final year student from architecture stream. He was best known for his hero worship of Shahrukh Khan.

"Guys, come on... start dancing," Mustafa yelled. A moment of trepidation filled the air as the first year students kept looking at each other. Mustafa ordered Puneet to bring his music system. He made him rush when he saw Puneet just about managing to drag himself, as he did not want to miss the fun on the hostel terrace. As Kiran was the closest, he started dancing first, followed by others. Ballu and his friends' dance looked like they were playing cricket. Ballu danced moving his hands rapidly as if he was bowling and Chetan danced as if he was batting followed by Aman who danced as if he was guarding the wickets standing behind Chetan in the normal wicket-keeping fashion. It was one of the funniest dances, the seniors had ever seen. The seniors were so happy with the dance that they singled out the five dancers and asked everyone to cheer them for a second round.

Aman wiped some of the sweat accumulated on his forehead with his hands, and started to dance followed by his friends. They changed roles but the 'cricket dance' had its share of popularity even amongst the first year students. Actually, the dancers were laughing as well thinking that the joke was on the rest of the group.

Taking some deep breaths after a marathon session of laughter, Hemant asked, "Are there any gays in this batch?" After hearing the question, fretfulness and unease took over from laughter and amusement. Some of the first year students were more worried about the fact that the final year students had the keys of the shutter, which protected them from their friendly predators.

As per the plan, Ballu made a peculiar face and hastily fainted near the edge of the terrace. While fainting, he shouted his heart out. "I am fainting. I am fainting."

The seniors who were treated to the earlier slapstick act, found the performance funny.

Some of the senior rushed even as Ballu had just managed to limit his fall near the edge. The boys' hostel had managed more than its share of nuttiness but no one had fallen from the terrace until now. "Do we tell people around us that we are fainting?" Mustafa asked while rubbing his palms.

Everyone was scared when Ballu did not move for some time as he managed to hold his breath for a longer time than expected. Riyaz started to weep and this made sure a sizeable crowd gathered near

Ballu who was fantastic in his act. Riyaz asked if he along with Aman could clutch Ballu to his room. Aman also mentioned Ballu's fight with epilepsy attacks. Seeing Dev and Chetan stare, Aman requested to take help from two more students to tug along.

"Size does matter," shouted someone from the crowd.

The rest of the first year students had to imitate Ballu and his cricket dance.

"They can't perform like their peers. Tomorrow we will call the *sardar* fellow again for his cricket dance," Ashish said, scratching his goatee.

Riyaz thanked Ballu as Chetan poured accolades on a soul stirring performance.

"We need to make a different plan tomorrow or practise our cricket dance. I am sure we will be called again for our cricket dance," Ballu whispered as he wiped the sweat on his face using his shirt as an easy substitute.

Ragging normally happens during the weekends and nothing boisterous happened for the next four days. It was almost a week now without ragging and first year students were so happy that some even persuaded Ballu to teach him the famous cricket dance. "What cricket dance? Are you guys crazy? Cricket and Dance are two different things," blasted Ballu even as Aman could not control his laughter and urged the students again.

"He is famous in Mumbai for his cricket dance. Offer him money; I am sure he would be more than glad to teach you people. After all, he invented this dance form and it's almost similar to salsa apart from the curves."

The first year students were living dangerously on the edge and knew that they wouldn't be able to evade the inevitable for long. Next Saturday, around two in the morning all the first year students were called yet again.

The fully clad first year students knew where to go this time and took their own sweet time to get ready. One of the seniors had to come all over to the ground floor again to remind them. Saturday nights, actually early Sunday morning after a big round of drinks was the most preferential timeframe.

They formed a straight queue just near the stairs leading to the terrace. The seniors were sitting exactly at the other side, near the tank. Seeing the students, there was an uproar amongst the seniors. "Where are the cricket dancers?" asked someone, making a loud noise. Ballu, who tried to hide behind Sameer was pushed by Ajit.

"You are so fat; you won't be able to hide behind that emaciated guy," Hemant said, smiling directly at him.

As expected, a session of cricket dance was arranged for the amusement of the seniors and the other first year students. Dev took the umpire's role in the cricket dance as Ballu was the only one who was not in good spirits while the act was going on.

After a repeat session and also making sure that everyone had put their hearts into dancing, all first year students were asked to name three negative points of the their room partners.

Most first year students tried to be suave and told general negative traits, which did not match the level of interest set by the 'Cricket Dance'. People may appear sceptical about their room partners when they are not around, but every hypocrite soul makes a naïve remark when asked the same questions in their presence.

Comments ranging from their hygiene sense to their loyalty towards the fairer sex rallied.

Hungry for excitement, some of the final year students discussed some more things.

It was still around half past three and with no sign of rain, no one was in the mood to let go a luminous opportunity to have some fun at others' expense.

"Someone please come forward and speak for five minutes on a topic. You come here, the one in blue shirt," Hemant said, pointing at Aman.

Aman was hesitant to come forward, but when he saw his friends cheering for him, he set his foot forward.

"Speak about Indian Girls," Rakesh howled and made himself comfortable in the open space behind Raj.

"Yes, yes," people continued in chorus.

Aman asked for some time to prepare for the topic. Mustafa made a weird face before nodding in agreement against the popular verdict. Seniors may be plain superiors for the first year students, but they are classified according to the time they have spent in the college or the hostel.

"As our college uniform has lots of blue colour in it, everyone would wear only blue coloured underwear from now on. Also, add our hostel community to your Facebook account. I hope everyone here has a Facebook account," Mustafa said, carefully scrutinising everyone. Ali whispered something to the person standing near him. Mustafa walked straight towards him and repeated the same announcement.

"Sir, I don't have a Facebook account," came a twitchy whisper from the group standing next to Aman. Bursts of laughter followed the proclamation.

"Please come forward," Mustafa said while throwing his cigarette butt.

Ali stepped ahead and repeated that he did not have a Facebook account.

"Make one as soon as possible. I don't want any excuses," Mustafa thundered, staring at the crowd behind Ali. Ali was asked to speak on the same topic after Aman.

Getting restless, Mustafa enquired about Shahrukh Khan's new movie, titled 'My name is Khan'. Everyone was aware of Mustafa's hero worship of Shahrukh Khan and people who were smoking near the tank asked him to shut up.

"What is your branch?" asked someone. Aman who was not sure if he was asked the question, made an uncertain face.

Aman stood up when asked about his branch again.

"Classic Milds," he whispered in a squashy, boyish tone.

"What? So you think all this is funny."

Aman made a nervous face when he saw Mustafa coming towards him.

"No sir, you had asked about my brand. I smoke only Classic Milds."

"Idiot, I asked your branch as in mechanical or computers?" Ashish said controlling his laughter. The first year students didn't get the joke or acted naïve.

"Electronics!!"

"You are one of those who performed the cricket dance, right?" someone asked from the crowd. As per the plan, Ballu gave a wide-eyed expression and with some saliva dripping from his mouth, fainted again. Everyone was in a state of shock and Ballu was surrounded by all the first year students. Making a sad face, Aman asked if he and Riyaz could take their ailing friend to his room.

"Shut up and stand there. Last time, you people took him and never came back. We have to be harsh now," Hemant thundered as the helpless first year students took their seats.

"Has anyone seen him faint earlier?" Mustafa enquired with a bated smile.

The sudden silence gave the answer. The only people who responded were Aman, Chetan, Riyaz. Dev was busy taking to someone and did not realise the tumult.

"That's outlandish! He faints only while ragging, that's an obsolete deception."

Ballu who had managed to hold his breath was feeling desperate. The adventure continued until about five in the morning and then the first year students were asked to march to their rooms. The Facebook and the dress code warnings were repeated before they dispersed. Sundays are the worst as ragging may take place anytime if the so-called seniors are not enjoying their siesta. Ragging is directly proportional to the time available with the seniors. A water cooler was kept exactly outside the shutter near the rooms allotted to the first year students. It was risky to venture out of the aisles, as seniors were known to throw water bottles at them to have them filled. Filling the water bottle was not the issue, it was the jeopardy involved in delivering the bottles to their rooms, which was like an open provocation.

The lunch was served from half past twelve until two in the afternoon. It was almost quarter to two and Hemant had just woken up when someone knocked his door ad infinitum.

He walked to the aisle with a towel wrapped around, and exactly at that instant, Ballu finished his lunch and walked towards the water cooler, which was visible even from the top floor. Hemant was happy to find someone, as the first year students just would not come out of grill which formed their protective shell.

"You!" he shouted, pointing at Ballu.

Ballu knew someone was shouting and for a moment thought of running to his room without looking up, but was sure of getting caught somehow or the other.

Feeling frightened, he looked up to find Hemant staring at him.

"Is the mess open?"

"Yes, sir."

The suffix 'sir' was to be added after every senior's name as per the instructions provided to them. Ballu replied in confirmation without even looking up.

"Go and bring two plates for me. Tell them my name..."

"I have finished my lunch, sir."

"Do what I say," he shouted, gesturing with his hands. Ballu cursed his sense of timing, as he was late to follow his friends for an early dinner to escape the pleasantry intentions of the senior students. Ballu asked for two plates informing them about Hemant's request. To his surprise, the mess workers gave him the plates without even asking any questions. Instead of going up, he took the plates to his room and explained the entire scenario to his friends. Yesterday's ragging was still afresh in his mind and he suddenly spat in one of the plates. He asked his friends to follow him, but most defended their stance of not spitting on food giving divine explanations. Ashish and Ballu spat more than thrice. Ashish looked frustrated and blamed his seniors for all their quandaries. Ballu was not sure of Hemant's room but managed to get there asking directions from a few senior students.

"May I come in, sir?" Ballu asked politely which was quite unlike him. Seeing plates in both hands of the dancer, most laughed their hearts out but some accompanied him to Hemant's room for a fresh bout of fun but were asked to leave.

Hemant welcomed him and ordered him to join. As he went to brush his teeth, Ballu sat on the corner of the huge bed and neatly differentiated the plates.

Hemant who had excused himself for brushing his teeth, took a long time and returned only after taking a bath. As soon as he entered the room, he threw the wet towel on the chair and said a small prayer. Ballu felt relieved to see him praying and regretted the idea of spitting in the plate but now one of them would have to feast on spit flavored food and he decided, not to do so. "This is your plate and that is my plate," Ballu declared.

Rubbing a green coloured cream all over his body, Hemant was ready to eat when he saw Ballu staring at one of the plates. “Good. You will eat from my plate and I will eat from yours, now.”

Ballu was stunned, made all possible excuses, and even tried puking, but Hemant made sure he ate from the same plate. “Babaji might have punished me,” he told himself while eating from the unfortunate plate. After finishing, Hemant asked him to deliver the plates to the mess again. Coming to his room, he put one of his fingers in his mouth and added some more trying to puke. “What happened? Is everything alright?” Aman asked showing his counterfeit concern. Ballu was in no mood to discuss about the event and kept thinking for some time. He got up abruptly and rushed towards Mustafa’s room. Asking directions, he managed to get to his room to find it locked.

He ran towards to the TV room adjacent to the hostel mess. Senior students never allowed first year students to come to the TV room so Ballu was anxious and thought twice before entering the room taking god’s name. Mustafa was surprised to see him, but more was to come. “Can you come out for a moment sir, if that’s possible?” Ballu said managing a smile on his face.

Mustafa was angry but calmed down when Ballu apologised.

“Sir, I know you are a Shahrukh Khan fan like me.”

Mustafa was pleasantly surprised but nodded in accord. “I have a deal for you, sir. It’s related to Shahrukh Khan,” Ballu whispered softly as he was not sure if Mustafa would entertain his offer.

As it was about Shahrukh Khan, Mustafa had to agree.

“What’s the deal?” he asked leaning on the pillar nearby.

“I have an original autograph of Shahrukh Khan. I will give you that autograph if you people spare me and my four friends,” Ballu continued shuddering.

“You are smart. You should try to enter politics.”

“I would give the autograph in the evening,” Ballu said, checking his watch.

He felt relieved after the small talk deliberately took Mustafa’s permission to go.

He ran when he came near water tank, slowed down coming to his room, and knocked repeatedly to have Aman open the door in a rather irritated manner.

“What?” Ballu got in and closed the door immediately confirming privacy. He told the plan to get a stunned look from his room partner who declined his offer. “No problem. I will have Dev, Chetan and Riyaz in the plan and you can continue the cricket dance and other antics every weekend.”

Aman thought for a moment and agreed on a condition.

“What’s the condition?” Ballu asked giving an immersed look in desperation.

Aman left the room and shared the plan with his friends even as Riyaz had vanished after the lunch.

Dev was ecstatic when he heard the plan and hugged Aman for sharing such an important hearsay. They leaped towards Ballu’s room in no time to see Ballu praying near the picture of Babaji.

“Come on, let’s give the autograph to him and escape this step motherly treatment.”

The problem was that he did not have any autograph and had to make a counterfeit. When Ballu told them about this, they declined to be a part of the deceit. “You cowards, had I managed the autograph you would have sided with me and now when I have to imitate the signature, you are stabbing me.”

Dev smiled and requested them to give Ballu an opportunity. Ballu took a pencil and tried to sign like the superstar as others feasted on the fruits and snacks, which Ballu’s mother had bought for him. Even after a hundred tries, the signature looked phony.

"With love, Shahrukh Khan," he managed to write somehow. He took a pen, rewrote it, and tore the page even as his heartbeats increased with every minute.

"Wrap it in a gift paper. I have some fancy wrapper covering a new book. Shall I bring it?" Chetan asked, desperately waiting for an answer.

Getting restive, Mustafa visited the ground floor in the evening. "Sir, sir, yes sir, no sir," were the words, commonly heard in the passage of the ground floor near the grill.

"Where does the cricket dancer live?"

Amit guided him to his room. Ballu who was sleepy after a double round of lunch and didn't even bother to open the room in spite of the repeated knocks.

"Ballu, it's me."

Ballu rushed to open the door as he heard the words and shouted, "Yes sir, welcome sir."

"I thought of reducing your stress of coming to my room. You had told me about the autograph you wanted to gift me," Mustafa said as he tried to be courteous even when it was not actually required. Ballu thanked his stars for keeping the autograph ready.

Mustafa checked the pictures on the wall and complimented on his choice of posters.

Ballu took the page wrapped in golden paper and handed over to Mustafa. For a fan, it was a magical moment like owning a piece of history.

"You are my favourite senior," Ballu swanked while gifting the autograph.

Immensely impressed by the gesture, Mustafa asked him to lock himself and his friends in their rooms when someone orders them to come to the terrace. He also promised to check what more can be done and requested them to ebb at weekends. Mustafa hugged Ballu and thanked him for giving him the greatest gift of his life. With teary eyes, he humbly took leave.

Ballu called Aman in excitement. Aman could not believe the incident, but thanked him. "I know you could do it. You have a fake personality, so making a fake autograph is no big deal," he said and asked for Bill Gates's autograph. Ballu smiled and he asked him to lower his volume. Dev and Riyaz had seen Mustafa near the first floor and hugged their friend for his dicey accomplishment even without confirming the episode.

❖❖❖

4

DVD Player!

They won't believe you if you tell that you were just eating at the bar.

It was a pleasant Monday morning, coupled with bright sunshine – very different from yesterday's scanty yet incessant rain. A fearless Ballu was ready to tackle a bigger problem called 'regular attendance'. Yesterday's sham triumph made him feel on top of the world. Even after jogging and other forms of morning pastimes, he was ready for college earlier than his classmates were. Ballu had managed to smuggle Dev's DVD player to his room with apposite permission. Zeroing to his favourite track, he increased the volume taking full advantage of the fact that his friends were busy with their chores. Going alone was fine as far as his breakfast was concerned, but he always took someone or the other when it came to having his lunch or dinner. With a good supply of fruits from the orchard coupled with his mother's outgrown treasure still intact, he would skip his dinner when it came to going alone. Dev was popular for his DVD player amongst his peers and somehow the news reached their seniors who were furious about this.

Ballu and his friends were walking through their college grounds when Riyaz realised that Ballu was the only one wearing something similar to their college attire. "Did you try to wear our college dress, today?" he asked inspecting the apparel. Ballu declined showing his black coloured trousers. Ballu had even managed a blue coloured underwear, just in case. He whistled his way to his classroom. The classroom was big enough to accommodate at least hundred students even if they sat with ease. Ballu was happy to be surrounded by his pals, as hostel students outnumbered the day scholars when it came to attending the initial lectures. Many new faces sprung up even as the whole of first year students, irrespective of their courses, had assembled in the classroom. The course was similar for all the streams in first year engineering but the lectures were as boring as they used to be in his junior college. Scarcity of good-looking girls combined with a session of mathematics made the class look more like a gathering of genuinely non-interested inhabitants. When his friends told him about the attendance permutations, he bore a stunned look. "Eighty-five percent is huge in any form of an equation. Actually forty percent is fine as that's what is required to scrape through."

Ballu managed his serenity throughout the lecture even as the professor disappeared, without noting the attendance for the session. Ballu was enraged when told that the same professor took the attendance strictly during the last week.

"One hour of torture and no credits. How do you expect us to prove our eighty-five percent attendance?" he argued with one of his colleagues. He managed to attend most of the lectures sacrificing his siesta, pleasure and interest. Ballu had made friends with some senior students with the help of the trust he generated due to the charade autograph. "Whatever! At least it made someone in this big bad world happy," he told himself while praying.

He was surprised not to see the DVD player in Dev's room on a lazy Friday evening. Yesterday's torrential rain made way for a pleasant day today. "Oh my god! Where is the player that I had returned yesterday?" Ballu shouted as if his whole life depended on the existence of the DVD player. The face with all those added superfluous emotions was a treat for his friends.

"A senior student came and took it to watch a movie."

"Who?" Ballu changed gears to sound harsh.

"I don't know. The half bald guy who asked for gay people took it," Chetan said checking his new hairstyle in the small mirror fitted nicely near the window. Ballu was shell-shocked as the DVD player formed the only source of entertainment apart from the never-ending talks at Riyaz's place. "I can't believe it. You people could have made some excuse to avoid the barter." Ballu sat on the folded bed sipping his tea. "Let's go to the Mango Orchard." Chetan's face gave the answer and his words just repeated it. "Seniors have asked us not to go to the Mango orchard." Giving a desperate expression, he threw the white plastic cup through the window. He kept on looking at the flight of the cup as it travelled to the ground gradually. "Let's go to that side of the hostel." Enthusiasm was at its worst.

Chetan showed his collection of pictures to calm Ballu, but he was in no mood to stray away from his plan. He dragged his friend insisting that he accompany him for the escapade. Ballu sprinted to his room to bring his digital camera and managed to persuade Riyaz and Abhijeet for the small adventure. Riyaz was excited to come along and Abhijeet was keen to alleviate his loneliness. Chetan was just not interested in the exploration but to his horror, the power-cut destroyed his happiness. "You are so unlucky," Chetan bawled when the power-cut happened just when Ballu entered his room. Ballu laughed as he took a piece of cloth and wiped his camera clean. "The power won't return till late night, so let's click some pictures near the foothills, behind the quarters." In spite of the ongoing power cut, the futon of bulbs near the cooler was flaunting with all its might. Riyaz played with the buttons to check the source of electricity. "The futon may be an emergency." Devoid of power, the hostel looked more like a movie set of an old horror movie but the small halogen bulbs managed to disturb the calmness created by the antagonistic darkness.

The hostel was known for long power-cuts and this made for a great opportunity for the students to explore everything around the hostel. The only side, which was not popular with the students, was the side adjoining the servant quarters. Unlike the mango orchard, they were never forbidden for going there but somehow no one was ever seen near the servant quarters. A lot of smoke used to appear from the quarters in the morning due to the burning of wood churned with the hard firewood available near the foothills of the mountains nearby. Burning of wood for cooking and other chores was a major source of the redundant smoke resulting in pollution of the small yet beautiful, evergreen neighborhood. Riyaz peeped to check and Ballu repeated the same from the other side, near the tap. They were sure that the seniors may get bored and there was every possibility that they might be called for fun.

Ragging is fun for the predators and it gelled the victims. With Ballu in their group, the possibility had multiplied in recent times. In a short span of time, Ballu had gained a lot of notoriety amongst his peers and fame amongst his seniors. Ballu kept the digital camera's empty handbag in his room and neatly hid the camera in his pullover. He hated to part with his belongings but it was quite different when it came to living in a hostel. He never wanted to leave Mumbai in the first place, but his father was keen to make his son aware of the worldly sense with some left-handed treatment in the hostel. His father was sure that his son would not be able to cope with the rugged hostel life but it was vital to make a 'man' out of the bubbles of pubescence. A man is not a byproduct of time, but a result of intelligence and anticipation being screwed up to aggravate the level of patience. The area adjacent to the quarters was a stark contrast to the sumptuous hostel facilities. At times, when it would pour, the hostel was the only source of illumination for the entire area, right from the foothills of the mountains until the playground. The famed mango orchard had no alternate source of power and it was known to house a whole lot of weird species of reptiles, which entered the hostel premises at the drop of the hat. Snakes were amongst the host of common visitors to the boys' hostel. These reptiles were in more need of shielding that the students living in the hostel who were known for their malice, even as killing and setting snakes on fire was a common site in the monsoons, in and around the hostel. Decrease in the level of illumination proved propitious for the boys for they could escape the hostel without being noticed. Eluded of concrete pathways, the area around the hostel was at its aesthetic best. Nights demonstrate the beauty of a place and monsoons give an idea of the condition of the same place like it was some years ago. Monsoons show the poverty of a country but it brings the best when it comes to the countryside.

Ballu cleaned his trousers as he ran towards the crowd of saplings, and uprooted something in order to make some space. Riyaz and Abhijeet posed while Ballu showed his photographical skills. After taking some more pictures, he handed the camera to his friend. While posing, he slipped and fell on the saplings near the bushes. Abhijeet could not control his laughter and slipped as well. Riyaz checked the sole of his shoes and sat down comfortably on the fresh green grass. Ballu was about to stand when he realised that something struck his hand. He checked to find a big firecracker near the bushes. Mistaking it for a live bomb they all started running but came back laughing when nothing happened. Ballu would never leave an opportunity to show his valour even when he could do without it. He picked the cracker and threw it in the air to catch it again. "Fire cracker in the month of July. That's weird," Ballu shouted as he confirmed the dampness on the cracker.

They clicked some more pictures with the grasslands as a striking backdrop near the bushes and clicked some keeping the sunset as the background.

Ballu was still playing with the cracker as they came towards the hostel when the memory card of the camera gave some errors while clicking pictures. Ballu grew so fond of the cracker that he kept it safe in his locker.

Concerned about their budget, they rejected Ballu's idea of eating out. Life had come to a standstill without the DVD player. Dev and Aman were busy playing chess in Aman's room. Ballu hated chess for he lost to all his cousins on a trip to Kashmir as a child and stopped playing chess after that fateful day. He tried to hamper their concentration but they were in no mood to even consider the fact that Ballu was present in the room. "Chess is a slow man's game," Ballu said and managed to grab their attention. "It's a slow game for fast thinkers," Dev insisted, making a move on the chessboard. Riyaz summoned him to his room sharing his hatred towards the game. Apart from Aman and Dev, most of the first year students were present at Riyaz's room. The room seemed filled with students who had used up all the space available, be it the flipside of the suitcase or the space behind the door.

The talk nineteen to the dozen continued simultaneously with the game of chess in the other room. People who declare that gossiping is a feminine quality should have come to Riyaz's place at night, especially during weekends. Dogging, the all-new male bitching was in full flow, and they discussed about everyone present in the room, and then thrashed their seniors. Even the professors were not spared.

"Dev is a great guy with a golden heart. Everything about him is perfect," Riyaz asserted and everyone seemed to have agreed.

Ballu continued spitting his venom and did not even spare his new friend. "What is so great about him?" It's in human nature fuelled with ignorance, for we take pride in opposing anything and everything, keeping the person in mind rather than the subject. Ballu still remembered the first day of ragging when a senior had asked, "Has anyone seen him faint earlier?"

Apart from Dev, everyone from his group had raised their hands exhibiting support. An anomaly remained in his heart for him. Ballu and Chetan hopped from this room to their room to Dev's room trying their best to distract the chess players. Aman took pride in playing chess even if it was just a game of sixty-four moves for others. Even at half past twelve, the game was going on with full surge. The tardiness of the game could be gauged by the fact that more pieces were on the chessboard rather in the basket, which was used to keep the defeated pieces. Dev's side looked more depleted than Aman's as their concentration augmented with every move, irrespective of its importance.

At two in the morning, most of the first year students gathered at Aman's place surrounding the players. Some people not only have a charming personality but also have a calming effect on others. The point can be further explained if we carefully observe Jesus Christ's portrait who was known for the calming effect he had on everyone. If his portrait can generate such calmness, we cannot even gauge the amount of serenity he might have poured upon the people he met.

"People who are lucky in love are unlucky in chess," Riyaz said as he gifted a fresh round of chuckles. Some more movements on the chessboard and Dev was in a fix as another of his trusted lieutenants bit dust on the chessboard, tilting the game towards Aman. Aman still maintained that the game was evenly poised and Dev was very much in the game. Watching the scanty and midget black pieces against the lofty pieces on Aman's side of the chessboard, it looked more like a case of David fighting the goliath. Considering the choices we make, life and chess are almost similar.

A smart move by Dev and Aman was in a state of hara-kiri. Everyone present checked all possible permutations and combinations possible in the chess book but failed to tackle the move. The smile on Dev's face showed his anticipation for victory but he insisted that there was a move, which could save Aman's throne. Scratching his head, he tried to move one piece at a time and gave up on the condition that Dev would share the solution first. Dev made the move for his opponent and continued the game in a display of true sportsmanship. Aman complimented his friend's spirit, which was short lived as just after a move, Dev made the final budge to impede Aman's movement on the chessboard. A second highly witty move and Aman and his friends gave up this time. His friends celebrated the win but Dev only managed a gullible smile on his face. "Man, you are a genius," Aman proclaimed. Everyone agreed and cheered for the man of the moment. "What's so great in it? It's just a game," Ballu said making a counter comment to Aman's statement of admiring Dev's intelligence and sportsman spirit. Most of the first year students had left by now leaving Ballu and his gang in his small cozy room. Ballu excused himself for a moment and showed them the firecracker, which he had found near the bushes. When Aman requested him to show the firecracker, Ballu was just not ready to part with his prized possession. "What's so special about the useless fire cracker?" Aman asked as he sat on the floor to check something under the bed.

"I have an idea. Let's see if this fire cracker works or not? What do you say?" Chetan asked, taking the cracker from Ballu and checked its size. "It's a big cracker capable of making a loud noise, if we manage to explode it."

Ballu took the cracker from him and brought out the thread from the cracker, which seemed to be stuck inside. Dev and Chetan tried checking their bags and lockers to find a matchbox without much luck.

"Do you have a matchbox?"

"If I had a matchbox, wouldn't I burn this world?" Riyaz said with a smile, but frowned abruptly as he got a cold shoulder from his friends.

Chetan even tried to check with his colleagues in the adjacent room but did not disturb them when he saw the lights switched off.

"When you want to find gold; go to a goldsmith. That way, if you want to find a matchbox go to a smoker," Riyaz said seeing his friends' mad rush for a matchbox.

The commodity called matchbox is more like a pen, inexpensive but important. Everyone in this busy world has asked for a matchbox or a pen at some point of time in his or her life.

Aman gave his matchbox claiming that he has only two matchsticks left. "Don't worry, we will light it with a single matchstick and you can claim the other one," Dev replied as he checked the illuminated but vacant passage in their wing.

"Let's celebrate Dev's victory after a splendid game of chess. They made a boring game look interesting," Riyaz who really looked out of senses today managed a small shout.

"Let's celebrate our friendship instead," Ballu cheered as he threw the fire cracker and caught it again.

Ballu checked it thoroughly before putting the firecracker near the grill. He lighted one of the matchsticks but the cracker just would light and that left them with the last matchstick. "I won't part with the last match stick as I want it for lighting my cigarettes."

Ballu cleaned the cracker again and asked for the matchbox. "No man, why can't you understand? I have to smoke."

After some discussions, Aman lighted a cigarette and passed on the matchstick, which was still burning. Ballu tried his best but could not light the cracker. "You are a hopeless ass," Riyaz said. "How will we light the cracker now?"

Getting desperate, Aman took the cracker and lighted it with his cigarette. It took some time but exploded giving out a thunderous noise. Aman who managed to light the cracker was so stunned that the cigarette dropped from his grasp. Feeling scared, everyone ran to their rooms even as Aman switched off the lights in the aisles. Ballu rushed to the loo and managed to get to his room before some students entered the passage creating a chaos. Not only the ground floor but also people on the upper floors were dazed to hear the noise.

It woke some students who ganged again at Riyaz's room for a new round of dogging and gossip. The warden who was fed up of the intrepid yet hopeless students rushed to the ground floor initially. He opened the grill and knocked every door in the wing.

Initially he singled out Ballu's room, and knocked the door continuously.

Aman who was still smoking in his room near the window was surprised but still did not stop his smoking. "Bastard, throw that cigarette. We might get caught for the cigarette if we managed to scrape through," Ballu said while folding his blanket.

Aman continued his smoking spree even as the knocks on the door increased.

The warden who seemed lost in the passage managed to find the switch but somehow even the small tube light was not interested to show her colours.

The full moon could be seen from their room and Aman seemed frustrated and started taking big puffs exuding the half-white, half-golden cigarette creating a bundle of smoke.

Ballu who looked concerned about the noise had started his round of snoring which sounded real even when considering the fact that he was taking Aman's case left, right and centre. Aman threw the cigarette and raised the speed of the ceiling fan to drive away the aerial left over of his smoking spree. The amount of smoke seemed colossal even for the fan so Aman had to open the other side of window, which was not opened even once, until now.

He used his hands to clear the smoke but only managed a weird form of dance instead, even weird than the famed cricket dance. Getting anxious, he opened the door to find the warden fighting with Abhijeet about the tube light.

"What's your problem? Why do you people switch off the only source of light in the passage?" he asked candidly.

"Sir, the light flashes directly on my eyes from the ventilator and I cannot sleep due to this," Abhjeet confronted, as his voice grew louder in the passage. "Everyone has problems with this light."

After some arguments with Abhijeet, he rushed to Aman's room, which was left wide open. Aman was nowhere to be seen and Ballu increased the speed of his snoring tunes when the warden came in to check. "Yes sir," Aman said getting into the room.

The warden wore a suspicious look as if smelling something. "Do you smoke?"

"At times," Aman thought for a moment and replied. "Were you smoking now?" he asked again. "Yes, sir." The fearlessness in Aman's eyes might have worked for him as the warden requested him to stop smoking or at least abstain from it while in the hostel.

"Don't let me catch you smoking or else I will throw you out."

Aman nodded in response. "Did you hear a loud noise?"

"Yes, I heard something of that sort. What was it?" Aman asked, lowering his voice innocently. Aman pushed the chair offering him a seat but the warden seemed uninterested. He moved his hands closer to Ballu who had stopped snoring for a moment as if giving them scope for a conversation. "Is he sleeping?" He asked, pointing towards Ballu as the snoring started again with a greater vigour.

He was sure that the first year students might be involved in the noise but moved out of the passage. The darkness outside was a complete contrast to the mock illumination inside the hostel premises. The warden checked the main transformer to clear his suspicion about the noise.

Just when he closed the grill and was about to go, he heard some prangs of simultaneous laughter. The vacant aisles, which were closed from outside seemed impartial. He moved towards the stairs, connecting the ground floor to the TV room.

The echoes increased as he moved closer to the TV room. He switched off his torch to avoid giving any admonitions of his arrival. The door of the TV room was not closed but just pushed aside blocking the view. He took a deep breath and opened the door to a shocked crowd who looked bewildered as they stood up. The warden was dazed as he looked towards the television. Students, who had grouped close to the television set, were enjoying a porn movie. The warden's sudden arrival made sure the students never had the time to switch off the television in time. "I can't believe it. You people can stoop to such low level to enjoy life."

None of the stunned students managed to find the remote to switch off the TV. "Give me the remote," he shouted as he switched on the light of the room.

The crowd looked bigger now with some of the students enjoying the session from a remote view, adding to the numbers.

One of them managed to find a remote and handed it to the warden as insisted.

The warden tried his luck and increased the volume instead. The superfluous sounds ensured a chortle amongst everyone in the room. The movie was in full swing with a group scene enacted by some Caucasian performers.

After some more trials, the warden managed to switch off the main supply going to the television.

"This is ridiculous... cheap gross-group carnal pleasure in the hostel."

"Sorry, sir."

"Shut up. This might be going on for a long time. It's good that I caught you red-handed, and Naren you...."

Making a sad face, Naren tried his level best to hide his face moving behind pillar.

Naren who was the current university topper began to cry gradually.

"Whose DVD player is this? Men will be men, they will always think with their..." he did not complete the sentence on purpose.

"Sir, it's Dev's player," came a voice from someone in the crowd.

"Dev, who is this rascal?" The warden banged the torch against the wall.

"He is a first year student," Rakesh said in a distressing tone.

"First year student... I can't believe it. Where is he? Is he amongst you people now?" the warden yelled while taking a head count.

"Forty-six people watching porn and our university topper is amongst them. Shame on you people. You should have watched porn in your rooms instead."

The warden managed an occasional glance around the room as he checked the CD cover, which had a sleazy photograph pasted on it. The television was college's property so he confiscated the DVD player used for the untimely gratification. The news spread like wild fire and generated bouts of laughter instead of trepidation. Dev was shocked when he was made a scapegoat for the incident and was called at the hostel office, the next morning.

"See, I had told you," Ballu said when Abhijeet told them about the incident.

"What! We won't be able to watch movies. That bastard won't return our CD player now," Ballu said rubbing his spectacles with a soft cloth.

Dev was as stunned as their peers were, but laughed his heart out when he came to know about Naren. "Is anyone coming with me to the hostel office?" he asked vehemently when the thought of the DVD player came to his mind.

Everyone made some excuse or the other leaving Ballu with Dev.

"Take Ballu with you as he had brought the firecracker responsible for the noise, leading to the scene yesterday."

"Let's make a story first and then go," Ballu replied, checking something on his mobile.

After the breakfast, Dev and Ballu were seen standing near the hostel office.

The warden came late, giving a concerned look. "Come in. You are my heroes."

"Yes, sir. You had called us."

"How is your business going on?" the warden asked and banged his hand on the table.

"Business! I don't understand sir," he sighed and stepped aside.

"Should I inform your mother? You were acting so naïve that day."

Sensing trouble, Ballu introduced himself again and reminded the warden that it was Dev's DVD player. Dev dropped his face enacting a mourning scene.

"I was not able to switch on the DVD player to check it yesterday," the warden said as he kept the confiscated CD wrapped in a plastic paper.

"Is it Indian or Caucasian?" the warden asked checking the cover.

Dev looked up but could not gather the courage to speak.

"I didn't get the question, sir," Dev said looking eye to eye.

"I mean, is the porn movie Indian or entirely Caucasian?" he looked up and asked unequivocally.

Ballu and Dev kept quiet for the next minute as the warden repeated his question.

"I don't know. The seniors asked for the DVD player and I was not able to refuse," Dev clarified in a voice soaked with raw emotions.

"Don't you people have any Indian flicks? Aren't you fed up of watching these emotionless foreigners?"

Ballu wanted to laugh desperately but managed to hold his desire. The warden asked him to give him in writing that they would be expelled if caught again.

Dev and Ballu had to agree in spite of the fact that they were not amongst the starcast of the carnal episode.

Overall, it was a session of mixed emotions as the warden handed over the DVD player after Dev signed the warning letter. The warden kept the CD insisting on checking it. Ballu and Dev could not hold for long and burst out laughing, coming out of the office.

❖❖❖

5

The Marathon!

Happiness is not in things, it's in us.

Just two months into the long journey and Riyaz, Aman, Dev, Ballu and Chetan seemed inseparable. In addition, each was born on an important day. Ballu was born on India's Independence Day, while Aman managed to come in this world on the first day of the year. Riyaz was born on eighth of March, celebrated as International Women's Day while Chetan was born on the most important day when it came to Indian sentiments, for he was born exactly on the day India conquered world cricket. He was born on Twenty-fifth June, when India was crowned the world champions in cricket. The luckiest of the lot, Dev was born on twenty-nineth of February, a leap year. Dev easily surpassed everyone in terms of popularity.

"He is so lucky that if you push him into a river, he will come up with a fish in his mouth, even if he doesn't know swimming," Abhijeet summed up when Dev flipped a glass bottle accidentally and it was still intact. It was strange that the perfume bottle remained in one piece, even after a fall from a height.

"He is god's man. He can do anything and everything. He was rightfully born on twenty-nineth of February, a one in a thousand possibility," Aman said while giving his take when Sonia admitted her infatuation for Dev. Sonia was more popular than all the first year girls put together but somehow Dev was never interested in her.

"Are you gay?" she asked, when Dev rejected her proposal. Ballu who tried his luck on every second girl in his batch failed miserably even when it came to starting a decent conversation. Ballu was the only one who doubted Dev's credibility and justified his actions. Overall, mostly everyone had gelled and apart from some incidents of ragging, it was a pleasurable and one of a kind experience for everyone.

They named their group, 'ABCD' rightly so honouring their initials. They even made a community called 'ABCD' in Facebook with five members and the numbers in the community never changed. To add to the excitement of the first year students, the college arranged for a mini marathon, which would start from the hostel premises and end near the strawberry plantations. Initially only the first year students were allowed to take part in the marathon, but after a round of discussions, everyone including the teachers were to be a part of this year's marathon. Last year's marathon had to be cancelled because of the heavy downpour in the month of November when the foundation day of the college was celebrated. With prize money of twenty-five thousand, everyone seemed more than interested.

Almost everyone filled in the forms and the necessary entry fee to participate in the exciting event. The third Sunday of November was chosen for the marathon. There were speculations of a Bollywood star being invited either to flag off the event or at the prize distribution. Rumours are at their creative best when people have a lot of time at hand. November is a busy month considering the submissions and the start of the preparation leave. All hostels have their peculiar rules, some for the heck of it and some for luck. Most of the students of this college abstained from shaving from the onset of the preparation leave until the examinations were over and done with.

It was more like a custom here and people blindly followed it. Photocopying the seniors, many of the first year students also managed to keep their goatees decorated with thin and thick layers of hair.

Ballu who always sported a beard was the happiest amongst the lot who copied the tradition. "If we avoid shaving, there is a greater chance that we might clear the examinations," Hemant replied when asked about it.

Ballu managed to smuggle his laptop in the hostel even as laptops were not allowed for first year students as an outlandish measure undertaken by the hostel authorities. Ballu even managed to augment his already huge collection of voyeuristic pictures. He even had a revealing picture of Sonia taken in the cafeteria, when her undergarments were visible for a moment.

His laptop made him at par with Dev in terms of popularity, but Dev had the humane touch, which the ignorant Ballu lacked. Not only was he immature for his age, but also as a typical Leo, he thought highly of himself thereby getting into dim arguments.

He kept a password for his private folders on his laptop but shared his voyeuristic pictures with Aman who had promised to do his bit to add to his already massive collection.

The first year examinations were to be held after the second, third and final year semester exams, making the first year students richer when it came to receiving extra time for preparation for exams.

Ballu had skipped his lectures again on a busy Monday due to his growing attraction towards his siesta. Swirling his towel, he entered the room and just as he was about to lock the door, it seemed like someone was resisting the effort. Ballu used all his might and closed the door. Someone knocked the door as he was about to undress.

Adjusting himself in the mirror placed exactly opposite the door, he opened the door to find his warden staring at him.

“Sir,” he sighed.

He loosened the grip of his towel, which he had wrapped just seconds before opening the door.

“Don’t you attend your lectures,” he asked.

“I do.”

It was half past eleven and Ballu was amongst the very few students still at large.

Ballu welcomed the warden in his room, managed to get the towel off, and wore a comfortable pyjama. Ballu was more concerned about his laptop and he threw the towel on the laptop managing to cover it in time. As the warden was checking the posters on the wall, Ballu collected the laptop and kept in his locker seeing the warden deeply engrossed in checking the Bryan Adams’ poster.

“How many people live here?” he asked looking at the string, which went from the window towards the flipside of the door. Ballu gave a surprised look on a bizarre question. “Is he out of his mind?” he asked himself. “Two.”

The warden moved closer to the window and counted something. “One, two, three, four... six. A lot is going on behind my back these days, I feel,” he sighed.

Ballu felt a bit irritated but managed a smile on his poker face.

“How come there are seven underwears planted on the rope,” asked the wide-eyed warden.

Ballu had anticipated the query and was prepared for it.

“Except for the black one, all are mine,” Ballu said looking at the string.

“Two people, seven underwears, it seems something is cooking here.”

"I like changing my undergarments every now and then, so have a huge collection of it."

"How come most of them are in the colour blue?" he asked trying to read the brand name.

"My favourite colour is blue. Therefore, I bought all my undergarments in blue. Even the one I am wearing is blue," Ballu smiled adjusting his pyjama.

"But the brands are different. Tell me the truth. How many people are living here?" the warden repeated his question while checking the different shapes and sizes of the under garments. The warden had a nasty but effective habit of confirming the number of people residing in the room. "Parasites" was the term used for students staying illegally in the hostels. Many local students used to team with the hostel students to enjoy their weekends or night outs at the hostel, which seemed a good backdrop for the parties.

The warden literally touched one of the under garments to check. "If I catch any of your friends in the hostel after nine at night, I would expel you from the hostel on fraudulent grounds."

Ballu nodded in agreement and the warden left but instead of turning to the right, he turned to the other side to check the connections in the washroom. Ballu thanked god and changed into his college attire. Just as he was about to lock the door, the warden came in again.

"College?" he asked.

"Yes sir, I don't like to miss my lectures."

"Today is Monday and you don't need to wear your college clothing. Am I right?"

The warden still seemed immersed in the posters flaunted in the room.

"I like my college, my college dress and as you saw, I even have my under garments in blue colour, matching the college uniform,"

Ballu replied moving out of the room. He locked the door and kept the keys on the ventilator.

"Why are you keeping the keys there? If something happens, who will be blamed?" he asked to add more irritation to the exasperated fellow.

"You are absolutely correct, sir," Ballu jumped to find the keys and hurried towards the mess. He returned in about ten minutes and kept the keys near the ventilator after confirming the exit of the warden. Not only the warden was known for his irritating ways, but he also had an uncanny habit of giving advice unasked.

"Study, study and study," was the mantra he gave to the students after reading a note pasted on Naren's study table.

Ballu and Sonia both came directly after the lunch break. "Oh my god! How come you and Sonia both missed the early lectures?" Abhijeet inquired scratching his head.

"We had some fun earlier in the day. Do you have any problems?"

Lectures are the last thing on the students' mind on a pleasant Monday afternoon. In the midst of the last lecture, even the professor seemed lethargic and ended the harangue a bit earlier. It was just fifteen minutes, which seemed to be saved but it gave a huge psychological edge as the professor had already insisted about it in the initial stages of the lecture. "Relieved" would be the only word, which would describe Ballu's pain that was equally shared by everyone around. The fairer sex was known to grasp every word but the results were quite contrasting at least for this college, as the percentage of male students who passed was always higher than their *salwar-kurta* clad competitors.

The gloomy part of the marathon was the fact that only hostel students had participated in it baring a few day scholars. The women's marathon had to be cancelled at the last moment due to the negligible response shown by the girls. There were two more interesting things associated with the marathon. First, a starting point and an end were given with no maps serving as guide. 'Take any shortcut you want,' was the slogan penned for the marathon. "First prize twenty-five thousand and second, a mere ten thousand – this is not fair," Ballu argued being cocky that he would be amongst the top three performers of the mega event as per the hill station and the college standards. The main glitch for the marathon was the fact that it clashed with the first match between the archrivals, India and Pakistan. The students were so passionate for cricket that many of them opted out of the marathon even after paying the non-refundable amount. "India is playing Pakistan, had it been any other country, I would have participated. Anything for cricket," Riyaz said when asked about his participation. "I think that will leave the marathon with meagre runners. God bless the marathon." Ballu was the happiest when he came to know about the match. "I can do anything for twenty-five thousand." Ballu was planning a website for his collection of voyeuristic, sexy pictures. "Even after making a website, I would be left with ample money."

The light in the room kept troubling Chetan as he sat on the other side of Ballu's bed to avoid the reflection coming directly on his eyes. "Take a pillow and make yourself comfortable near the corner."

The room, which seemed to be cleaned just a while ago, now had footprints all over the floor. The extra carpet used for maintaining cleanliness seemed attached against the window for drying.

Ballu had an excellent opportunity to clear his doubts, as Aman and Dev were busy playing chess in Dev's room even as Riyaz was playing cricket with his fellow first year students in the small passage brightly lit with the help of tube lights.

"You cannot post pornographic content on a domain purchased in India," Chetan warned his friend when he heard of the idea.

"What are you saying? Are you nuts? There are hundreds of websites with pictures of nude Indian women."

Chetan who was trendier when it came to technical stuff pertaining to computers disturbed Ballu's dreams of opulence. "These Indian websites have an American domain. American domains are domains purchased in USA which don't have any stringent laws when it comes to adventures of adult people."

Ballu looked confused and shot a new question to his calm and composed friend who took pleasure in answering the naïve questions. "My pictures are not fully nude; some show the undergarments of women, that's it."

"I have seen them. Some even have the faces of the owners of those undergarments," Chetan explained.

"What! Where did you see the pictures?" Ballu asked giving a wide-eyed look.

"Dev did it. I don't know."

"But it's password protected." Ballu felt embarrassed to acknowledge his collection. "I will have to change the password again, I feel."

The starting point of the marathon was the hostel gate and the winning barricade was set up near the strawberry plantations, which was around five kilometres away.

"I have an idea. Let's go through the Mango Orchard. It will save a lot of time and who knows we might earn all the prizes at stake. Adding all the prizes, it comes to around forty thousand."

Dev and Aman laughed on the idea. "What happened?"

"Let's win first. Stop dreaming. Do you think the seniors will leave you if you win the race?"

"I think most of them will opt for a less monetary, more interesting option," Ballu sighed looking at the heap of clothes which were spread all over the bed.

"It's India versus Pakistan and also the exams are just round the corner. Who will leave that for the bloody race?" Ballu had different views contradicting the popular verdict. "We can catch the match in the last stages after the marathon as well."

The group made a few more plans after dinner at Riyaz's place on the preceding night to the marathon. Somehow, only the first year students looked excited for the event. The ragging seemed over as the seniors and the first year students appeared friendlier now and apart from the occasional filling of water bottles, everything seemed under control.

"I heard our seniors ask us to complete their journals during the submission times."

"What are you saying?" asked a concerned Ballu who had his own journals still incomplete. Apart from Chetan, mostly everyone stopped shaving in the hope of passing the first semester exams.

It was a pleasant Sunday afternoon and everyone was ready for the marathon. Students saw their professors for the first time inside the hostel premises. A banner was pasted just outside the hostel entrance highlighting the prize amount. The preparations could be seen even from the windows of the rooms at the ground floor. As advised by Dev, Ballu had a light breakfast but drank lots of water to compensate for it. Water bottles were filled, and kept neatly on the benches supporting the huge banner. Even after a formal invitation was given to the girl's hostel, not even a single representative of the species had come to witness the epic drama called 'Marathon'.

"We will miss an exciting match," Hemant said, confirming something on his mobile.

"Sachin is playing with his full flow as India had won the toss and elected to bat first."

The warden announced the prize amount first as a concerned crowd gathered near the fig tree close to the entrance. The instructions were read again and a pamphlet with the instructions written on it was handed to every participant. There was still an hour left for the event and most students were watching the match, which unfortunately was getting interesting with every ball. "I thought these bastards might skip the marathon for studying, but most of them have turned up," Ballu said looking at the crowd that seemed to be increasing every minute. No Bollywood star was seen at the event clearing the week old rumours. "Maybe, there would be someone at the prize distribution, next Sunday," said someone from the crowd gathered at the venue.

The only controversial rule was, 'anyone caught talking on a mobile would be disqualified'. Barring a few, most didn't carry their mobiles.

Exactly at 1 pm, the final announcement was made. Ballu and his gang wore white T-shirts combined with white shorts. 'Eighteen till I die' was the caption on Ballu's T-shirt.

To avoid the heat, most students were seen in white shirts disturbing Ballu and gang's plan of getting noticed. The parking of the hostel was cleared to give more space to the runners.

It looked like more people had gathered for the event than the entries received. A head count was taken and after a brief discussion, the marathon was to be started. Not many had seen the college principal and this was a brilliant opportunity as he shook hands with every contestant.

"We will run in a group and that way we all can win the marathon by romping home exactly at the same time," Ballu suggested while drinking some water.

"There is no rule which states that the prize money will be shared. They will be compelled to shell out individual prize money for the joint winners."

To keep Ballu quiet, his friends hesitantly agreed. The principal was gasping for breath after the marathon session for shaking hands with everyone. Resting for some time, he drank some more water and decided not to take part in the marathon on health grounds.

The grimace was clearly seen.

"One less competitor," shouted someone from the crowd. A loud roar of laughter followed. Many of the professors opted out at the last moment making the students happy. "I can't even imagine running with these oldies."

The score of the match was announced through the loud speakers yielding a round of clapping and hugging by the crowd.

The stage was set and the professors and some students cheered them from the other side, near the shade.

A whistle, followed by a complete chaos, and the marathon started. Taking a right turn, almost everyone entered the mango orchard. Ballu was shocked but followed them to the mango orchard through the broken fence near the locked entrance of the mango tree.

There was no sign of any guard and absolutely no fortification today. "Maybe the hostel authorities might have taken prior permission from the orchard owner," Aman said taking some big steps to match his friends. The orchard was filled with students in no time and some tried their hand at plucking some pomegranates, which the fruit laden trees had to offer. Aman who was very regular with his jogging knew a shortcut to a farmhouse near the mango orchard. Chetan asked for water and Ballu threw his bottle towards him. Unable to match the running and the jump, the bottle fell from his hands. Ballu made a gloomy face watching most of the students jumping the fence to get to the other side of the mango orchard. "Chetan, do you remember the farmhouse near the orchard?" Aman asked taking some deep breaths with his hands over his knees. Chetan recollected something and asked everyone to take a right turn from the guava tree. Ballu never wanted to follow them but it was the only chance they had, as most of the students had surpassed them, at least by a few metres.

They turned towards the right side again after the initial turn. "If we pass the bushes through the fence, we land near the stream."

"Stream?" Ballu and Dev both seemed surprised to know that they were close to an actual stream. "Let's go for it."

Aman was the first to cross the fence. The sharp edges had bruised his legs. He used his spit as an antiseptic for the wound. The rusty fence had scratched his skin making a small wound pouring a lot of blood. "Take a tetanus injection when you reach the hostel," Chetan yelled at the top of his voice.

Chetan managed to get past the fence, without any casualty followed by Dev. Ballu was the last and the fence was held split wide open by Dev and Chetan. Aman was more concerned about the wound as the blood seemed inexorable. Ballu tried his best to tackle the edges but the last of the edges made a sharp cut on his leg. Aman and Ballu had the same wounds, exactly on the same leg.

"We are partners after all," Aman said, as he drank some water and poured some on the wound. "Never pour water on a wound oozing blood."

"Oh my god! It's hurting like hell." Dev gave his handkerchief but Aman refused as he was panting for fresh air. Dev forcefully used his white coloured handkerchief to wipe the wound. "It looks more like a piece of modern art," Chetan said as Dev showed the white handkerchief, which had shades of red added to it. Ballu repeated his plan as they climbed the pillar of stones near the foothills. It seemed more like a scene straight from the episode of National Geographic channel as they saw the opening leading to a beautiful stream. "It's dangerous."

"We will hold our hands firmly and using the big rocks, go through the gap," Aman suggested while kicking the rocks to check the balance. "It's our only chance. The rest of the students might be halfway through," Ballu said and even turned around to confirm. "No one is following us. But are you sure that we can reach the strawberry fields from here in less than ten minutes?" Ballu asked as he drank some more water. Aman and Chetan were the first to pass through leaving Dev near the rocks. Ballu who looked exhausted urinated near the rocks. "See that bastard. First he drinks water then waters the plants with his infected fertilisers," Aman said, as he could not control his laughter.

Ballu managed to pour some water and washed his hands before helping Dev.

As per the plan, Dev was to come first followed by Ballu, but on Ballu's request, Dev gave him support to go through the gap. Chetan sustained even as Aman was still checking the wound. Ballu took a lot of time crossing the path even when supported from both the sides. Dev scrapped through the gap easily without much support. Chetan grabbed the water bottle from Ballu and kept it in his pocket. "The stream is behind this big maroon rock. We can see it from that side," Aman said pointing towards the layer of big rocks.

They ran towards the rock and helped Aman climb the rock first. Dev was literally on his fours to give support to his friend. Aman was tall and knew the amount of pressure, which Dev might have to carry for he had kneeled down for firm support. Aman climbed the rock after some initial struggle and stood on the big rock. He dusted his pants and saw the stream. A happy heart helped his friends to climb the big rock, which posed more danger than the rusted fence. The rock was big enough to carry the weight of all the four friends.

It was so nice and refreshing to be able to see the stream from the rocks. "We should have brought a camera to click some pictures before we move ahead," Ballu said wiping his sweat from his brow with his T-shirt, which he used as a makeshift handkerchief.

"I should have joined your morning jogs, but you never told me about the stream or the strawberry fields. Also does anyone know the current score?"

They ran when Dev informed them about the time. "Run, man run."

Ballu looked exhausted but the thought of money made him run faster. The stream, which looked miniscule from the rocks, seemed like ocean to the boys. Ballu dipped his hands and touched the water, but looking at the blunt rocks, he stepped aside. "It's dangerous, one mistake and we may create some news in tomorrow's local newspapers resulting in declaration of a holiday for us," Chetan mumbled as he checked the drops of water falling from the stream. They rushed from the side of the stream to a makeshift room, which housed an old transforrner. Crossing the hut, they reached the other side of the stack. The pink strawberry fields were waiting for them. The sight of the strawberry fields was a vista to watch. They jumped and found a small boulevard through the rocks to the pink fields. All of them were running holding their hands imitating kids from the kindergarten. The happy-go-lucky group was just a mile away from glory. As decided, they would put the winning step simultaneously. The strangest part was that no one, not even the seniors who lived here for quite some time, managed to be acquainted with this shortcut.

"Who cares? We will party after the win," Chetan screamed as he patted Ballu.

The air seemed to make a lot of hullabaloo but the boys cheered each other for a master plan enacted comprehensively. "Yes, we have done it," roared Ballu adjusting his small turban, which was a perfect contrast to the colour of his clothes.

They could see the final lap towards the barricade. They could even read the print on the barricade. Some people were seen near the barricade. It was a straight road for victory, just some metres away. The joy was short lived as someone running with full speed came from the last turn to the barricade and sprinted towards the finishing line. Ballu could not believe the sight and gave a perfect wide-eyed expression. There were some airborne banners as some people were waiting with water bottles for them near the barricade.

Completely exhausted, they were just around ten metres away from the barricade, when a second gentleman came from the turn and sprinted towards the finishing line. In a trice, even the first runner-up place was taken by someone.

They were so near the finishing line that they managed to recognise the people who took the first two positions. Chetan was speechless as was Dev who just would not move.

They still had a chance to finish third but were not sure if someone would come from the turn leading to the barricade.

Out of a sudden, Ballu sprinted towards the finish line. He gave all his might and collapsed after finishing the race. Just after him, a group of students came from nowhere and sprinted towards the finish line. The people, who were cheering, lifted Ballu and sprinkled some water on him. Dev, Chetan and Aman were more shocked to see that their friend had betrayed them. "I can't believe it. The bastard deceived us," Aman said, as he showed no interest to cross the finishing line. "It's all over boys."

Chetan and Aman walked towards the finishing line followed by Dev. One thing was sure, had Ballu never sprinted towards the finishing line, someone from the crowd would have been crowned the third runner up. "At least, someone from our group would get something," Dev murmured dusting his shorts. "Five thousand is a substantial amount. We could have a big party after our exams." Chetan praised Ballu's effort as well.

They checked Ballu who had managed to sit down but could not look up.

Dev congratulated Ballu and he hugged everyone. "I had no option left; I had heard the crowd coming. It's our prize, not just mine."

Forgetting about the marathon and the winners, people were seen engrossed in some long discussions about the match. Someone in the crowd had managed to smuggle a pocket radio through the marathon. "Great man, India is playing well and our Ballu won the race," shouted someone from a distance.

❖❖❖

6

Prize Distribution

Jealousy is nothing but feeling alone against smiling enemies.

The marathon was a huge hit amongst everyone; be it the hostel or the college.

As for the cricket match, even after posting a challenging total, India lost by a whisker.

Ballu climbed the popularity charts amongst his peers mostly due to the posters which were almost everywhere to glorify the winners. Professors also congratulated him for his astonishing win. Aman was quite upset by the episode and would talk with Ballu, only when it was absolutely necessary. The prize distribution was to be held at the college lawns and placards congratulating the winners were pasted all over the college.

To celebrate the victory, Ballu was ordered to perform his cricket dance with his friends on the terrace again. The best part was that none of his first year friends were present while the performance was staged. Aman wanted to walk off but managed to support the notorious dance troupe. Ballu knew that he had betrayed his friends' trust and promised to employ all the money for a big party, which he would host after the exams. "At least, I managed a podium finish," came a typical Ballu style blunt answer to all the questions about the marathon. The advent of the last week of November proved decisive for everyone.

Settling rumours of a postponement of the exams, they got pre-poned by a week instead. Riyaz was the happiest of the lot and even hugged him thrice for his victory after the dance. Ballu joined his gang at Riyaz's place making himself comfortable on the bed. "Oh my god! I haven't even completed my submissions. I won't clear these exams... I feel," was Ballu's reaction to the announcement.

"I have some important work to be done, so I will make a move now," Dev said as he tried to find his slippers within the huge pile generated due to the number of people in the packed room. Just as Dev left the room, many more realised the time and followed Dev.

"That's crap. You didn't realise this earlier," Ballu said, adjusting the pillow.

Dev smiled and threw a banana peel on his friends.

"I will be back in some time. Let me know if you people are planning to watch a movie tonight," Dev said while closing the door. As there was no Internet connection available, Ballu's laptop was used as a substitute for Dev's DVD player.

"Yes, we could watch something in the horror genre. Have you seen that movie?"

"Which?" Aman asked, interrupting him.

"I am not getting the name, but it's really a very good horror movie. It's name starts with the alphabet 'T', I guess," Ballu said, closing his eyes while trying to remember something. He looked more like a person absorbed completely in meditation.

"The ring, I got it. It's an awesome movie. I have the original DVD, what do you say?"

"Let's go for it then. But after a smoke," Ballu was not amused by Aman's smoking instalments, which interrupted many interesting session of talks.

"Call me, if I am not here. I would be at Dev's place."

Chetan and Aman went for a smoke even as Riyaz insisted on taking a short nap for some time.

Ballu never smoked in the hostel fearing the seniors who had warned them against it. Ballu practised chess as he dreamt of defeating Dev one day. Whenever Ballu met a confusing move or anticipated defeat, he would adjourn the game giving any of his lame excuses. Later, he was seen playing with the switch of the tube-light in the passage. He searched his pockets to check for his mobile and his heart stopped for a moment fearing the worse... losing a thirty thousand worth mobile would be a big loss, considering his father had warned him while purchasing it. "If you lose it, don't ask for another one," he still remembered his father's words. "Oh my god! No one would return it."

He rushed to Riyaz's room who had strangely left the door open.

"Hey, did I leave my mobile here?"

There was absolutely no response from Riyaz, who had kept a pillow over his head to get even with the noise generated by some people playing in the passageway. Ballu pulled the blanket, which Riyaz had draped.

"What happened?"

"Man, I lost my mobile phone."

"Great, now if I find it, I won't give it back," Riyaz wrapped the blanket again.

"Shut up! I am serious. My father will kill me," Ballu said, pulling out the sheets under the bed even as one of sheets seemed stuck.

Ballu started his search from the other side of the room and reached the side where the bed seemed camouflaged with the wall besides it.

"Where were you gone before coming to my room?" Riyaz asked as he checked the cupboard.

"I was playing chess on my Laptop."

"Did you check your room?"

"I had the mobile when I was in your room. Don't you remember Akash playing with it?" he said, checking something under the bed sheet.

"Did you ask Akash?"

Ballu was irritated.

"He had given the mobile to me, I remember it clearly. He had squeezed the mobile in my pocket when he was unable to slide it."

After a round of frantic search, they used their common sense and Riyaz grabbed his mobile phone and dialled Ballu's number.

"I don't know what happens to my common sense when I am surrounded by fools?" Riyaz said as he dialled Ballu's number and it got disconnected automatically.

"Same is the case with me."

An extremely irritating tune burst out to disturb the silence, which had prevailed after the brief argument. The mobile was stuck between the gap created by the table and the locker.

Ballu rushed to the gap and removing the sliver ornament from his elbow, he put his right hand in the gap. He could not grab the mobile and had to use his left hand instead.

"Got it," he shouted, looking upwards.

"What?"

"My mobile. Stop dialling the number, it's vibrating as well."

"I really can't understand this, how did the mobile manage to go there?"

"Either someone had kept it there or you might have tried some of your tricks which backfired on you."

"Shut up!"

Ballu checked to find a lot of calls which he missed during the mobile's stay in the congested fissure. He thought for a while and remembered the golden rule made famous by a recent blockbuster movie.

"No one will give you a 'missed call' to convey anything even remotely connected to your profit."

In addition, whenever Ballu had called any unknown numbers from his mobile phone, he had to either part with his money or happiness. The last time he called a local number in Mumbai, he had to shell out around two-thousand rupees from his pocket money to save a friend from his debts and so on. His hostel mates were no different. He called on an unknown number and had to give his digital camera. It was more than fifteen minutes, and still the smokers were nowhere to be seen. They used to smoke in the bathroom earlier, but three boys coming out of a bathroom could arouse unscrupulous suspicions, so they managed a bigger, airy space to smoke.

Ballu knocked the door as he saw a lot of illumination in the room coming through the ventilator as compared to the contrasting darkness in the passage. Dev wanted to hide something but as the knocks increased, he threw a blanket on the bed, opened the door, and turned towards the bed trying his best not to have Ballu venture this side.

"Hey, are you busy?"

"No. I was just packing something," Dev said as he sat on his bed.

"Shall we play a quick fire round of Chess?" Chess was the last thing on Dev's mind.

"Hmmm," Dev took a long time to agree. "But our rule stays. The move has to be done within five minutes. Open this locker and take the chess board from the first shelf."

Ballu unenthusiastically agreed, but asked, "Do you have a magnetic chess board?"

"I have the normal wooden board, but Raghav has it. It won't be a good idea to wake him up, I guess," Dev said, spreading the bed sheet evenly on the bed.

Dev arranged the chessboard on Chetan's bed to flag off the game. Ballu requested to have black pieces, as the white ones weren't lucky for him.

"Hmm! That's fine."

The game started and like his idol Bobby Fisher, Ballu played out some of the weirdest moves on the chessboard. "Now you will see," he said, looking up from the chessboard.

Dev still was more concerned about the book under the bed sheet.

"Did Sonia really ask you out, or was it a rumour?"

"She didn't, actually," Dev tried to change the direction of the conversation.

"I have a sexy picture of her. Someday, I will show you."

"What are you saying? Show me now."

"I will show you only if I lose the game."

"No, please show it now," Dev insisted, as he could not hold anymore.

As Dev insisted, Ballu showed a picture on his mobile, which seemed to be edited.

"How do I know that it's Sonia in the picture?" Dev asked, as he looked at the picture displaying a woman's cleavage.

"It's up to you, I have one more in which her undergarments are visible."

"What! That's awesome man."

Within the next fifteen minutes, Ballu had lost most of his pieces and defeat loomed large on his face.

They heard some knocks on the door and Dev rushed to open it. Ballu smoothly moved some of the white pieces and threw them into the basket, which was kept nearby. As soon as Chetan and Aman entered the room, they burst out laughing. "Ballu is playing chess... I can't believe it." Suddenly, Aman pulled the bed sheet from Dev's bed.

"What's this?" Aman shouted, as he saw the red book along with some boxes.

Dev who had managed to hide his personal red book from Ballu was not surprised but tried to divert the conversation without any luck.

"Did you see Sonia's pictures on Ballu's mobile?" he asked. Sonia's picture reminded Ballu of his hidden folder and he exploded, "Dev, I wanted to ask you something? How did you manage to open my hidden folder?"

Dev was in jeopardy of letting his secrets pop out one by one.

"You should make a difficult password. You had the spelling of the word password. I tried it and it worked," Dev said, trying to get past Aman who was standing in his way.

"What is this red book about? Is it your personal diary?"

Aman asked while checking the red book, which had something scribbled on the cover.

"Yes, that's my diary."

Aman handed over the diary and checked the white box. It had the words 'Magic Box' printed on it.

"So are you a magician?"

"Nopes. It's used all over the world," he replied, taking the box and pouring something from it. Some chits came through and some got stuck in the narrow opening.

Chetan appeared surprised even as Ballu kept thinking of a bizarre combination for a password to his hidden folder.

"That means, Dev had already seen the pictures and was acting innocent," he told himself.

Everyone was eager to know about the magic box and pestered Dev until he bulged.

"You people might have heard about the Magic Box in some of the old Irish novels."

"I don't read books, so I am out of it."

"Neither do I," Aman replied while trying to fix his mobile which seemed to be split into two.

Dev told them about his 'Magic Box' and the fact that it should be made of our favourite colour and that was the reason he made it in white, as he wanted peace of mind. The colour white denoted peace.

Ballu wrapped the chess game and shouted, "I drew with Dev."

"Okay, okay."

"What does the colour black symbolise?"

"Fearlessness, I suppose," Chetan chipped in while playing with the football near the cupboard.

"Correct."

"And what about brown?"

"Brown is the colour of the humble man. People who like brown are grounded and quite down to earth in their scheme of things. We should put our ideas, our best photographs, memorable events in life, first crush, first bike, first mobile and other significant details written on small chits in the Magic Box. We should also use a big chit with the headline 'dream' written on it."

"Dream? I didn't get that part."

Everyone seemed fascinated and got engrossed in the Magic Box. The name itself commanded interest.

"Dream may be something like buying a car, and then we need to come back first of every month and write down about what all we did this month for our dream."

"It sounds childish. I cannot believe that a twenty-year-old can do such a thing," Ballu said, collecting the chess pieces from the basket.

Ballu excused himself from the room stating quiescent reasons.

Aman jumped and closed the door. "Good, the bastard went away. He deceived us in the marathon."

Dev continued, "I also write the praises I receive on the chits and put them in the Magic Box. Some people write thanking notes of their dreams," he said, showing some chits.

"Thanking notes! What's that now?"

"For example, if you want a Mercedes, we can thank god for giving us a Mercedes. It creates a positive effect and the negative vibes are removed."

"Oh, that means, when you check the Magic Box next month, the car will come out from the Magic Box," Aman joked gifting a round of chuckles.

Chetan seemed curious that Dev did all this stuff from the start of the semester and he never came to know.

"Can I see the chits?"

"Sure," Dev opened the Magic Box and gave the chits to Aman.

Aman and Chetan smiled as they read the chits. "Dev looked really very cute as a child," Aman said, checking Dev's photograph as a child.

Looking at the stack of chart paper near the window, Aman requested if Dev could help him make a Magic Box for him.

"Sure."

"I mean, I want to make it now," Aman insisted on present tense.

"Sure."

"What's your dream?" Dev asked making himself comfortable on the bed.

"I want to be a manager of a big company, earning a million per annum."

"You people will laugh when you hear my dream," Chetan said taking the pen.

"Cool, I want to marry someone like Katrina Kaif."

Like millions, Chetan was head over heals for Katrina Kaif.

"I will make the Magic Box in the colour Black, but we don't have black coloured chart paper," Aman said while checking the various chart papers.

"We will have to buy some black chart paper when we go to the market, next Sunday."

Dev helped Chetan and Aman make their magic boxes in white coloured chart paper for the time being, even as Ballu was busy deleting some of the less revealing pictures from his laptop.

The week was not as busy as it should have been in terms of the lectures in college.

As Ballu had won a prize in the Marathon, he attended some more lectures as he gained popularity out of the event. The function to felicitate the winners of the Marathon was to be held on twenty-eighth of November. Ballu was more excited than all the first year students combined, but never showed his excitement.

"When I receive the prize, you can stand near the podium and click as many pictures as you can, okay?" Ballu asked expecting a response, which came after a brief silence.

"Yes sir," Abhijeet replied as he checked Ballu's digital camera.

Ballu prepared earnestly for the mega event and even requested others to attend it.

"Sure, I will host a grand party after the exams," he promised to every query thrown at him.

It was a bright morning on twenty-eighth of November and the prize distribution was postponed by an hour owing to the adjustments, which were to be done in the college lawns.

"It's your lucky day man," Abhijeet said, when he saw Ballu strolling in the passage.

"I know. Actually I would have won the marathon had it not for the shortcut taken by some seniors," he boasted when asked about his second runners up position.

Ballu had feasted on butter-chicken and showed symptoms of a stomachache but the thought of taking the prize and the money involved made him concentrate more on the event.

He was in the washroom for more than five times and remained there for quite some time on each occasion.

"I can't believe it. It's troubling me like hell," he declared to a rather surprised crowd gathered at their favourite hangout.

"Wait for me please, I will hop and come in a moment," he requested, rushing towards the washroom.

"Sure, I will be in your room or do you want to come to my room?"

Ballu was in no mood to answer and covering his mouth with his hand, he ran to the washroom.

"What a relief!" he sighed.

Dev tried his hand at Ballu's guitar until then. Ballu came in after a long time and apologised.

"Are you okay?" Dev asked keeping the guitar on the bed.

"Will you do me a favour?"

"Sure." Ballu made a weird face while pressing his belly.

"I will let you know if I am able to go to the event, but if I miss; kindly collect the award on my behalf. Is that fine with you?" Ballu asked taking some deep breaths.

"That's fine. But will they allow me to collect the prize on you behalf?"

"Why not? Keep your phone free."

Dev wasn't convinced enough, but agreed when Ballu insisted.

Ballu excused himself and rushed to the bathroom again.

Aman was not interested in attending the prize distribution and decided to go to the college library instead, which was open during the preparation leave.

Chetan and Dev were seen near the college in about an hour.

Riyaz was nowhere to be seen and was later found playing cricket on the terrace. After the initial excitement, baring a few, most of the hostel students were not even seen at the college campus. Abhijeet took the digital camera and tried his luck at clicking the scenic beauty, testing the piece.

"I will collect Ballu's prize on his behalf."

"What are you saying? Are you sure?" Chetan asked looking shocked at the revelation.

"Good. Make sure you collect the prize money as well. We won't leave that bastard."

The event was a low profile affair as the posters, which were stuck everywhere were torn apart and the event started a bit late than scheduled.

"Where are the rest of the people?" Abhijeet asked as he clicked some pictures. He seemed smitten by the digital camera and used more than three fourth of the memory.

The stage only had a small poster pasted on the wall and some professors on the stage.

"It's a pleasure to have you all here," screamed the principal.

"Where is Ballu?" Abhijeet asking as he cleared the flash with a piece of cloth.

"I don't know. His phone too is switched off."

Abhijeet tried calling his friend desperately as he was sure that the prize for the third position would be given first.

The foundation day was celebrated in the library and some saplings were planted.

The hype supporting the event died out in the first hour itself.

Gauging the scarcity of the event, college authorities called the students from the library to be present for the occasion to add some credibility to the event.

After some jokes and introduction, the prize distribution finally started.

The final set of rumours were also dead, when not even a single celebrity was present for the occasion.

"That bastard had lied."

"Who?" Abhijeet asked checking the screen of the digital camera.

"The warden, he told me that Amitabh Bachhan is coming today."

"And you believed him?" The entire crowd burst out laughing.

"Please, maintain the decorum," an announcement was made through the loud speakers.

The crowd was silent for a moment and the noise level increased after some more announcements.

"And the third prize for the Marathon event goes to... Balwinder Walia."

Dev smiled and ran towards the podium, eagerly cheered by the crowd. All of a sudden, Ballu appeared from the foyer through the library and entered the podium.

It was strange for Chetan who was on the podium with Ballu rushing from the other side. The smile on Ballu's face was missing and it was more embarrassing for Dev. One of the professors standing behind the principle knew Ballu as well as Dev.

Dev could not believe that Ballu appeared out of nowhere and landed directly on the stage.

"Yes, what do you want?" asked a senior professor standing next to the principal.

The professor recognised Ballu as his poster was displayed on the banner behind the stage.

Dev was closer to the principle on the stage, while Ballu had halted abruptly adding some more confusion to the muddle. Ballu was always a bag full of contradictions.

"Are you Balwinder Walia?" the professor shouted keeping his hand on the mike to avoid his voice being amplified.

A stunned Dev was not able to show any emotions. Ballu used his hands to convey even as the students cheered the commotion.

"Are you deaf? Can't you hear? Are you Balwinder Walia?" he repeated, coming closer.

"No sir."

"We are looking for Balwinder Walia. Why the hell are you on stage?"

"Sorry, sir."

"Rascal, is this a joke going on?" he yelled on the mike this time. The rapturous crowd went quiet for a minute even as Dev took a right turn towards the college library.

Ballu came forward and apologised for the incident.

"That's fine. These scoundrels take pride in making fun of their professors," he said, shaking his hands vigorously. The principal wasn't amused and handed over the cash prize even as the committee was confused whether Ballu was to be given a trophy or not. After checking the names on the trophies, they confirmed that the third position was not to be awarded any trophies, just the certificate of merit.

"That bastard should not have done that," Chetan said, dialling Dev's number.

Abhijeet had even managed to click many photographs of the chaos, in the time being.

"What was he doing there?" asked a puzzled senior student.

"Not sure, maybe they were enacting something straight from a movie."

The humiliation was huge as the senior professor taught Mathematics to the first year students and had known Dev as a sincere student. Ballu tried his best to convey his message, gesturing with his hands but Dev was shell-shocked to even understand this.

Dev managed to escape the college premises and ran towards the hostel. As more and more people started to call him, he switched his cell phone off.

"Something is wrong," Chetan said as he ran through the entrance of the college towards the hostel.

After taking his prize, Ballu jumped from the stage into the crowd directly who lifted him in celebration.

"Party, party," someone shouted from the crowd.

"They have given me a cheque which would take around three days to be credited," he yelled, as he was unable to hear anything in the celebration.

Ballu had done this on purpose to teach his friend a lesson and acted naïve when Aman and Chetan questioned him.

"That's fine, it happens. It's a big day for him, don't spoil it," Dev said, sitting on the chair in his room.

"I had a stomachache and had asked him to collect the prize on my behalf. But after you people were gone, I felt better and had to take the shortcut through the canteen."

"Why was your cell phone switched off?" Chetan asked, with an awkward smile on his face.

"Calm down, I can understand the situation. Believe me, it was unintentional."

"Let's go for a smoke Chetan," Aman suggested checking the number of cigarettes in his packet.

Dev took the newspaper and began to cut a part of it.

Ballu closed the door rushing towards it.

"Slap me as hard as possible. I never understood your greatness, man."

Dev was shocked to hear this and kept the newspaper aside.

"I am really sorry," he repeated with tears in his eyes.

Dev rushed and hugged him. "Ballu, you are making me feel embarrassed. Stop crying."

"You will have to forgive me first."

"You haven't done anything. It was just a lack of communication."

Dev hugged him as they smiled, even as tears kept falling from his eyes.

Just as they were about to sit, somebody knocked on the door.

Dev asked Ballu to wash his face as he opened the door. The warden ordered everyone to come to his office. Ballu washed his face and ran towards the warden's office.

The warden was busy reading some documents when the boys entered the cabin.

"Yes sir, you had called us."

"I saw hair in the washbasin today," he said as he stood up.

"Is that so unusual?" Dev asked making a mockery of the warden's question.

"I mean, maybe someone might have shaved or cut his hair," Abhijeet said, staring at Ballu's beard.

"It's not facial hair or hair from a person's head," the warden yelled.

"Then?" someone asked. The warden was irritated as hell, but the students laughed their hearts out even as the warden warned them against repeating the act.

Later, Dev even helped Ballu make a 'Magic Box' for himself.

"I want it in the green colour. However, what does the green colour signify? Also please don't tell anyone about this."

❖❖❖

7

Facebook Friend Requests

Social networking sites are capable of doing what even the saints could not do.

Ballu was so fond of his guitar that he would never let anyone touch it. It was almost six in evening and Ballu had finished his guitar practice. Light filtered through the rusty iron windows making it clear that the bachelors' room was untidy as usual with clothes and socks thrown all over. Clothes were fine but it was strange to see six tc seven pair of socks thrown all over the room. The white bed sheet seemed as if it had not been washed since ages and had turned to pale yellow. The big bed gave ample scope for recumbence. The strangest part about Ballu was that he used to be fully dressed while rehearsing on his guitar. The only thing missing would be the turban, for he would leave his hair open, which made him feel that some trance like feeling had taken over.

His mother collected the clothes, folded them and kept them inside the big steel cupboard, which had two guitars neatly kept in it. The door got stuck and resisting the piles of clothes filled inside it, she shut it forcibly. She opened the door and put her hand to check if it would take in some more. She took some clothes out and folded them again to make some more space when she saw some more clothes under the bed.

Analysing the heap under the bed, she shouted, "You have a million pair of shirts and trousers, still you move around half naked in your room." The statement proved contradictory during the practice sessions, as Ballu looked dapper unlike other times, when his so-called 'struggler' attitude showed even through the Kurt Cobain photograph pasted on the cupboard, which read... 'Whatever', followed by some question marks. The picture displayed his attitude, which never did him any good.

Gasping and panting, she tried to use the guitar as a stick to move the clothes. As soon as Ballu saw this, he jumped from his chair and screamed like hell. Shocked, his mother dropped the guitar, which left Ballu in utter bewilderment. "You should have told me, I would have done that for you. How dare you mess with my guitar?" The voice grew louder as he checked the strings of his guitar.

He kneeled and collected the clothes passing them to his mother.

He checked his guitar again, wiped it with a soft cloth, and kept it in the black coloured guitar shaped bag near the cupboard.

"I wanted to talk with you so you could pass on my message to Dad," Ballu grinned and hugged his mother.

"I don't have any money," she frowned and tried to stand, but her knee pain would not let her do so. Shrugging off, she took some more deep breaths and sat on the bed. Seeing Ballu check the guitar strings, she started crying, covering her face with her hands.

"I know I have always let you people down. However, someday, you people will be proud of me. Money is not I'm after, that's the reason I opted out of a job," he continued his vocal autobiography, which gainsaid his way of life.

"Dreams are more important to me than anything in this world. People are at their creative peak until thirty and I don't want to waste these years by working hard." Tears started rolling down his hairy cheeks. It seemed uncanny and quite similar to a scene straight from a mainstream blockbuster. His mother wiped his tears with her bare hands and reminded him about the fact that he catches cold as soon as he cries. "Why don't you try for a job in your field and give second priority to guitar? Make yourself busy in something and practise in the spare time, side by side," she said while squeezing his cheeks and smiled. He took a pillow and sat on it making his mother feel awkward. "Tired," he said answering his mother's unasked question. His eyes still showed some signs of wetness but leaked of honesty reminiscent of a toddler's eyes.

"If I do something all day as compared to just some hours a day, which of the scenarios should work?" Ballu asked pulling out his mobile phone, and connected it to the mobile charger, which was seen dangling earlier.

"Do what you want, but don't let your dad's name muddle up."

"This is my life and I am damn serious about it. It hurts when the most important people in your life think as if it's fun for me," he said innocently.

His mother felt uneasy and tried to get up but Ballu importuned her to sit down.

"I have absolute faith in god and my abilities. I want you to wait for five years. I have planned my life. It takes a lot of discipline, practice and hard work to be a rock star," Ballu exclaimed as he disturbed the strings of his guitar. His mother was so shocked hearing the word 'rock star' that she did not speak for some time.

The brief silence was perturbed by the sweet sound of the strings. Stunned by the sound, she enquired about Ballu's plans. Ballu was happy that at last someone was interested in his plans. As Ballu came near, she felt tensed and asked, "Why didn't you tell this when we sent you for your engineering course?"

"I have given enough indications of my dreams. The posters in my room are still the same. Don't tell me that you people never understood what they mean," he said and reminded his mother that it was his father who had gifted him an electric guitar when he was seventeen. Even in the movies, guitar had replaced the bike, while highlighting the strugglers aka 'the band of angry young men' and the posters in Ballu's room thumped this notion effectively.

Ballu wanted to speak but his mother interrupted him, and excused herself from the room. Just as he switched on his laptop again, his mother bought a glass of buttermilk and banged it on the table as she stared at him.

"I am only asking for five years and that too from my own life. Fortunately, I come from a rich family so why shouldn't I give it a shot?"

His mother sighed to show her lackadaisical attitude and excused herself again. Gulping the glass of buttermilk, he untied his shoelaces and pressed the enter button to wake his laptop from hibernation. Like millions, www.Facebook.com was his homepage so he never had to type in the website address to access it. He jigged in joy as he received a friend request through the website but his happiness turned into dust as he came to know that the person who had sent the request was not from the fairer-sex. The city was missing in the location filed and the profile picture just had light emanating from a source.

He touched his beard, moved fingers through it and made a bemused face. He opened the baffling profile and checked some more details. He checked the friend list of the person which only had a single addition. All of a sudden, he saw Chetan as the common link between the new profile and his profile. Immediately he dialled in Chetan's number and moaned as he got the busy beep. "Who is this moron talking to?" Ballu voiced a concern. In the meantime, he kept his pair of shoes in the shoe-rack behind the door and peeped from his balcony. A typical Mumbai evening with the hustle and bustle welcomed him. It was busier than usual due to the upcoming festival season. He changed into casual attire and made himself comfortable in the small chair. As usual, he visited profiles of his female friends to check their pictures and messages.

Facebook is like a second home where people garnish their profiles with almost everything. It's like people leading an entirely different life online which is completely opposite from their regular puppy-dog approach amidst the realities of the bigger blockbuster called 'life'. The state of their mind or what's exactly happening with them can be gauged by their profiles and the comments they get and make. Some people even click pictures just for the sake of displaying on these social networking websites. The phone rang and Ballu reached to grab it and failed as he had thrown the mobile phone on the other side of his bed. He had to get up and by that time, the ringing stopped. He checked the call list to view Chetan's number. He called him immediately and as expected got the same routine answer. When asked the reason for being busy on the phone, Chetan murmured that he was talking to the customer care of a credit card firm. Ballu laughed his heart out after hearing this, "You are marrying tomorrow and still talking about credit cards. I can't believe it. Give a call to Neha for a change."

Chetan confessed that he was talking to her and scolded him for interrupting their conversation. Still, Ballu invited him for a drink in the evening.

"I got a friend request from an unknown person and I saw your profile as the link between us," Ballu said in excitement.

Chetan told him that even he did not know the person and had just added to swank his list of friends. Ballu reminded him that the profile was of a guy and there was no reason to add an unknown person at least if it was a guy.

Chetan insisted that he would call him in an hour. Ballu laughed and agreed. After the call, Ballu tossed his coin and it came down as heads. Whenever it came down as heads, he assumed the answer as yes. Nevertheless, he told himself that he had not asked the question as yet and tossed it again which came down as heads all over again. Somehow, he was not in the mood of listening to destiny and out of an impulse, declined the friend request leaving a standard "who is this?" message. He continued checking his friend list and commented on a recent picture of Aman with a guitar. He laughed his heart out seeing the picture, as he knew Aman knew nothing about his favourite musical instrument. He emailed his picture while playing at a recent music festival. He was the moderator and the owner of many guitar and music communities on the website and checked for any relevant information about music festivals and get-togethers. In some time, he was seen playing his favourite tune on his guitar. He was mesmerised with the song, 'love is in the air' and played the tune with perfection. His mother peeped, found Ballu sitting with the guitar, and made a desperate face. Meanwhile, Chetan had his big day tomorrow.

Chetan was to marry his childhood sweetheart against his parents' wishes. He was always the no-nonsense man and took pride in everything he did. Inter-caste relationships have their share of artificial yet logical problems. Chetan came from an aristocratic South Indian family while his would-be wife Neha came from a simple middle class Marathi family. With royal looks personified, Chetan had class written all over him, but fell flat for Neha's simplicity. Neha's family had somehow agreed to the match, but Chetan's side threatened to disown him. The recent events made him tense and the stress was easily visible on his face. On his insistence, Neha agreed for a court marriage. Neha's father had taken all possible precautions and even filled in the application a month earlier. Chetan never liked the typical Hindu wedding rituals and the matchmaking concept.

Neha's family had secretly matched their '*kundlis*' and settled for the day of marriage ceremony only after consulting many high profile pundits.

The Deshpandes were very happy to find a great son-in-law in Chetan who not only was well mannered but also looked genuine to the core.

Neha's family had their house decorated with lightings of all colours possible. The entrance of their ground floor adorned a floral look. It looked as if the flowers had taken over. The reception was to be held this Sunday at one of the premium lawns just outside Mumbai. Neha's brother who initially resisted the match changed his mind after meeting Chetan. It was outlandish on the part of Chetan not to inform his parents about his marriage. On Ballu's doggedness, he intimated his sister who promised to be at the reception at least. Somehow, Chetan felt nervous even as the most beautiful day of his life approached. He called Ballu and they agreed to meet at Prem's near Bandra, a suburb in Mumbai.

Chetan finished the call, opened the window and smiled as he saw some children playing cricket on the ground floor.

His phone started ringing again but he was in no mood to go and pick it up. He had two mobile phones and knew Neha would never call on the other number. After a brief silence, the phone rang again. Feeling irritated, he grabbed the phone and disconnected the call.

Aman who was to arrive that day was calling Chetan desperately. Checking the received call list, he dialled in Aman's number who also took his own sweet time to answer. Chetan apologised and requested him to come directly at their favourite hangout. Later he took the photo-frame kept near the bed and wiped the dirt which had formed a layer making the picture almost dusty in colour. Neha was seen wearing a black coloured sari flashing her thousand watt smile and it brought a small smile on Chetan's face. Even while ironing his shirt, he was constantly looking at the picture. He went and checked his drawer for something. Apart from Neha, he never gave the second mobile number to anyone. As soon as he dialled her phone number, his alternate phone started ringing. Already annoyed, he rushed to pick the first phone and it stopped ringing abruptly.

It was Neha who was calling him anxiously as his alternate phone was switched off for a long time. He called Neha who was so happy for the call that the phone almost slipped from her grasp, but somehow she lunged and managed to hold it with her ring finger intermingled with her little finger. Seeing her smile, her mother knew it was Chetan on the other line. Chetan and his friends were known for their uncanny ways and Chetan was no exception. He was so fond of his beard that he had stopped shaving and would only trim his beard. "If I ask something, will you give me?" she asked with a childlike beam even as Chetan knew the question. "Apart from shaving, ask anything from me," he said looking at her photograph neatly fixed in the pink coloured photo frame near the bed. He went near, lifted the photograph, and kissed it.

"Anything, are you sure?"

"Yes anything. You are the boss," he replied as he kept the frame.

"Will you stop watching cricket for me?" she asked breaking the words to make it less palpable for Chetan to guess.

"Sweetie, I will shave and come tomorrow. Are you happy now?"

Neha started laughing even as her laughter could be easily heard on the other side.

"I would never force you to do anything. I still remember what you said when we were in Goa," she continued in a tone which almost had him recreate the memories of their last vacation in Goa. Chetan did not remember what he said, hence requested her to elucidate. "Mutual respect and space are the pillars of a pleasant relationship. I only want these from you, everything else will be taken care by time," she repeated his words.

While talking, Chetan checked the newspaper when something struck him and he confessed. "We should change the date of our marriage."

"What?" she almost shouted. Her mother who was watching her favourite cookery show reduced the volume and tried hard to listen. Sensing this, Neha moved towards the balcony of her third floor apartment.

"Tell me! Did I hear it correctly or were you talking to someone else?"

Chetan apologised and reminded her of the finals between India and Australia which was to be held in Mumbai itself.

"Grow up dude! I can't believe it. Do one thing, instead of marrying me, marry cricket."

"I was joking. I love you, love you, love you," he repeated until eternity.

Obviously not at all amused, she changed the topic to their honeymoon. They were to leave for Bangkok via a direct flight from Mumbai on Tuesday.

"I always wanted to go to Switzerland. I had this fascination for the country even as an eight-year-old," she confessed.

"We have to buy a flat soon, so I arranged things according to our budget. However, I will keep this in mind. Some other day, some other time," he kept his phone and excused himself.

"Hello, hello!"

He searched for a piece of paper but did not find any. He took the newspaper and tore a small part of it. He tore it again into small pieces and took the bigger chit, wrote something on it and squeezed it in his wallet.

Neha had screamed her heart out and eventually disconnected the call.

She checked the signal strength and even confirmed the battery status before dialling Chetan's other number. Chetan dialled in her number from the first mobile phone and got an engaged tone. His other phone rang and he picked it up promptly this time, as he was sure that Neha would call him.

"Where did you vanish?" she enquired in a polite manner.

"You told about your Switzerland dream, so I wrote the dream on a piece of paper and put it in my wallet."

"Hmm! I didn't get it."

"I wrote the message to be reminded about your dream as and when I check my wallet. That would make me work hard and would jog my memory about saving money," he said even as Neha giggled for a long time hearing the words.

"I love you, sweetheart," Neha whispered making sure no one could hear her.

Chetan did not hear and asked her to repeat.

"Nothing. I will have some food and call you in the night," she said while disconnecting the call.

Chetan had met Neha on Facebook after they passed out from school, even as Chetan went on to become an engineer while Neha pursued her Diploma in Business Management.

The wall clock made a small noise to signal the end of another hour. It was eight and Chetan called Ballu to check if he had arrived at the permit room.

Ballu had even started drinking as he waited for his friends. As instructed, Chetan went to the airport but Aman took an auto and reached Prem's, their favourite hangout since college days.

By nine, all the three were seen at the Prem's. Chetan looked at the tattoo on his right hand for a moment and emptied his glass on the small plant housed nearby. The waiter and the group of people sitting besides them in the last row felt it to be odd.

"Love and money can make a man do anything. God be with my friend," Ballu uttered.

"Shut up! I have to get up early tomorrow so I will smoke instead."

Ballu who was already drunk stood up and called the waiter. He called him by his name. "Mohan, come fast man," he said. The waiter politely introduced himself as Santosh.

"If you are Santosh then why do you come when we call Mohan?" Aman asked, keeping his glass down. The waiter had no answer and asked for the order instead.

Aman ordered some vodka and Ballu repeated his order for rum. Aman looked at Chetan to check if he wanted something but he declined taking a deep puff.

Ballu borrowed Chetan's lighter and lighted a cigarette. Aman pulled Chetan's T-shirt to check the tattoo but Chetan shrugged off.

"Lover boy, show us the sign of love."

Chetan felt intimidated and showed the tattoo, which read "Neha" written neatly in the colour blue. "Is it original?" Ballu asked while returning the lighter.

"It's permanent, like my feelings. She has my name printed on her right hand." After a brief silence, Chetan lighted a cigarette again.

Getting restless, Ballu stood up and shouted for Santosh this time.

The manager, who witnessed this hubbub, came forward and offered help.

"First tell me what your name is?" Ballu demanded.

"Mohan," the manager showed his batch which had his name and title printed on it.

"So Mohan, where were you when I called you?" Ballu asked repeating his words.

The manager knew that Ballu was quite drunk, so he apologised and took the order again.

He made sure that the order was on the table in the next five minutes.

"Who proposed? Did you propose?" Ballu tried whispering in Chetan's ears, but his loud voice could be heard even from the first room, which was around two metres away.

"No," he thundered.

"Then, did she propose?"

"No," he said.

"That's interesting. Neither you proposed nor she proposed so someone else proposed, right?" Ballu whispered and started laughing, but stopped unexpectedly and apologised.

Chetan looked at his watch and confirmed the time again on his mobile phone. It was quarter to eleven but the wall clock showed half past ten. Like many permit rooms and restaurants, even this had their wall clocks set at least fifteen minutes behind the standard time to provide a psychological excuse for the customers to drink more. Some permit rooms don't have any wall clocks displayed for analogous reasons.

Chetan gave his cigarette and excused himself. "Show your tattoo again. Can I get a small photograph of guitar painted on my body as well?" Ballu asked while pouring soda in his drink. Chetan smiled and going ahead, reminded them to be at the collector's office by half past ten. Aman stood up, hugged Chetan, and was soon followed by Ballu. "I love you. If you have any problem in life, you can call me. I will come. I am not drunk," Ballu hugged Chetan who looked embarrassed at the scene being created.

Ballu and Aman continued their drinking spree while discussing about Chetan's marriage. "Actually I don't like this court marriage. It does not have the charm of a celebration. I haven't seen any lavish marriages involving South Indians in spite of the wealth that these people possess," Ballu exclaimed. Their discussion came over to Neha now. Aman and Chetan worked in the same company and it was Aman's sister, who had introduced them. Incidentally, Chetan's girlfriend and Aman's sister both shared the same first name. She also had played cupid for them. Aman reminded Ballu about the nonsense that he uttered while he was drunk.

"I am not drunk," he said and called the waiter again.

"Do I look drunk?" he asked one of the waiters. He did not allow the waiter to speak and asked for his name first. He introduced himself as Santosh.

Ballu felt strange and stumbled. "How many people with the name Santosh work in this bar?" he asked and sat down in Chetan's chair.

"Three," came a quick answer.

"That's strange, very extraordinary actually. Please call all the people with the first name Santosh," Ballu said while putting his arm on the waiter's shoulders and smoked his cigarette, which formed a part of his other hand.

The waiter smiled and freed himself. "See, I told you I am not drunk. But you people just don't believe me. Ask Santosh." Ballu was about to fall when Aman pulled him over to their table and made sure Ballu did not order any more drinks.

On the other hand, Neha was busy reading her emails. She was feeling restless not to find the email that had the first love letter, which Chetan had written.

She called Chetan and pleaded to have the email forwarded. He confessed that he might have deleted and offered to write it again. Both laughed and Neha had to agree when told that he would be happy to write the letter all over again. Neha insisted on writing the same old letter.

Chetan promised that he would call in ten minutes once he finished writing the love letter. He took more than the time promised but came out with a masterpiece. Love can make a Shakespeare out of a clerk, they say. He typed the email in bold capital letters. He even drew some small butterflies in Microsoft Paint and pasted it in the email. Apart from cricket, he was so crazy for butterflies that he drew small butterflies in every love letter of his.

My Dear Neha,

When the heart is full of love, the eyes will show it. Just look into my eyes and you will know it. "Just one glance, and you make my day". Heart likes what it likes; there is no logic in it. Love is a triumph of dreams over reality and you are my only dream.

People come in your life for a reason or a season or lifetime. You be my reason spreading fragrance in this season and all my life.

If I get your smile, I don't need the flower. If I get your voice, I don't need the music and if I get you, I don't need the world. Don't place me in your eyes, I may fall as a tear, place me in your heart so that every heartbeat reminds you that someone, somewhere is always there for you. To tell you the truth and make this long letter short, I am head over heels crazy for you.

Love is in the air, love is here and there. Just turn around and see, you will always find me.

Yours, truly yours,

Chetan

He sent the email and called her to find her phone busy. Neha was so happy reading the email that she almost cried. Getting restless, he called again and succeeded this time around. It was almost one in the morning and Chetan proposed her again, reminding her of their first date. Happiness crept in and it showed on her face. Adjusting his pillow, he crawled to the other side of the bed to have a view of his girlfriend's photograph.

The small beep reminded her the time and she reminded Chetan that it's just about twelve hours left for their marriage. While discussing about their forthcoming Bangkok holiday, Neha interrupted Chetan as her mother screamed from the adjacent room. The anxiety was on both sides, evenly matched by Chetan who seemed restless and switched on his I-pod and tried listening to some hard metal songs, but romantic songs were the flavour of the day for the would-be bridegroom. Love had made the prosaic engineer into an uncanny sugary candy-man. In about ten minutes, the darkness in the room signalled that sleep prevailed over anxiety. He inadvertently could not change to his favourite dotted pyjamas and evidently slept in his jeans and white vests. The politically correct son of an equally politically correct father was at his wayward best. Chetan's beautifully cleaned room had a pair of shoes errantly kept on the dressing table, while the plastic holders which were specially made for keeping mobile phones were unoccupied. One of his washroom slippers was missing and its other twin was seen on the dressing table. The air conditioning was left unused, strange for the month of April even as the window, which was never seen open after nine at night was split wide open showcasing lunar beauty at its best.

Suddenly the gentleman responsible for the mayhem got up, looked at the wall clock above his bed and went towards the kitchen. It was half past two but the clock in fact showed quarter to three which was the case of all the clocks in his house which were kept a quarter ahead of actual time to create an illusion filled scarcity of time for accelerating things. Taking a water bottle from the refrigerator, he emptied it in no time. He threw the empty bottle on the kitchen ridge. Coming to his bedroom, a serene silence welcomed him but he was in no mood to waste any more of his precious and scarce sleep. He seemed unaware of the mess he created and fell on his bed. Sleep took over and all in all, he was in high spirits after a long time.

❖❖❖

8

Cricket Vs Marriage

During a match, people may catch the telecast even at the expense of love.

Like Ballu's guitar, cricket proved to be Chetan's bonafide, omnipresent and startling companion. A game thrives on cohorts and same was the case with cricket. Chetan was born on the day when the Indian team conquered world cricket and was deservingly crowned the world champions.

Chetan had a good collection of newspaper cuttings of many important events, which also included the newspaper, printed a day after India triumphed. 'A pinnacle of glory for a cricket crazy nation. India is crowned the new world champion,' were the headlines of the next day's newspaper, which remains, attached to the memories of millions of Indians all over the world.

His father passed his hobby of collecting paper cuttings to him.

Chetan was also passionate about trekking as was evident from the many trekking communities he shared on his Facebook profile.

To know a person, check his Facebook profile thoroughly, they say. The day of his marriage somehow collided with the finals of the ongoing triangular cricket tournament played in India. India managed to beat New Zealand to book a berth in the finals alongside Australia. Chetan could not believe the mess he created in his bedroom. He gave a confounded look when he realised that he had worn his jeans while sleeping last night. He made some important calls even as it was getting late. He cleaned his bedroom first and moved to the hall next. Checking his hairstyle in the bedroom's oval shaped mirror, he switched off his alternate mobile phone after typing a message. He thought of shaving but the dearth of time made him rush for a shower instead. After an hour or so, he looked dapper in his grey blazer. He patted his hair and made sure he looked exactly similar to the big photograph displayed in his hall. He had his breakfast, digested the sports page of the newspaper first, and then moved towards the initial pages. Many of us, especially men read the last page first as the last page is dedicated completely to sports. He reminded Ballu of the venue again and even dictated the address to him. Aman had called him earlier and as decided, he was going to pick him directly from their favourite saloon near Bandra. After checking his look again in the mirror, he switched off all the lights and the air conditioner. Locking his house, he rushed to his bedroom. He wanted to update his status on Facebook from single to married but managed to control his emotions. People flaunt their adulation when their admiration reaches its peak in the glory of love. He thought for a while and changed his status to 'engaged' as he still had some hours left to conclude his bachelorhood.

To check the latest updates of the match, he opened Facebook homepage again. Such was the vogue for cricket in the subcontinent that the 'live score' would be updated in a small window near the right hand corner of the Facebook homepage. 'Three hours for the match' was the status of the match and it had a link which could give us a possible player combination and some trivia about the match.

He really wanted to go for a shaven look today, but the paucity of time lead him to a trimmed beard instead. Hurriedly he switched off his laptop and after locking the main door rushed towards the small bus stand near his apartment. He boarded the wrong city bus in a typical movie style confusion when the two buses halted one after another at the crowded bus stop. The bus conductor stared at him and laughed when Chetan asked for a ticket.

"The bus doesn't go towards Bandra. You can get down at the next halt at Andheri circle," the conductor said as he gestured to the driver.

Chetan smiled and asked for a ticket till Andheri substation.

"No problem sir, get down and look for a bus going towards Bandra." Clothing initiates an impression and character holds it. When Chetan insisted, the conductor gave a ticket charging the minimum fare possible for the short journey.

Chetan stood out from the rest of the commuters in terms of his spruce dressing sense in the otherwise scruffy and crowded bus. Monday morning doubled up with the usual office going people and the rush of public made the bus look horde. The big, red, dusty bus halted a few feet ahead of the bus stop and the rush made sure Chetan could not take the money which was due. He smiled when he noticed this and waited for the next bus. This time, he enquired about the destination with some people who managed to keep their hands out of the several windows of the bus. He sat near one of the vacant seats available near the rear end. Some people gave him a suspicious look as he moved to the seat near the window. He took his ticket and while checking it, he realised that Mumbai bus tickets had inspirational and interesting thoughts printed on it.

'Love is the triumph of dreams over common sense,' read the line printed on the bottom of his ticket. He smiled and checked his pocket to find his earlier ticket.

He could not believe when he checked the lines mentioned on his earlier ticket. Apart from the colours, the lines were exactly similar on both the tickets. God has his own ways to make his presence felt in our lives. He sneered at the little boy who was constantly staring at him. His mother lifted him and took his seat while giving him seat next to the window. The boy had his water bottle in his hands and was neatly dressed in his school attire.

He turned and started his continuous gawk at Chetan. Feeling amused, he smiled at him and even waved his right hand to grab his attention.

The bus conductor shouted on some schoolchildren who were blocking his way and this reminded Chetan of his destination. He excused himself through the small crowd ahead of him. Even while going, the little kid was still staring ad-infinitum.

Chetan winked and waved at the kid as he got down. He was the first and the only person to get down from the wrong side of the bus. He thought he might be looking funny or something and for confirmation, he even checked his face in a mirror of a bike parked at the other side of the road. He checked his trousers and his suit as well. He had to walk a small distance to reach his favourite saloon. Mondays are different from other days, they say and this was evident by the number of people in the saloon. He took the best position available to view the television fitted on the wall near the washbasin. He moved forward and managed to change the channel to check any news of the final match. Most cricket matches are sold out a day before in the Indian subcontinent. Like millions, Chetan also did not understand the logic behind a final match being played on a Monday, as Sundays are the best and most convenient occasion for a cricket match, leave alone a final match and that too between India and Australia.

He looked out of the artistically made glass windows of the saloon and saw some police officers patrolling the area. The stadium hosting the final match was just a mile ahead. Cricket and Amitabh Bachhan are the only two obsessions that can halt a billion people simultaneously. This was evident from the number of people near the giant screen fitted specially for the finals near the saloon. Police officers were guarding the area, who managed the crowd even before the start of the match. The vacant seat reminded him of his turn and he whispered something to the man adjusting the grand seat. He got his already trimmed beard trimmed again. He wanted to share the news of his marriage with Salim, who was the owner of the saloon as well as his friend but managed to control his enthusiasm.

He made up his mind not to share the biggest secret of his life.

Even when he submitted his papers at the registrar's office a month ago, he and his would-be wife had decided to make the ceremony private.

"Is anything special today?" Salim asked as he ogled at Chetan. Chetan turned around to greet his friend after checking himself in the mirror, which covered the entire wall.

He thought for some more time and was about to confess when the newspaper heading reminded him of the finals today. "I and some of my friends have bought tickets to the finals and it's the first time that I will see a live match," Chetan exclaimed in excitement.

Somehow, his friend was not ready to digest the fact that a man could watch a match dressed in a blazer. Chetan felt he could not hold much and asked him to come with him. Salim lighted a cigarette as they sat on the bench just outside the saloon. He asked his employees who were sitting on the bench to start cleaning the floor inside.

Salim asked the same question again putting his right hand over his friend's shoulder.

"I will marry my girlfriend today," Chetan said in a soft voice as he tried to avoid the smoke let out by the cigarette. Salim was so happy that he hugged his friend and apologised for the smoke, which was seen all around them. Seeing the nervousness on Chetan's face, he had already sensed trouble and talking with Salim decamped his anxiety.

"Is it an inter-religion or an inter-caste affair?" offering his cigarette, he asked. Chetan thought for a moment and declined.

Salim could not understand if the answer was related to the question he asked or for the cigarette. "We belong to the same religion, separated only by languages," Chetan sighed.

"You are well settled and a level headed person, so I don't think it would have been a big problem for you to impress her parents," Salim said, adjusting the bench to have a more comfortable position.

"The script is already written, it's just the drama which is pending. I haven't even informed my parents as they are against this match. My sister informed that they are looking for a suitable South Indian match for me." Chetan said looking at his watch. He took a cigarette from Salim's cigarette case lying on the bench, lighted it and suddenly threw it away.

"Not today," he shouted as he waited for a response from his friend.

"Yes, that's true. Smoking is injurious to health," Salim said and started laughing. Chetan joined him to laugh their hearts out.

Cigarette had started their friendship. Both shared the same brand of cigarette and even had the same brand of lighters. Most smokers are quite particular about their brands and go to any extent to maintain their brand loyalty.

They talked for some more time as Salim wished him luck and even offered his phone number in case of an emergency.

Aman honked as he saw Chetan and waved the bouquet he had bought.

Chetan had specially ordered a combination of white lilies and red roses for his bride. Salim waved at Aman and hugged Chetan wishing him luck.

It was a bright Monday morning and Chetan managed an extended leave for another two weeks in spite of being on leave for most of the month.

Aman was not as lucky as him and managed only a day off while Ballu never had any problems when it came to taking an off. He used to prepare for musical fests, television programmes and all other music related events all year round. He managed something, which very few of us could boast of. He was the one who submitted documents, visited lawyers on Chetan's behalf as he had all the time in the world. Aman gave the bouquet and Chetan kept it on the rear seat of the car. "Cheer up dude; it's the biggest day of your life," Aman said looking at his tensed friend. Chetan smiled as he slipped his hand through his pocket to open his wallet and glanced at his girlfriend's picture neatly squeezed through the two covers. "Don't mind, can I ask you a question?" Aman asked as he tried hard to concentrate on his driving. "Ask two!" a standard, quick reply came.

"If you have agreed, Neha and his parents have agreed then why are we opting for a court marriage. If you love someone, flaunt it," Aman exclaimed as he slowed down near the turn.

"I am happy that they have agreed but somehow I did not want to go for an extravagant wedding without my parents involved in it," Chetan replied, staring at the traffic signal, which proudly flaunted drivers' least favourite colour, similar to the colour of their car. The traffic signal gave an opportunity to check his documents.

Chetan crosschecked each document and even confirmed the marks of stamp on it. Marriage is a meticulous affair when it comes to documents even with the consent of the people involved. Chetan dialled Neha's phone number, which gave an engaged tone. "She might be busy with her friends," he told himself. The colour green is a welcome sight for car drivers and this was evident on the faces of the drivers. The match and the swarm of people gathered near the giant screens made the scene worse in terms of traffic. It was still a couple of hours for the match and people had bought snacks and were enjoying their stay on all sides of the giant screen. They still had to pick Aman's sister from her boutique next to railway station.

They did not have to wait for long as she had managed to walk till the first turn. More than the time, she was excited that she knew the bridegroom as well as the bride. When it comes to marriages in India, people are divided into two distinct categories as in people from the groom's side and people from the bride's side.

Chetan greeted her and opened the rear door. She kept the bouquet and the transparent carry bag neatly as she made some space for her on the already cramped seat. As Aman's sister and Neha shared the same name, she always reminded Chetan of his 'would-be' wife. Chetan managed to calm his nervousness as soon as he saw Neha. Such is the magic of love that a strange range of emotions erupt even when we see something which is remotely related to our loved ones.

Chetan asked his friend to rush as he peeped out to check the traffic on the road. Aman smiled on Chetan's anxiety and asked, "Are you nervous?"

"Me? I am more nervous about the fact that we don't have much time. We have our turn exactly at twelve after the witness and other procedures start at half past ten."

Aman laughed as he was sure that the event would not even last an hour after the prescribed time. Aman's sister who was busy on her cell phone managed a moment and agreed with her brother.

"You did not wear your trouser suit?" enquired Chetan as he saw his friends outfit.

"I wore simple clothes so that people could identify the bridegroom."

Both laughed their hearts out as Aman managed to look smart and dapper even in his simple combination of white shirt and black trousers.

Ballu managed to reach the scene first even ahead of the bride and her troupe.

Neha was still on the phone even as Chetan had called twice in between.

"India will lose today, I feel," Chetan admitted as he checked the headlines on the local newspaper kept near his seat. "Yes, India would have fancied their chances had it been New Zealand instead of Australia. Let the better team win," Aman pitched in. Aman was not known to follow traffic signals but managed to do so when Chetan was around. Aman and Ballu hated him for coaxing them into following traffic signals. At last, they managed to be at the collector's office on time. The collector's office, which was also called as the registrar's office, was in the heart of the city and still managed not to be swarmed by people. How many of us know the reason for having a collector's office or how many of us have visited it ever? Answer to this question gives the reason for the vast portion of parking space still available in the parking lot of the collector's office. Ballu whistled seeing his friends enter the parking area. Ballu had brought a couple of friends along with him, one of whom was a professional photographer. Ballu was seen in formal clothes after a very long time. He insisted that it was a big day for him as well when Aman teased him on his dressing sense.

"Chetan is my younger brother," Ballu said as he embraced Chetan.

"You are younger to me by two months.'

"Okay. I am sorry. Chetan is my older brother," Ballu defended his stand. He asked his photographer friend to start the proceedings by clicking some pictures of the three friends. Neha was not amused by this and remained busy on her cell phone. Even while having their pictures clicked, they discussed about the forthcoming match. Ballu was ready to bet a thousand bucks on India as he fancied an upset Indian win.

The happy-go-lucky Ballu was known for losing more bets than all of his friends combined. "If India wins, you will get married in the next six months," Chetan said while checking something on his cell phone. "Shut up! Whatever happens, I am not going to get married for the next five years." Everyone including the photographer started to laugh after hearing the timeframe in the announcement. "You still have ten years to mature, so you could wait a bit longer," Aman said as he clapped to grab the attention of the photographer.

As soon as they saw Neha and her family, they stopped and rushed to greet them.

Neha looked fabulous in her dark green sari, while her mother sported the sparsely embroidered maroon coloured sari. Green was the flavour of the day as most of the women present there had something or the other in the colour green. The bride was wrapped from head to toe in the colour green along with green coloured bangles and sandals.

The warmth of togetherness could be smelled in the air. It was more like a backdrop of an Indian movie being shot. The word 'crowd' which is synonymous with government offices was not to be seen at the registrar's office and apart from Ballu, Chetan and Neha's father everyone was here for the first time. The registrar's office was a popular place when it came to giving directions but not many have a reason to go past the gate of the office.

Neha's brother wore a blazer, which matched Chetan's clothing in terms of the colour combination.

In spite of some repeated caveats by Chetan to keep the occasion a private affair, Neha's parents managed a small crowd of relatives, which even included some of her father's colleagues. Chetan felt a little sad as it reminded him of his family.

His sister did not even bother to call him since yesterday. Neha's brother Nilesh hugged his 'would-be' brother-in-law and introduced him to his relatives. One of his aunts even commented that he looked more like a film star than a software engineer. Chetan managed a persuasive smile as Neha's father welcomed him.

Exactly at half past ten, they entered the registrar's office but they were asked to wait outside to avoid any sort of interruption to a small meeting going on inside. "I know these people. Our time would come after the lunch as I have checked with a friend of mine who works here," Neha's father explained.

Everyone agreed when Ballu asked if they would be interested in joining him to the office canteen. The registrar's office canteen was well kept compared to the government standards. The clean environment hinted the scarcity of people visiting the office or the canteen in general. Ballu asked an elderly waiter to have three tables joined to accommodate everyone. Nilesh introduced himself first and later introduced everyone to his brother-in-law and vice-versa.

"Let the couple sit together," Ballu teased his friend while sipping his tea.

Even after all kinds of adjustment, Chetan was sitting in the corner near the shutter while Neha managed a seat besides her uncle, towards the other corner.

Chetan managed to type a message without being noticed and sent it to Neha via his cell phone. 'I really wanted to shave today, but didn't manage the time for it,' it read.

Neha smiled at him and blushed when her mother caught her innocent emotions. Chetan was happy to find a television in the canteen. The match was just about to start.

"India won the toss and elected to bat," shouted someone from the counter.

Nilesh excused himself to check the proceedings in the office as most of the people present there discussed the match. Most favoured an easy Australian win but wanted India to give a tough fight. The registrar was busy solemnising a marriage ceremony when Nilesh enquired about the lunch hours and got to know about the floating concept prevalent in government offices. There were fixed timings for everything as displayed on the blackboard near the entrance, but the timings could be extended or stretched depending upon the amount of bribe involved or the influence which some people manage. The peon sporting a complete khaki uniform asked him to meet the assistant registrar if they wanted to speed up the proceedings.

Nilesh was happy to know the more convenient options and rushed to the canteen. Chetan who was not very happy about the crowd that his in-laws had created, forged a smile on his face. When it came to Chetan, it was very difficult even for his friends to distinguish his emotions from his facial expressions.

However happy he might act, it was Ballu who managed to catch his counterfeit emotions, which Chetan never admitted. At around half past twelve, the registrar called the bride and the bridegroom to his office. The registrar's office had a provision of a makeup room. The women were the first to utilise the facility followed by the men. Ballu tried to find Chetan who had switched off his mobile phone. When he came to know that even Neha was missing, he was sure that the couple had managed some privacy in the dressing room. "I am hundred percent sure that he is with her in the room," Ballu whispered. "Shut up," shouted Aman as he pulled his mobile out and dialled Chetan's number. Ballu knocked at the door even as the crowd was getting impatient.

"Give me a minute please," Neha shouted even as the shout was reduced to a mere whisper to the people standing near the door.

"Can't he wait till the honeymoon?" Ballu asked even as Neha's parents felt embarrassed and knocked the door again. After a brief silence, Neha came out first followed by Chetan, both of them smiling like cherry cats after a brief flush of romantic moments.

Strangely, no one dared to ask them about the issue and rushed towards the assistant registrar.

The assistant registrar asked Chetan to submit all the documents with the clerk.

“Also please switch off all your cell phones and maintain the decorum of this office,” the registrar screamed when he saw Ballu talking on his phone.

Somehow, the office looked teeming with people who specially came for the occasion. Even if it were a court marriage, the scene reminded many of the so-called ‘big fat Indian wedding’, which was the source of many Indian movies. Ballu and Aman were to sign as witnesses so they were asked to visit the duty office with their original driving license or their PAN card for identification. Following the instructions of the registrar, they went into the duty room but were asked to come from the other side as this side is closed after half past twelve. They were happy to see no one in the queue.

Ballu laughed when the clerk asked for his PAN card. “I am unemployed by choice so no PAN card for me. I can show my driving license instead,” Ballu said as he took out his wallet. He just could not find his driving license and emptied the wallet on the ground to confirm. Aman sensed an opportunity and sneaked ahead and he showed both the documents to the person at the counter who took a Xerox of the documents as a proof.

Ballu was still searching for his driving license. “I have donated my eyes. Can I show my donation card as it has all the information?” Ballu asked showing a red coloured card.

The clerk made his point clear in a stern voice this time.

Aman called his sister and she showed her documents instead of him. The clerk tore Ballu’s form and made Neha fill a new form.

It was almost one pm and the registrar had a word with his assistant and requested everyone to be present after the lunch, exactly at two.

Nilesh and his father pleaded to have the ceremony squeezed before the lunch, but the registrar pointed towards a small wooden board, which displayed the lunch hours. Nilesh checked the big clock on the wall, which exhibited the current time. They even confirmed the time by checking the time on their wristwatches. Chetan and Neha were fine with the decision. "The bride and her groom are fine so we will meet exactly at two."

The relatives looked irritated but the bride's father managed to calm them down.

This time everyone adjusted to have the bride and the groom sit next to each other.

Chetan exchanged his place on the wooden bench with Neha to have a better view of the cricket match, which was being aired on the television fitted on the other side of the wall. Sensing the attention that they had managed, they were neither talking nor exchanging glances, which they were known for. Neha in the meanwhile adjusted her green coloured heavily embroidered sari as she removed a bangle from her right hand and put into her left hand instead.

A five star hotel was booked for lunch after the marriage ceremony so no one bothered to eat much at the office canteen. Ballu had his tea again. Neha's father gave an eerie look and asked, "How many cups of tea do you manage?"

"Around four which may extend to six or seven if I am practising music."

Neha's father was happy to find someone who shared the same passion, as he was known to imbibe more than ten cups of tea everyday.

Ballu introduced himself as an upcoming musician and Mr Deshpande patted his back wishing him luck when he heard the musician part of his introduction. Aman went and requested the waiter to increase the volume of the television and the waiter amplified it immediately. Chetan had made plans of watching the match after the marriage but the delay had dented his hopes of watching his favourite stars bat. He wanted India to bat second as that might give him an opportunity to enjoy the match in his style.

Like most Indians, Chetan was more interested in watching India bat instead of seeing them bowl. The small black and white TV was surrounded by onlookers who made it difficult for people seated on the benches and chairs to have a view at it.

It was strange that no one had complained about the size of the television or the fact that it did not illustrate any colours other than the plain black and white. Just as the first ball of the match was bowled, Nilesh rushed into the canteen. He came in exactly at the stroke of two with a message from the assistant registrar. Chetan managed to see some more balls being bowled but was requested to be at the office as soon as possible.

Therefore, by half past two after almost everyone had their turns of using the makeup room again. People were ready for the ceremony but the news of India struggling with their batting in the initial part of the match crept in and contaminated the general mood. Neha could not believe her ears when Chetan mentioned his displeasure of missing an opportunity to see the match live in a stadium.

Aman and his sister signed the necessary paper work followed by the bride and her groom. As they were marrying according to the Hindu marriage act, the registrar read some verses from the Bhagwad Gita, the sacred book of the Hindus.

The bride's father opened the gift-wrap and presented the rings to the bride and the bridegroom. The diamond-studded rings sparkled as people took their mobile phones out and started clicking pictures even before the rings were exchanged.

Chetan's ring had many small blue coloured diamonds fitted in the gold ring while Neha's ring was a smaller version with less diamonds embedded on it. As per the instructions of the registrar, Chetan and Neha exchanged their rings while the giggles continued amongst the people surrounding them. The official photographer clicked some pictures from different angles followed by some pictures taken by Ballu's friend. Chetan smiled when the couple received a round of applause by the small crowd gathered in the room after the registrar announced them husband and wife. "India have managed a score of hundred at the loss of six wickets," shouted someone from the crowd. "Oh my god!" the registrar said expressing his disbelief on hearing Indian team's pathetic display yet again. Nilesh confirmed the score and a bout of silence followed as if they were mourning the loss of wickets. "I had predicted that India would lose," Chetan said, as he defended his stand. "The match is not over yet. Cricket and life are almost similar. Anything and everything can happen within a short period of time," Neha's father chipped in.

The women who were turned into a group of mute spectators insisted to have the ceremony completed. "It's our daughter's marriage. I can't believe that you people are more interested in the fruitless game of cricket," yelled the bride's mother and all the women shouted in a rare display of unity. "Do you get something if India wins?" she asked. The registrar came into his groove, completed the final round of the ceremony, and breathed a sigh of relief.

After the ceremony, the couple had to click innumerable pictures with all possible combinations of relatives and friends. By some means, Chetan managed a smile in every photograph they clicked. Smiles, gifts, hugs and wishes followed.

The couple who managed to look strikingly stunning till now showed their first round of weariness when they were asked to provide their thumbprints on some documents. Unable to catch the match, Chetan felt irritated but managed to look calm and composed even as Ballu and some of Neha's relatives ran to the canteen to check the score.

Neha's father gave directions to find the famous Intercontinental Hotel near Worli. On Aman's insistence, Chetan and Neha were the first to move in his luxurious red car. Everyone gathered near the hotel's lobby and moved to the garden area where the lunch was to be served. The lobby looked similar to a cruise party with the decoration and well-mannered staff who took pleasure in welcoming the guests.

Before the food arrived, Ballu and Neha's father had their share of tea. Chetan who never found pleasure in being the centre of attraction was seen enjoying the dinner and even managed to pull off some jokes.

Ballu was the only one who opted for non-vegetarian food as against the western style vegetarian delicacies ordered specially by the bride. "Change the status from single to married on your Facebook profile." Everyone erupted in rounds of laughter on hearing this.

After the dinner, almost everyone thanked Mr and Mrs Deshpande and Chetan in turn thanked Ballu and Aman for their support. Neha called Chetan aside to discuss something, which made her mother feel suspicious. Neha took him to the other side of the lobby near the pillar.

"What happened?" Chetan asked.

"If you don't mind, I want to be with my parents today and will directly meet you at the airport tomorrow at three," she asked fondling with Chetan's tie.

Chetan's smile made way for his no-nonsense expression on his face. "That's fine. Take your time but make sure you are at the airport by half past three. We won't be able to go as husband and wife for the trip, as the certificate would come by post later in the week," he explained, keeping an eye on his mother-in-law who was trying her best to hear their conversation. In fact, Chetan was happy that he could catch the rest of the match without being disturbed.

Neha smiled and even explained this to her parents. Chetan had promised that he would allow her to use her last name even after marriage. Even if Chetan agreed to allow her to spend the day with her parents, he was not sure as to how would he cope with his loneliness later in the day after the match would be over? Neha and her parents left after the hectic day along with their relatives. Neha looked cheerful, thanked her parents for being supportive, and cursed the ongoing cricket match.

"Chetan is a man of honour. I appreciate your choice," her father said.

Neha was not sure as to what her father was talking about, but still nodded her head as she considered Chetan as her pride.

"He paid the bill for the lunch and never asked anything from us."

Neha was happy to hear the comment about Chetan and thanked him for being so wonderful. Meanwhile Ballu thanked his friends who doubled up as photographers as well and went along with his college friends.

❖❖❖

9

The Match Continues

On its day, a cricket match seems colossal when compared to our lives.

People flooded the giant screens placed especially for the cricket match. The traffic came to a standstill due to the giant screens and the crowd it generated. Chetan tried his best to check the score but missed it as replays were being shown on the giant screens. He reached his house along with his friends in the evening after dropping Aman's sister at her friend's house.

Chetan thought of informing his relatives in Mumbai, but avoided it on Aman's insistence. The first thing he did was to turn on his television set to catch the live telecast of the match. India played as expected and their innings folded with only one-ninety one runs on the board. "These idiots couldn't even play the full quota of their overs. They were bundled out within forty-five overs. Does anyone want to bet?" Aman enquired while changing the channel as the match had halted for the innings break.

Ballu thought for a while and grabbed the calculator kept near the table lamp and tried some permutations and combinations even as Chetan excused himself for some time.

"India can win. How much do you want to bet?"

"Let's go for the losers pay option. If India wins, I will pay for our dinner and drinks and you do the same if Australia wins," Aman said as he made his point clear while settling himself on the royal black sofa.

Hearing the word 'losers pay', Ballu tried some more calculations utilising everything he could grab, from the calculator to his fingers and so on.

During their college days, Ballu was known to have lost most bets while playing snooker through the losers pay option. Confirming his calculation, he took the bet but insisted on paying only for the dinner and not the drinks.

"Come on man, you have a job. I am unemployed; I have to manage the whole month."

Aman gave an awkward smile trying to remember the last time when Ballu had paid for the drinks. When Ballu insisted, Aman agreed for the gamble, as he was sure that India would never be able to defend such a modest total.

Ballu scrolled around for the match, which started a bit late without any specific reasons being given. Chetan changed into his favourite pyjamas and made himself comfortable, sitting on the white marble floor.

"Take a comfortable seat. Consider it as your house," Ballu joked seeing his friend sitting on the floor.

"So our hero will spend the first night of his marriage alone."

Chetan smiled and mentioned that it was he who insisted that Neha should spend some more time with her parents. "So what's the plan?" asked Aman checking his watch.

It was half past six and they had ample time. Chetan could not control his laughter when Aman told him about the bet. Ballu insisted that India had a chance, which brought some more smiles on his friends' face.

"It's a pity that we are watching the cricket match on TV when it's being played in the same city, just some miles away."

"Thank god we are at least watching the match for I thought we might miss it because of my marriage ceremony," Chetan replied, giving Ballu a playful clap.

In the meantime, Australians were going strength to strength without losing a wicket and had a good opening stand.

Getting bored of seeing his team perform badly, Ballu stood up, yawned, and suddenly out of the blue, the first Australian wicket fell via a brilliant catch by Sachin Tendulkar. Ballu jumped and tried touching the hanging lights in ecstasy.

Aman explained that Australia needed only one-twenty runs in twenty-five overs with nine wickets in hand which seemed more like a run of the mill task as per Australian standards.

Indian spinners were faring better than their fast bowler counterparts.

After the drinks break, Australians managed not to lose any more wickets and were fine even if they did not make any runs as they were ahead of the asking rate by miles. Ballu stood up as he remembered the earlier Australian dismissal but without any luck this time. "Try yawning to get a wicket," Aman insisted as he moved closer to the television. Ballu smiled and yawned, and all of a sudden, the Australian captain was declared out, leg before wicket. Ballu danced in joy pulling his shirt and jumping in elation.

Some more Australian wickets fell as they were unable to read the 'line and length' of the Indian spinners. In the next two hours, the equation titled slightly towards the Indian side. Australians now required sixteen runs from four overs with two wickets in hand. Ballu seemed overjoyed and reminded his friend about the bet every now and then.

Chetan made some fruit juice and offered it to his friends to ease out the tension.

"See what we missed. Had it not been for my marriage, we could have easily booked tickets and watched the match live at the Wankhede stadium," Chetan said as he sipped some juice.

"When I applied for a leave, TT uncle was certain that I opted for a leave just for the match," Aman replied stretching his arms in exhaustion.

Brett Lee pulled a mighty six over the head of the fielder stationed at the long on.

The umpire signaled a no ball even as the Indian skipper and the bowler were seen arguing with the umpire.

"Six of a no ball! India has lost it. Ballu, be ready to pay the bill."

Ballu tried standing up, yawning and jumping but it just did not work. As he sat down, a cruel mix up had both the batsman at the strikers end and the ninth wicket fell, increasing the excitement of the match. Three runs were required of the last over with a wicket in hand. The match still could swing in anyone's way. That's the irony of the game, which is almost similar to life where we could see its generosity for a moment and the very next instant we are left to face the vindictiveness which it offers.

Ballu went to the washroom between the advertisements.

The Indian contingent tossed the ball to their most trusted lieutenant, the veteran Anil Kumble. They were taking their own sweet time adjusting the field.

Ballu entered the living room and looked at Aman who gave a grave look unlike sometime ago when he made fun of the Indian team and

Ballu in particular. Kumble swirled a full toss, which was handled stylishly by the batsman but brilliantly saved by Yuvraj Singh at point, which stopped the tail-enders from taking a single.

Kumble asked Yuvraj to move towards the backward gully instead of fielding at point. It seemed that the ball had slipped and it was not as per his manoeuvre.

"The old man has gone mad. There is no fielder at point area. I can't believe it," Aman said as he showed his discontentment at Kumble's decision. Kumble changed his stance to bowl from round the stumps. He flighted the ball even as the batsman tried to clear the fence and was bowled while doing so. The entire stadium erupted in ecstasy even as Chetan missed Neha's call as his cell phone was lying in the bedroom.

India had defeated Australia by two runs.

Ballu danced in joy and hugged his friends. Aman and Chetan were happy and celebrated by gulping the fruit juice.

"I knew India would win. Cricket is a game of glorious uncertainties," Ballu said as he increased the volume of the television.

Chetan excused himself and checked his cell phone to see three missed calls from his wife's number. He called her and apologised even before she could speak anything.

"That's fine, sweetheart."

"I was tired, so slept for some time," he insisted.

Neha laughed on hearing this and asked the score of the match.

"I will have to check. I am in the bedroom now."

"India lost the match. I just saw it on television. I am so happy that India has lost," she shouted with excitement.

Chetan knew his wife was teasing him, but agreed and even cursed the Indian cricket team. Ballu came dancing to the bedroom but moved out seeing his friend busy on the phone.

"Missing you like hell, sweetie."

"Same here. Darling, it's so annoying not to be with you," she whispered.

"Shall I come there or do you want to come here?"

Neha blushed as Chetan could hear her giggling even through the phone.

Chetan told her about the scenic beauty and shopping malls of Bangkok and Pattaya rekindling the memories of his last year's visit to Thailand.

"Have you packed your stuff?" he asked kicking something with his leg.

"I have to buy some more clothes tomorrow. Should we go for a round of shopping tomorrow morning?"

Chetan thought for a while and agreed looking out of his balcony. It was dark outside but life was still busy in the lights.

"What's the plan for tonight?" she asked checking the time.

"We will go for dinner in some time and Aman will pay as he had betted against India and lost."

Neha smiled and said, "I knew you were watching the match and that was the reason you didn't pick my call. Right?"

"No, I did not watch the match. I just checked a message from him."

"You can't even lie properly."

"Leave all that. What are you wearing now?" he asked as he entered his bedroom.

"Shut up! Go to hell. Men will be men."

"I mean, it's quite cold out here so wanted to know if you are wearing your pullover or not. I care for you, baby."

Neha blushed and blew a kiss for him.

They talked for some more time as Aman and Ballu were getting bored in the living room waiting for the post match presentation. Aman was happy about the result of the match, as he knew Ballu would never pay the bill even if he had lost the bet.

"Should we change today's location of the party?" Ballu asked scratching his beard.

"Ask Chetan. It's his day today," Aman replied switching off the television.

"What? You lost, so you will have to pay for the dinner and the drinks."

"Drinks! Are you crazy? The bet was only about the dinner."

Ballu switched on the television as the presentation ceremony was being aired.

"Do you want to bet on who will get the man of the match?" Ballu asked, expecting some negativity.

"Yes, I think Anil Kumble would be the man of the match." Aman said.

"Even I think that way. We will bet with Chetan instead."

Just as they took his name, Chetan came into the living room.

"Where are we heading guys?" he asked arranging the bookshelf.

"Let's go to Prem's," Aman insisted.

"On the last day of my bachelorhood, I went to Prem's and you want me to go to the very same location on the first day of my marriage."

"As Aman will pay, let's go to a disco or else should we try a night club?" Ballu said playing with the car keys.

"It's cold outside, so if you people want to change or want any sweaters, you can have mine," Chetan said as he checked his pullover. Ballu tried all the pullovers but did not like any and decided against the idea. “It’s quite warm now, but it really gets cold after twelve,” Aman insisted as he took a green coloured jersey along with him.

In the meanwhile, Anil Kumble was awarded the man of the match award for his fine performance with the ball.

Aman informed his sister that he would be late and gave her strict instructions to be at her friend’s place until he picked her up from there. Ballu called her mother who requested him to be at home by eleven pm. As instructed by Chetan, Ballu did not even tell his parents about Chetan’s marriage. Ballu insisted on driving the car and Aman had to agree considering Ballu’s naïve face. Even during the journey, they were not sure about their destination. After a brief discussion, which included scrutinising some more restaurants, they reached Prem’s by nine, failing to reach any unanimous decision.

Ballu who did not have a proper driving license for four wheelers managed to take them safely. Unfortunately, a group of collegians already had taken their favourite place near the second last bench. They adjusted themselves near the other side of the permit room. Chetan ordered beer for everyone. Aman who avoided drinking beer on most occasions agreed just for the sake of his friend.

Sounds of cheers were heard after the drinks were served. “Cheers to Chetan and Neha for their guts to go for a love marriage,” Ballu exclaimed while sipping some beer. The best part was that everything ended in a smooth way even when the list of the people to be invited for the extremely private ceremony swelled. More than anything, Chetan did not want his relatives in Mumbai to know about the wedding.

Ballu had a round of regular rum for he believed that you are not drunk until you consume rum. Ballu who had an army background found it easier than others to coagulate with rum. “Vodka is for style, whiskey is for frustrated people, beer is for kids and rum is for men,” he declared when he was requested to go for a substitute to rum, some months ago in one of their friends’ bachelor party. The wacky part seen in millions of frustrated people is their loyalty towards useless things and their sudden disbarment of the same brand when times upturn. As they take pride in everything, men are known to contradict their own words in the later half of their lives.

Ballu was out of sorts after a few drinks and was known to create nuisance irrespective of the place. He took the beer bottle and emptied it on the money plant kept neatly near the end of the table. When asked for a reason, he proudly defended his stance shouting, "We are men."

Chetan kept himself busy talking with someone on his cell phone and Aman had to bear all the aerobatics, which his friend tried with the glasses, and the ceramics placed on the table. It was usual for them to pay for a glass or two, which Ballu would smash to smithereens when drunk.

"You know what will Chetan do on the first night of his marriage?"

Aman turned around as he lighted a cigarette.

"You are a spoilsport," Ballu yelled, as he made sure Aman was listening to him.

"What?" Aman asked in a rather irrational tone making sure he showed his annoyance.

"Nothing! Today is his first night after marriage and he is with us."

Aman tried his best to subdue his laughter but had to smile on hearing this.

"Do you know what Chetan will do on his second night?"

Aman lighted a cigarette and asked, "What?"

"Nothing as he would be flying tomorrow."

Nowadays, his mean yet witty side called Coyote would only pop out either when he would be drunk or when he would be alone.

Chetan joined them and after a round of drinks they debated about the famous Shiney Ahuja's rape case floated by his maid.

Ballu liked debates as debates brought open the philosopher 'Coyote' in him who was known for hitting sixes rather than taking singles.

"Every man is a Shiney Ahuja, it's just that he got caught," Ballu shouted.

Such was the elation of the comment that people sitting on other tables also burst out laughing. The word "cheers" echoed in unity amongst everyone around.

Chetan felt irritated and excused himself to the small airy balcony of the restaurant. Layers and layers of smoke were seen through the balcony even though it was well aerated. Chetan talked for some time with his sister about the day's proceedings and she promised that she would be present for the reception later in the week. Even taking to her made him feel at ease.

Ballu gulped his drink and declared, "I will pay the bill today."

"Sure?"

"I have booked a new sports bike. Actually my maternal uncle will gift me a brand new sports bike so I will pay the bill."

"Okay. We don't have any problems. Why don't you pay for the people who cheered for your silly jokes as well?" Aman suggested after the public gave a huge uproar.

"Good Idea. I will pay for everyone," Ballu said as he poured some soda in his glass.

Another round of applause followed as people rushed for giving orders and cheered Ballu. Feeling a bit embarrassed, Chetan decided to leave and was flanked by Aman. Feeling their absence, Ballu joined them as he insisted on paying, so made his way to the bill counter.

"You could have paid from your table itself," the manager at the counter hummed.

"I will pay with my card, so came here for security reasons," Aman said taking his credit card out.

Ballu was angry as he heard this and pushed his friends aside and in the tussle fell down. One of the waiters checked and confirmed that the stout man was unconscious. Apart from Aman and Chetan, everyone else stood and came forward to help him. Aman and Chetan maintained a calm composure even as people lifted Ballu and put him on a couple of chairs, as a single chair was just not enough to hold him. The manager sprinkled some water on his face and put an onion slice near his nasal opening, but Ballu was in no mood to regain consciousness.

Aman took Ballu's wallet out to confirm something. He checked the wallet thoroughly and laughed his heart out. Chetan took the wallet and put it back to its original place. He paid the bill to celebrate his marriage even as Ballu was still unconscious. People helped them to clutch Ballu to their car.

Chetan took a sharp left turn from the magnificent display of fountains near the Railway Station and reached his apartment instead.

Ballu regained his senses and confirmed the status of the match.

"What match?"

"India won it some hours ago."

"You idiot, you wanted to pay the bill and I checked your wallet to find only eleven rupees in it," yelled Aman who was angry on his public display of repercussions of alcohol consumption.

"What! I had more than three thousand rupees in my purse. Where is my money?" Ballu said, showing his desperation by throwing the keys. Aman burst out laughing and made himself comfortable on the small chair near the bed. Ballu pulled out his wallet and managed to pull out some neatly folded notes from it.

Aman wore a stunned look when he checked Ballu's old, half-torn wallet even as Chetan brought some water for his friends. "I keep some cash for emergency purposes in the small gap in my wallet."

Chetan smiled and picked up some clothes lying on the floor, which Ballu had thrown on the floor.

"You people carry on. I have to go for a bout of shopping with Neha tomorrow morning. Also, I have to pack everything and catch the flight in the afternoon."

Suddenly Ballu got up from the bed and started searching for something frenetically. He realised that he had parked his bike at the registrar's office. "Can you drop me to the registrar's office? Ballu requested.

"Now?" Chetan asked as he folded the clothes before keeping them neatly in the steel cupboard near the bed.

"The office might be closed now. I will drop you home and you can collect the bike tomorrow," Aman replied after a brief pause.

"I don't even have the parking coupon and will have to fight with the watchman tomorrow."

After his friends left, Chetan called up his wife for a brief session of an extremely personal dialogue.

Next day, after shopping endlessly, the couple had their first fight when Chetan had to shell out his money to pay the bill.

"What! I can't believe it. Eleven thousand rupees for this piece."

Realising his folly, he apologised keeping in mind the thought of their honeymoon.

With everything all set, they flew for Bangkok later in the day.

Even Aman had received the weird Facebook friend request. Aman accepted the friend request and send out a message asking for a proper introduction. Ballu had reminded him about the mysterious person who knew almost everything about them. In the meantime, Ballu received a reply for his message, which was more in the format of a puzzle. It ended with A, B, C and D for Dev.

As soon as he read the message, Ballu could not control his happiness and shouted. "Yes, yes, yes."

His mother came in to check after hearing the noise and found Ballu standing on his bed. He smiled as he saw his mother and sat down comfortably.

"Nothing as such, India won the match yesterday so was happy about it."

His mother was fed up with the antics of her son. After Ballu's sister's marriage, the house wore a deserted look and this was a major reason Ballu was getting out of hand, as he was very close with his sister.

After making sure his mother was nowhere around, he locked the door from inside and made himself comfortable in his bed. He opened the window as he switched off the tube light which was making him uncomfortable.

He checked the message again and rushed to open his suitcase from the cupboard.

He kept the guitar near the table for a moment as he opened the suitcase to spill out everything that was inside it. After a frantic search, he found a small red coloured book.

He kept the suitcase back and locked the cupboard, kissing the small book.

The small half-torn book was his 'slam book' and he started reading it as he sat on the bed with folded legs.

It was his dearest friend Dev, the eccentric genius who was known for his stirring ideas. Dev had sent him a message on his Facebook profile. Dev had a Facebook account earlier and like many Asians deleted it to make a new account. 'A, B for Ballu, C and D'... Ballu replied to the message.

He was so happy that he dialled Chetan's number, but stopped when he realised that his friend might be out of the country for his honeymoon. He was not sure of the time difference so tried calling Aman, who disconnected the call as he was in his office. "Will call you in five minutes," he sent a message. Aman excused himself and rushed to the washroom near his cubicle in his firm. All the nostalgic, evocative moments flooded Ballu's futile mind reminding him of his glorious days of college. Four years of graduation are more saccharine than our entire life put together, they say and this was evident looking at the wetness in Ballu's eyes. It was more than fifteen minutes and Aman still had not called, but Ballu simply did not realise this as he was engrossed in checking the slam book After Riyaz failed in his first year engineering course twice, forcing him to take admission to a course in Bachelors of Business Administration, the group of five shrunk to an even number of four. The group was called 'ABCD' and they used to sign off in similar fashion, the same way like Dev signed off at the end of his message.

Aman almost forgot to call Ballu and rushed to break out when he checked his mobile phone again. The slam book made him check his suitcase again to look for more 'objet d'art' as he called his memory box in the heavily guarded cupboard.

He opened the first album of his college reminiscences and the first picture was their group posing especially for the moment on their hostel terrace. Most students, who have had an opportunity to live in a hostel in their college days, might agree that people are more emotionally attached to their hostels than their college.

Aman made himself a coffee as he dialled Ballu's number. The ring tone disturbed the tranquillity, which the moment had gifted. Ballu followed the sound and found his phone lying under the bed, near his shoes. He sighed as he took the phone and sat on the bed still keeping an eye on the fleeting disarray created by the albums scattered on the bed. "Hmmm, tell me," Ballu sighed as he balanced the mobile between his neck and his right shoulder.

"You had called earlier. Is everything alright?" Aman asked.

"You won't believe when I will tell you something very interesting."

"I have never believed you, so tell me quickly," reminded Aman sipping his coffee.

The breakout room did not have proper luminosity so Aman switched on the lights.

"You told me about the unfathomable friend request you got on Facebook, right?"

"Yes, so what happened to that request?"

Ballu paused for a moment as he adjusted his pillow, making way for a better posture and yelled, "It was Dev. He replied to me, as I did not accept the friend request. I will send him a new invite."

Jumping with joy, Aman stood up and gulped his coffee at one go.

"Are you sure? It might be someone else and how do you know it's D?"

Dev was also called D by most of his hostel mates.

"He had signed exactly like our group used to when we were in our college. A, B, C and D for Dev were the words pasted at the end of the message," Ballu told with excitement, compelling him to change his stance again due to back pain.

Aman was damn happy and it showed on his face even with the abstemious Spartan look. "This week has been so lucky for us. Does Chetan know about this? Message him; I am sure he would check his Facebook account," Aman said while shifting the phone from his left hand to his right hand.

Ballu shifted from his bed to his chair and switched on his laptop, which was in standby mode. As always, the first thing that popped up was the Facebook homepage.

He was typing a message with both his hands as his shoulder was supporting his mobile phone.

After typing the message, he checked something and laughed. He literally laughed while checking the status on Chetan's profile.

"Chetan has changed his status from being single to married," Ballu mumbled still trying to control his mirth.

"That's more like Chetan. He is smitten by his wife. Actually both are smitten by each other," Ballu said as he opened Google and looked for more pictures of a Honda CBR.

Ballu informed Aman about his new bike which would arrive next week.

"It's a Honda CBR, manufactured in Japan."

"Send me a picture of your bike. Ballu, you are one lucky ass, I must say," Aman said pitching in some humour.

Ballu messaged his newly wed friend to post some pictures of their holiday.

"I am not sure if Chetan would like this or not but I have asked him to post some pictures of his honeymoon," he said checking his Facebook account.

Ballu who was known for creating pun when he played with his words felt his friend would misunderstand his message of sending honeymoon pictures and rightly so, deleted the message after reading it again.

He replaced the earlier message with the regular, predictable 'bon voyage' and a congratulatory message. As Aman had to rush, he excused himself promising a call during his lunch hours.

Raghu called Aman in his cabin to make a graphic presentation as he was known for his expertise in it. Aman obliged taking some notes and assured him of a sample graph in an hour.

"I can play an entire tournament of TT in an hour. I want it in flat fifteen minutes."

Aman rushed to his desk and switched on his alarm. He then made a rough graph with a pencil on a piece of paper and after carefully inspecting it, completed the rough sketch in ten minutes flat, but unexpectedly Raghu was nowhere to be seen. Still, he was sure that Raghu would believe that he made the presentation in ten minutes flat.

Ballu in the meantime checked Dev's Facebook profile thoroughly to find some very interesting points. Dev was part of a community in Facebook, which believed in life after death that had a slogan, 'I will come back from my deathbed to fulfill my wishes.'

He was a part of some more communities dedicated to god. Dev was always known for his faith in god even during his college days. The green dot near Dev's name blinked and Ballu messaged him to check if he was online.

"Are you online?"

Dev had added Ballu to his friend list and to his chat list. "Hey!"

Ballu's happiness knew no bounds when he got a reply from his dearest friend who had literary vanished after graduation.

"Where are you? How are you? What's your number? Are you in Mumbai? Can we meet?" Ballu bombed him with a series of questions.

"I am quite far off from you all. No, I am not in Mumbai."

"Give me your number, I will call you right now," Ballu insisted.

"I will give you my number in some time. How are Aman, Chetan and Riyaz?"

Whenever Riyaz came into picture, Ballu showed his remorse, of not being in touch with him. "I don't know the whereabouts of Riyaz but Chetan and Aman work in the same software company."

"Riyaz is in Miami, Florida but I have lost contact with him," typed in Dev.

"You just missed Chetan's wedding by a whisker. He married Neha this week," Ballu showed his excitement for Chetan's successful romance.

"Neha? Aman's sister?" Dev wanted to confirm to let his confused mind know.

Ballu smiled at the comedy of errors and replied, "No, she is Chetan's wife with the same name and coincidently she is a fast friend of Aman's sister. Both share the same name."

Ballu typed and typed, unable to understand why suddenly Dev had gone offline.

"Shit," he shouted as he typed in three to four similar messages one after the other.

"Are you there?" he asked as he confirmed his offline status.

Not sure if Dev understood the confusion, Ballu typed in the exact details again via a big message with lots of bold letters in it. This week was damn lucky for him and his friends. He was happier to meet Dev than the combined emotional worth of Chetan's marriage and his new bike. Facebook had given him the biggest gift of his life.

"I should have asked for the number," he told himself as he punched his fist in the air. Ballu took his guitar and played something on it keeping an eye on the laptop, just in case Dev might appear suddenly out of the blue. He had a million questions for Dev but did not want to bother him. Aman was getting anxious by the minute and settled himself on his favourite chair near his desk. His chair was different than others' for it had an extra cushion stuck on a piece of metal, which sprouted out, from the upper side of the chair. As he was using his office computer, the homepage had to be his company's web portal. He opened Facebook.com to check his messages and could not find anyone who matched Dev's credentials. He had to check Ballu's messages to find Dev. "I am back!" were the headlines on Dev's profile.

Aman who was always focused when it came to work, could not resist checking Dev's profile on the social networking site, Facebook.

"Hey man, where were you these days?" Aman typed as fast as he could when he saw Raghu coming towards him.

"Sorry, I am really sorry."

Feeling suspicious, Aman opened the taskbar, closed Facebook and opened the slide, which he had prepared. He pulled a chair and gave his seat to his manager.

Raghu was an old-fashioned manager for whom respect came before work.

"I have always admired honesty and hard work," Raghu mumbled adjusting his glasses. He was more than sure that Aman might have made the presentation ahead of time. He used his pen to crosscheck the formation of points on the screen and said, "Perfect, I will copy and send it to Mr. Iyer. Don't worry, I wouldn't delete your name, the slide will still carry your name even if I have to rework it."

Aman was happy and turned around to check if people had heard Raghu's comments.

"I forgot to ask you one thing. How is Chetan? Also come to my cabin, I wanted to confirm something."

Aman knew the questions and he prepared himself for it. Chetan had warned him against it, but he was left with no option and with the internal job posting just round the corner, he could not afford to lose the faith shown by Raghu.

"Also before going, we could squeeze a TT match in the evening. What do you say?" Raghu asked, playing an imaginary table-tennis shot.

Aman nodded in agreement, "Sure sir, but I don't play that well."

"That's the reason I asked. I don't like to play with good players, it hampers my confidence," Raghu whispered as if making sure no one hears them.

Raghu hated cricket like anything and blamed its emergence for the reduction in table tennis' popularity.

Aman's cell phone, which was on vibration mode started to make noises signaling the arrival of a call. The silence on the floor was sufficient for Raghu to gauge the source of the sound. "Go ahead, take the call."

Feeling embarrassed, Aman disconnected the call and switched off his phone.

"Should I send the presentation to you now via email attachment?" he asked curiously. Raghu thought for a while and replied, "No need, after our discussion we can do a net meeting and share the files. I don't want to trouble you a lot."

Net meeting was the best method when it came to sharing attachments in corporate offices. Aman was stunned as when someone does not want a proof that something was sent or received or in case of attachment bigger than the size limits, only then the application was used. He was relieved when Raghu showed him the size of the file, which was more than twenty megabytes, which was the maximum limit of traffic, which could be sent or received through emails. Raghu ordered him to be in his cabin in the next five minutes. He closed all the sites and presentations, which were opened. In addition, he closed the site through which he had downloaded his presentation even as he had simply changed the ranges and values. He was relieved that Raghu had not checked the source site. Before heading to his boss's cabin, he switched on his mobile and checked the last call. Ballu had called him and he was fed up of his sense of timing. He switched off the mobile fearing someone else might call him during the course of the meeting.

❖❖❖

10

Weekend Shifts

A weekend is capable of defeating an entire season.

Three months into their marriage, levelheaded Chetan and his naïve wife were very happy with the advent of the New Year. He had applied for a loan for a new flat, but the bank was taking a longer time than expected to clear it. He managed to convince his wife to stay at the same rented flat until their loan got sanctioned. The flat looked so different from what he had while he was a bachelor. Not only the curtains and bed sheets were changed, but it had the fresh and an elegant feel of togetherness added to it. Marriage not only brings out a social change, but it is deeply rooted to our hearts. Money was an important factor after marriage as Neha had stopped working for quite some time now. The nameplate on the apartment was altered to have Neha's name added. The nameplate looked more like addressing people involved in a 'live in' relationship. Neha was still using her last name after Chetan supported the idea.

The living room looked fully furnished as against the bare look it carried before his marriage. After scanning the entire list of programmes available through all the channels, Chetan zeroed in to his favorite channel. At any point of time, Star Cricket beamed replays of old, exciting matches, when live matches were not available.

Chetan opened his secret album to add some more photographs. He checked the album thoroughly before putting the pictures in it with some notes scribbled behind the snaps.

"Neha, come here. I have something special for you," he said as he walked carrying the album with him. Neha was cooking something while listening to her pocket radio.

She was so immersed in cooking that she did not even realise Chetan's presence in the kitchen. "Hey, are you okay?" he yelled. It was nothing less than a shock for her. He switched off the radio and decreased the speed of the gas. As Chetan was a pure vegetarian, Neha limited her non-vegetarian intake considerably even as chicken curry switched to plain paneer curry for the couple.

"Look, what I have in store for you," he whispered kissing her cheeks.

Even after their long romance, Neha still used to blush on purpose, as Chetan liked it. "Come to the living room after you finish your cooking. We will enjoy an old cricket match today," he said pulling the album even as Neha resisted.

"Shut up! You had promised to watch only live matches or else I will lock all cricket channels," she threatened in her childish accent. Chetan smiled and nodded in agreement.

"Why don't you try some mutton curry?" she asked.

"Are you crazy? I am a Brahmin," he defended his stance keeping the album on the fridge. "Now you know, how I feel when you force me to see cricket." Neha's tricks had worked and she continued her anguish.

Chetan disappeared taking the album with him. The match appeared to be at a very interesting point when Neha entered. Wearing a green coloured kurta, she looked so homely yet elegant that Chetan complimented her on the choice of clothes, but hated their prices.

"The reception pictures have turned out better than our marriage pictures," Neha murmured softly as she went through some photographs.

"Yes, we do look happier in these pictures than our marriage ones."

"Hmmm," she sighed.

"Do you know why we look happier during the reception?" he asked taking her hand.

Neha stood up, sat on Chetan's lap, thought for a moment, and questioned, "Why?" Chetan tried to put his hands across her as she resisted his move and bit his hand in a playful manner.

"We look happier as we had just finished our honeymoon. The stress made way for calmness."

"Hmm; so we need to go there again, I suppose," she replied hugging her man.

They chatted for some more time on the sofa displaying the fracas nature of the couple, as they were known for it since the initial stages of their romance. The discussion moved to Neha's unemployment which annoyed her, but she concealed her anger in the wake of a romantic moment. After a passionate round of kissing, the couple moved to the marble flooring as Neha switched on the television and scanned through the channels, eventually sticking to an old romantic flick called Chocolate.

"We have a training scheduled later this week and most probably it will keep me busy for the next three-four weekends as the trainers will fly from Bangalore for the training."

The word 'weekend' ringed a bell and she asked, "Why weekends?"

Either love can make poets out of us or our common sense goes for a toss in the initial stages of marriage, and this was evident with the couple's conversation.

"This training would give me an edge over others and it can make way for a profound change in my cost to the company. Sweetie, money is a factor as most of my savings would collapse in the process of making a nest for us," he said as he caressed her neck.

Neha was fed up with her husband's workaholic nature, and on her insistence, he agreed to arrange a get-together of his office mates at their place. The insecurity in him shot up and he declined her initiative, but agreed when Neha cleverly substituted the affable option of a five star hotel.

"Actually, I want to invite everyone to our new house directly. Our new house would be bigger, and very different from this one bedroom, hall and kitchen." In spite of his verbal blows, she insisted that she was more than happy in their small bubble.

Chetan maintained a discrete life when it came to introducing his office mates to his wife and family. He had kept his marriage a secret for a long time until Facebook cleared the suspicion.

Even a charismatic personality could not make Chetan popular as he was always known as Aman's best friend and his straightforward ways never let him win trust of his office mates. Later, the training got postponed by a week, which gave him an opportunity to bridge the gap between his personal life and his official life. Resisting Neha's idea of celebrating hundred days of their marriage at their place, he arranged for a grander celebration at a suburban banquet hall in South Mumbai. The party was a great occasion to introduce his wife, whom they had only seen in Chetan's album on Facebook. Neha made sure she was introduced to everyone attending the party, even as Ballu joined Chetan's office friends at the get-together. More so, it was a great occasion for them to catch up with the rest in a different environment altogether. It's great to meet our office colleagues enjoying or rather trying to enjoy in a much more relaxed ambience.

"Oh! Therefore, everyone in your company has their official email address as their first name, and then a period followed by their last name at the rate your company's domain. That's interesting," she said, looking at Raghu's business card. Raghu was not only impressed by Chetan's wife, but appreciated her warm-heartedness more than anything. "You people don't have a lot of female staff in your office I guess," Neha said keeping her glass on the table. Plates were seen with cheese balls and crackers, chilli dip with Fritos, cauliflower and French dips, peanut butter balls covered with thin chocolate and crab salad on crackers and some slices of Wisconsin cheese.

"We don't have a lot of womenfolk in our office. Still, I have invited everyone," replied Chetan, confirming the representation of the 'fairer sex' in the party. Only two of his female co-workers had managed to be at the party, which clearly showed the dearth of women in the networking field or his company to be precise. Ballu was busy discussing something with Aman when he spilled his drink to a rather amused crowd. He apologised and bought another drink for himself. "No hard drinks, sir," the bartender replied when Ballu enquired about his favourite brand of beverage.

"Hmm, no party is over without a round of rum. No rum, no party," Ballu said, taking a sip from his cold drink even as the bartender whom he thought was listening to his crap, was actually busy in performing the famous 'bartender antics' with a couple of bottles. The bartenders are quite popular in the party circles for their tricks, which are greatly enjoyed by the partygoers. Ballu took his drink and whispered something in Aman's ears. "What! No man, I have to help my sister so don't count me in the plan," Aman replied, keeping the drink as he dialled his sister's phone number and suddenly disconnected it. "Just a couple of drinks, that's it," Ballu said showing something on his mobile phone. Aman was in no mood to listen and excused himself when his phone started buzzing. People were more excited to see an inter-caste marriage being successful as more often than not, marriages end up in a rather contemporary fashion, these days. Chetan was not very happy accepting the gifts and requested his wife to attend the guests as he went to have a word with the bartender.

The couple, who looked lethargic after the event, had managed to be in high spirits throughout the party. Along with Ballu and Aman, they were the last to leave the venue. Clearing the bills took a long time even as Aman excused himself and Ballu followed, both stating the exact same reasons. Aman stopped over at Prem's for a couple of drinks when Ballu insisted.

Chetan started his weekend shifts with half the time taken by training sessions and the rest in making reports.

"If I reject your call, then I would most probably be in a meeting," he said, polishing his shoes as he sat on the sofa. "That's fine, but finish your dinner on time," Neha replied as she adjusted the spring lever of the new Tiffin set, she had bought for him.

"Will Aman be there with you?"

"He will join just after a couple of weekends. He is in the other batch," he replied throwing the newspaper on the sofa.

Chetan combed his hair and checked himself thoroughly, standing near the mirror table. "Can I get a cup of tea?"

"Sure, but it would take some time," Neha shouted while rushing to the kitchen.

"Okay, that way I could watch some of the old cricket matches shown on Star Cricket," he said while looking for the TV remote control.

The remote was nowhere to be seen even as he checked the sofa followed by the table kept next to it. "That's strange, I am sure, I had kept the bloody remote on the table."

"Did you say something about cricket by any chance?" she shouted from the kitchen.

"No, not at all," he replied taking a few deep breaths and adjusting himself comfortably on the spongy seat. After a frantic search, he found the remote tucked inside the showcase. "Got it!" resting on the sofa, he switched on the television and scanned everything that it had to offer. Searching the entire market, the goldsmith has to stop at the jewellery shop. Chetan decreased the volume of the television as he found a live cricket match being telecast. Cricket is cricket, even if India is not playing. It was the famous Ashes tour of Australia, which had already generated a lot of interest in the cricketing world.

Making himself comfortable, he had just started enjoying England's batting when Neha interrupted. "Oh my god! You are watching cricket again."

"I was just checking something and found this match going on," he clarified.

"How come these players don't get tired by playing every day?" she asked furiously.

"India is not playing. It's Australia versus England."

"If India is not playing, then why are you so interested in the match?" she thundered, kicking the sofa in anguish.

"It's not about the country, it's about cricket."

"Darling, it's immature to be crazy for something as notorious as cricket," she said, looking up from the table.

Chetan seemed angry as he decreased the volume and turned this side to face his wife.

"Hmm, what did you say?"

"Have the tea before it turns arctic," she reminded her cricket crazy husband.

"I cannot explain it to you. You won't understand as you are too practical to value masculine emotions,' he said sipping some tea.

"Emotions, and that too masculine? Are you crazy?"

"Maybe I expressed it in a wrong way but I wanted to say something else."

The match seemed poised for a close finish and Chetan turned around and increased the volume. He dragged himself from the sofa to the small chair next to it.

"Your clothes may get sullied," Neha shouted.

"Hmm." He stood and made himself comfortable on the cushion again.

"Darling, we will discuss this after the penultimate over of the day is bowled."

"What? I am not shocked but sad at your reaction," she said while going towards the kitchen.

Her words fell on deaf ears even as Chetan was engrossed completely in the match.

He even increased the volume to make sure he could not hear anything apart from the telecast of the match. Cricket was cricket for him, even if that meant enjoying matches in which India didn't play. This was it, a software engineer earning a handsome salary having an extremely beautiful wife who was more than eager to please him, but nothing could come in the way of his cricket fervour. Cricket had taken over his world and left 'romance' at a distant second position when it came to adjudging the things in descending order with respect to his passion. It's not a very strange sight in India, but just three months into marriage and cricket had created a rift between them. He moved closer to the television to have a wary look at the scoreboard, which was being displayed. "I will have to test my eyes."

After the penultimate over was bowled the coverage stopped for a commercial break and he turned around and could not see his wife. "Neha," he shouted as he decreased the volume of the television. Adjusting the curtains, he checked the illumination in the room and switched on the small bulb behind the television. The bulb added to the enlightenment of the room and Chetan was happy for he could see things with ease now. "Neha, where are you?" he said looking towards the kitchen.

He rushed to the kitchen, which was filled with the aroma of the spicy curry she had made. "That's not bad."

He ran to the washroom and knocked at the door. "Sorry to disturb you at this juncture, but we need to talk," he said. With no response, he pushed the door to find the room vacant. "She is a kiddo. She will never understand my passions, even if it's trekking." The thought of the match made him rush towards the living room. The commercials were running giving him some time to dial his wife's number. As soon as the match started, he kept the phone on the table and made himself comfortable, watching the match. He wasn't even aware of the fact that the phone was still ringing. After some long rings, the phone got connected.

"Hello, hello," she shouted, but the loud noise of the match never allowed Chetan to realise this. It was the second day of test match and the last over of the day. As Shane Warne was bowling the last over, it generated a lot of hype and excitement.

The first ball had an appeal for a run out which was referred to the third umpire resulting in the stoppage of playtime. The beaming of replays gave him some time to switch on the laptop. Facebook was his homepage and it automatically signed him in. He went in the cricket community to bet for the match. Checking the odds, he made his bet on Australia. Betting was a nice addition to already famous social networking site. He chose Ballu for the bet, as he had bet for England, expecting an upset. He checked to find most of his friends had betted for Australia leaving very few options to bet against. "Ballu is an idiot, upsets don't happen often," he said and smiled when he realised there was no one to hear him.

Although Facebook never allowed money in the betting, people used to bet mostly for money or something else as friendly bets never yielded a good response.

The third umpire turned down the run out appeal and the play resumed. Somehow, England's bowlers managed to play the rest of the over without loosing more wickets.

"Shit, that was the best opportunity to put pressure on the England's tail-enders."

He kept the laptop and switched off the television. Out of the sudden, he checked the betting portal again which was flaunting 'eighty-eight percent to twelve percent' as the day's result. That was fast considering the fact that it was eighty versus twenty before the final over.

Checking his mobile, he realised that his wife received the call. "The duration of your last call was forty-six seconds," was the message it displayed. "Oh my god!" he shouted and ran to the kitchen. The bedroom remained the only place where he had not searched for his wife and he ran towards it. The door was locked which always made him feel irritated.

He knocked the door, which yielded no response. He knocked again showing his frustration. "I am getting late. It's already half past eight."

Boiling with anger, he dialled her number to have the call disconnected.

After a few more shouts, Neha opened the door.

"What! Is the match over?"

"No, I have left the match for you. Don't act like a bitch," he said, throwing his mobile on the bed.

"Bitch?"

She stood up and moved towards the chair near the study table.

"Now, don't cry. I am fed up of your tears," he said, making himself comfortable on the bed. Neha had always complained about Chetan's habit of sitting with his shoes on the bed or the sofa, but she was least concerned today. Realising his mistake, he apologised.

"Sorry, I am really sorry."

Neha smiled when she heard the words and hugged Chetan.

"You enjoy making me cry, right?"

"What are you saying, darling?" he asked and kissed her cheeks.

"Go and watch the rest of the match," she said, wiping her tears.

"The match is over. The rest of it will be played tomorrow."

She smiled with tears still falling from her beautiful brown eyes on the flawless skinned cheeks. Chetan kissed his wife again and lifted her with both hands carrying her till bed and kept her gently on the right side of the bed.

"I love you, sweetie," she sighed.

"I know. You never told me that you cooked curry and rice today."

"Hmmm, I learnt the recipe from our neighbour. She is also from Bangalore."

"You did this for me. I am honoured."

Neha hugged him tightly and whispered something into his ears that made him smile. "I know, I know."

"When would you come back?"

"Around half past one in the night. Will you be awake at that time?"

"Can't say actually, why?"

"A cricket match would start after I come," he said, kissing her hand.

"What! Cricket... get lost from here. I thought you have changed."

"Not that cricket. Cricket I mean, the match," he stressed on his word.

"What? You told me that the match has finished."

"I am playing. You will bowl and I will bat," he insisted.

Neha blushed and punched Chetan directly on his nose.

"You have a filthy mind," she said flashing a beautiful smile.

"I know, but it still loves you."

Chetan lifted his wife in his arms again and carried her till the living room. He switched on the television and scanned to get her favorite serial.

"You like this, right?" he asked increasing the volume.

"Hmmmmm."

"Call me, when you come. Don't just go on pressing the doorbell. I might be in the washroom or in the bedroom. Okay?" she said, giving the lunch box.

"Sure, I will call you when I leave the office itself."

"That's like a good boy," she said, kissing him on the cheeks. Unlike before, she never complained about Chetan's trimmed bearded look after the marriage.

"If possible, be awake till that time. I will try to come early."

Neha smiled and whispered, "I love you, honey."

"Bye, take care of yourself," he said waving his hand.

Chetan left for the weekend shift. It was the first time in his career that he would be at office on a Saturday. Feeling deadbeat, he took the lift even for coming down from the first floor. He called his wife and requested her not to open the door without confirming through the keyhole.

The weekend training and the reports kept him busy. The training part was done on Sundays and they had ample of time on Saturdays.

Neha also made herself busy by either watching television or having her dinner at her maternal home. She was always welcomed at her maternal home, for they took pride in having their daughter at their place again, even if it was for just an hour.

The training was cancelled for the next weekend due to the swine flu scare and that left Chetan with a lot of spare time at hand. Facebook and chatting were his favorite pastime when he was not making presentations. Chetan checked Dev's profile and dropped a message.

More and more people had the same message pasted on Dev's message board. "When are you coming to Mumbai?" was what Ballu had asked him.

Chetan maximised the Facebook homepage and made himself available for chatting.

"Angel-alone wants to add you in your chat," was a message displayed on his chat tool. He accepted without even checking the profile. "Angel-alone" seemed online and he jabbed her.

"Hey, do I know you?"

She took a long time to respond but replied at last.

"Hey, what's up?"

"I am Chetan, this side. Do I know you by any chance?"

"No, but we could know each other."

"Okay, I am a software engineer working in Mumbai. Where are you from?"

"I am also from Mumbai but presently in Pune."

"Great, I have a lot of friends in Pune."

Chetan turned the angle of the laptop so he could type in a more comfortable manner. "What else?"

"Nothing much, what's your name?"

"Disha."

"That's a sweet name."

"Thanks. You are quite good looking. I saw some pictures in your profile. Are you really married?"

"Yes, why?" Chetan smiled as he typed.

"Nothing of that sort. I just wanted to confirm."

"Can I see your picture, if you don't mind?"

"I will have to scan some more pictures as I have acquired a new look after coming from my London trip."

"London is a nice place, but too crowded on most occasions," he typed in.

"That's true, but it has got everything for a single lady."

"Your display name is strange. Alone added to the word angel. Does it mean something?"

"I am single. The alone part is just for fun."

"Fun?"

"Leave it. I will be in Mumbai next month. Where do you stay?"

"I will shift to Andheri soon. Hey, but I am married."

"You got me wrong. Nothing of that sort, pleaseeeeeeeee."

Chetan pasted a smiley and continued. They chatted for a long time and Chetan even gave out his mobile number during the online conversation. Later, Chetan excused himself to have his dinner.

"Dinner, at this time?"

"Yes, it's quite late, but I have to finish the paneer curry which my wife made especially for me."

"Paneer curry, that sounds interesting. Do you know the recipe?"

"Also we could visit the electronics market to check out the latest CDs and DVDs. What do you say?" Ballu said, smiling at them expecting a positive litter.

"Where should we put these DVDs to play them?"

Ballu insisted on buying a DVD player by contributing, but Aman and Riyaz vetoed the idea. They went for dinner as planned, but paid their share even when Ballu insisted on paying as per the discussion they had earlier in the day.

It was a lacklustre Saturday afternoon and no new plans could be made to fine-tune the budget. In addition, they were not too eager to listen to Ballu's plan who always managed to cut their pockets with his weird ideas. Riyaz and Aman were keen to explore the orchard in the dearth of a better plan on a Saturday afternoon, which would turn into a favourable evening in some anxious hours.

In spite of the name 'Mango Orchard', the orchard was filled with fruits of all kind. As many engineering colleges are located in remote places far away from the heart of the city, there is nothing much the pupils can do to pass time other than what is recommended by the hostel authorities. That's the reason most end up making the same plans.

In no time, they entered the orchard through the damaged fence even as the guard was seen fully engrossed in his midday sleep.

So now, there were at least twenty people in the orchard. "Ballu might have shared the plan with everyone," Aman told himself as he stared at the crowd. Ballu gave an uninterested look and tied his shoelaces. The Mango Orchard looked like a slice of heaven when compared to the half dug, half-spoilt concrete basketball court that could be seen even through the crowd of trees. The serene atmosphere along with the abundance of fruits every summer made it somewhat singular for the hostel students. The college authorities had tried all possible ways to acquire the orchard, but received the same answer in the typical arrogance of a politician.

The orchard owner and most of the people living on the west side of the hill station were against any kind of construction. Not just hotels, but they opposed even the recently constructed college which surpassed the green belt of banyan trees seen everywhere on the hill station.

Guava trees were more popular with students here. The small branch of the Guava tree was trying its level best to somehow hold Ballu. Ballu saw a full-grown guava and was tempted to try a jump but was not sure if the branch would handle his burlesque. The pain, which the pale looking branch was going through, could be gauged by the eerie noises, which could be easily heard. Ballu's brown coloured shorts along with his green coloured T-shirt almost camouflaged the guava tree, which seemed dwarfed by the big banyan trees surrounding it.

Ballu was slightly on the healthier side, but would always try his best to stay fit. Suddenly, he saw someone coming into the orchard from the other side. His weight and nervousness tumbled him over as he shouted. People started running in all directions. "You have to reduce, at least have mercy on the twigs," Riyaz shouted, showing his compassion on the full grown yet pitiable branches.

Ballu got up somehow and checked his pockets. They ran fast as they heard some weird sounds scorning from the trees. Riyaz ran towards the hut near the bushes even as Ballu tried to collect the guavas, which were scattered near the banyan trees. He heard something and ran as fast as he could towards the bushes. Aman whistled using both his ring fingers to let him know that he was hiding near the small hut. Ballu tried to whistle in return, but failed. He was never able to whistle, however hard he tried. Riyaz peeped out of the hut and shouted, generating a daunting reverberation. Ballu dusted his khaki shorts and tried to follow the rough sound of the whistle, but was still not able to gauge the source of the sound. Riyaz come out of the hut, and managed to drag Ballu inside. Riyaz took some deep breaths and put his hand to

"For the whole day?" Ballu asked and bit his tongue and threw a pillow at Aman.

"Actually I had gone to visit a friend in the government college near the bus station today." Aman showed first signs of nervousness when some other sharp bouncers were hurled at him.

"What about yesterday?" Riyaz asked giving a playful clap to Ballu as they saw their man being coaxed into their trap.

Aman tried his best to change the direction of the banter to a free for all topic about food and restaurants in their area, but Ballu insisted for an answer.

"This idiot acted so spruce in front of my mother, but I always knew that he too has a forced dual personality like everyone else."

Aman confessed that he went to see his girlfriend who studied in the government college.

"Girlfriend! Have you kissed her?" Ballu asked while blocking Aman's way.

Aman stared trying to find something in his pockets.

"Shut up, you ass," Aman thundered and threw a pillow at Ballu who managed to divert the pillow towards the floor. "See, if a man does not kiss a girl, she cannot be his girlfriend. Don't spoil someone's name by getting associated with her," Ballu continued.

Aman was angry as hell and pulled his wallet to show his girlfriend's photograph.

"It looks fake. She might be just a friend," Ballu said as he ran towards the door.

"What were you doing the whole day?" Riyaz enquired, pouring his suspicions.

Aman started laughing on hearing the question.

"I knew he was lying. Look at his face and compare that with the beautiful picture he showed," Ballu screamed as he stood at the door.

"You won't believe me."

"Don't worry, we don't believe you," Ballu said, keeping his mobile on the bed.

"I attended some of her lectures."

"What?" A combined voice spurt.

"I attended some of her lectures just to be with her."

"Do you think we are kids or something? The lecturers didn't recognise you?" Riyaz asked, checking the time on the wall clock.

"Admissions are still going on. Actually when the attendance was going on, the girl sitting next to me told her number, something like TMX 12 and I followed with TMX14. I swear I wasn't even caught," Aman said as he tried his best to persuade his covetous friends to believe him.

"For a change, try attending your own lectures. It will be more beneficial," Ballu said showing his witty side.

Aman threw the next pillow and shouted, "You shut up. I am better off than you. I have attended a lecture at least. Wait, I will call your mother and tell her."

"Also tell her that you attend lectures at different colleges by bunking your own," Ballu said, picking his mobile and pinching some more drollness.

Some playful exchange of words followed and they were ready to head to Riyaz's room for a big round of discussing the same things all over again.

Next afternoon, they were more than eager to go to the beautiful fruit laden Mango Orchard, but resisted Ballu's words. When his insistence grew then they agreed making him aware of their favour.

He checked pictures and messages for the next half an hour in his and his friends' profiles. No one was online for a chat so he logged off after sending some messages.

He was the only one in the bay area assessing Internet services. Walking a few steps, he turned around abruptly and ran to confirm if he had logged off from his Facebook account. Feeling a bit anxious, he pulled the cable and had the computer shut down completely. Library was filled with the usual hustle and bustle of students common during the initial days with even parents seen with their children. This college was huge with wide passages with people all the way in every corner. Even on the first day, he seemed lost more than homesick. Initial days were a mixed bag of feelings as he met some of his classmates and felt an ounce of conformability added. Even Facebook did not make him feel at ease.

"Why didn't you attend the first lecture?" asked someone. Ballu smiled and tried to divert the conversation towards a less susceptible topic. "Where is Aman?" he enquired, trying to look for him amongst his new-fangled friends.

"I was going to ask you about him actually. Why doesn't he come to college?" Bhushan asked checking his hair curls.

"What?" Ballu shouted giving a flabbergasted look. Bhushan used his fingers and curled his hair towards the other side now.

"He was only seen during the introductory lecture," Ashish explained hinting his astonishment as well. Ballu was more staggered of the lot, but excused himself when he saw someone.

He left in a very haphazard way from the library to the cafeteria and later to his hostel.

He cursed the college authorities for the long, unbounded way to his hostel.

He rushed through the aisles to his room and the warden who saw him looked at his watch to confirm the time. "It's none of his business," Ballu told himself, while opening the door.

Later that night, Ballu pushed hard his suggestion to venture out for dinner. "Man, I have to check my budget as well," Riyaz murmured as he pulled out his wallet and forced out everything. He counted the cash and put it back. Ballu offered help but thought otherwise, when Aman pitched his vulnerability towards money.

Riyaz asked Ballu about his rushing out of the library episode.

Ballu smiled, on being asked in the first place. He had seen the person whose account he had messed with. The so-called Mr DJ was waving at someone not even aware of the problems he would fall prey to in some time. Ballu offered to pay for everyone on a condition. "We would go to the Mango Orchard tomorrow. If you people agree, then I would pay for you all. Also I will pay only if the bill is below a small Gandhi," he said, sitting on the bed. The word 'Small Gandhi' made them go nuts.

"Every currency note has an imprint of Gandhi on it, so a five hundred rupee note is called small Gandhi and a thousand rupee note is called a big Gandhi," Ballu said, showing a sample five hundred rupee note.

Ballu snatched the note when Aman tried to check it.

"Shut up you fool, people will kill you if you insult Gandhi," Aman said checking his wristwatch. Ballu folded the note and neatly put in his pocket kissing it.

"Sorry, I would never insult such a great man. It's just our way of saying things in Mumbai," Ballu said as he checked his beard in the mirror near him. A small round of giggles followed after Ballu apologised. Aman changed his posture and moved closer to the locker to check something. Ballu enquired on Aman's impetuous disappearance from college.

Aman was sure he would handle Ballu and his questions but smiled when he saw Riyaz staring at him as if waiting for an answer. "I was in the cafeteria."

"Make sure you keep the keys on the window. I am leaving to check something important on the Internet," Aman said, checking himself in the mirror.

As soon as he heard the word Internet, the thoughts of checking his Facebook account ran through his mind. He did not want to show his desperation for checking his Facebook account, so he peeped from his blanket to confirm if Aman had left. Even after Aman was gone, he slept for some more time, as he could hear his friend talking in the aisle.

It was more than a week now since he had checked his Facebook account as his mobile Internet was also not being supported in the hostel premises. He had fought with the helpline, but they were adamant about the vicinity they support through the mobile Internet service.

Fifteen minutes were enough to take a bath, get ready and have his breakfast.

He had to fight for his breakfast as the mess timings did not match with the timings mentioned on the form.

"The timings have been changed some years ago, but still not updated on the hostel forms. No breakfast would be provided after nine from tomorrow," insisted a mess worker, giving Ballu his plate of breakfast. He set out for college, but rushed to the hostel again to take the USB cable along with him.

He knew the library was behind the parking area, but was confused and had to ask for directions. The bay area was full with students taking turns to access Internet.

Facebook and Google were the most popular websites when it came to colleges in this part of the world. As soon as the next lecture started, most of the students ran towards the laboratory and Ballu finally had an opportunity to access the Internet.

More than connecting people, Facebook is a platform for people to display their inner-self.

Nothing catches the exact mood of a person like Facebook does. Life is Facebook, and Facebook is life for the young generation.

Ballu looked for a computer, which could give him some privacy. He went to the computer stationed at the centre of the room and switched the monitor on.

To his surprise, the computer opened the Facebook page with someone already logged in. Someone had forgotten to log off from the website. It was a brilliant opportunity for him to have some fun. Unfortunately, it was a guy's profile but he was in no mood to leave a golden opportunity to have fun at others' expense. The profile seemed popular going by the number of testimonials written by people for him.

Only the acronym 'DJ' was mentioned in the name field which most probably might be an abbreviation for disc-jockey. He went through his albums, which indicated the colourful life that the so-called Mr DJ lived. He deleted all the pictures where he was seen with women around. The ever-fastidious Ballu was enjoying as he checked personal messages and even made fun of people's emotions by adding stupid quotes on others' pictures.

There were some sensuous pictures of Mr DJ and his girlfriend. Reading the romantic testimonial one could easily guess that this girl might be going out with Mr DJ. He replied with the most recent message in his profile.

"Would you like to rekindle the fun we had in Goa?" he typed in.

He could have done a million things when it came to utilising his destructive mind, but it was the scarcity of ideas at the right time that clogged him. Logging out of the profile, he logged in with his username and password now. He updated his latest pictures to his profile and checked his messages. The best part of Facebook is that you can check messages of your friends written on their wall to know what is happening in their lives.

3

Cricket Dance!

Ragging is fun, until it happens to you.

The college was famous for many other reasons apart from engineering. Ragging was one of those reasons; the boy's hostel was never out of limelight. Last year even their female counterparts were in the news for some ragging incidents.

Ragging is a horrible way of making fun of others' freedom but comes across as a hard paradox in movies or books. The problem with most outstation students is that they come to know the ground realities after they are wedged in. Someone told Akash about the murder which had occurred a few years ago as an alleged fallout of a ragging incident.

"Someone was murdered in broad daylight right in front of the entrance of our college," he said, keeping his mobile in his pocket.

He wanted to haul their attention towards the incidents of ragging, but his friends reduced the incident to one of the many rumours haunting the hostel life.

"I am more petrified of being ragged than meeting a ghost," Ballu said checking the time on his wristwatch. The scene looked straight from a novel based on student politics. Most of the first year students were sitting in Riyaz's room when Kunal reminded them about the ragging incidents which he had heard from the mess workers. They had managed to elude ragging due to dearth of senior students at that time of the year. The students had taken every possible space available in the room. The untidy room looked crowded more due to the luggage kept there. Riyaz's room was a favourite hangout for students of the first year and now with Dev and Chetan in the group, even the other wings had their share of representation.

Rajesh who was quiet for a long time stood up and said, "I will tell them that my father is a police inspector, thereby ensure my safety."

Ragging has been known to compose a bond of unity amongst the victims.

"I am also safe then, as I am a professional body builder and I see world wrestling episodes every day," Kunal made his point.

Everyone made some excuse or the other and Ballu was the only one left without any point.

"Let's see. I heard students are ragged only in the first month and we have managed a week without it. What if we stay overnight elsewhere?" Ballu asked, thrashing his fright.

Sometime later, a brilliant idea struck him while listening to his favourite song which had the lyrics, "It's fake, everything is fake." Ballu hatched a plan along with his friends and they even enacted it to be sure, even as Aman checked the authenticity of the act. After some trials, they were ready for the show. Everyone knew the first night in a hostel would be horrible but such was not the case here. Somehow, tranquillity made way for anxiety, even as a week had passed. All the first year students were happy about the fact, but knew that someday things will change and that too abruptly.

Ballu started laughing and swung quickly adding a second branch.

Chetan was furious hearing the word 'chakri'. He never gave his full or real name until and unless it was required. He tried making a cheery face and started swinging as fast as he could. "You are a *chakri,* swirl like one," screeched Ballu.

There are very few people in this world who are not happy with their first name and Chetan was one of them. It was really strange considering the hundreds of communities which have thousands of members on Facebook where people flaunt their love for their names. Dev apologised for letting out the well-guarded secret and told them that Chetan was the real name and Chakranarayan was the pet name.

He made an innocent face, but failed to keep an eye contact with Chetan. Chetan ran towards the branch to try swinging again. "Chakri," Ballu shouted as he tried to take a third branch and fell down. Everyone had a good laugh even as Ballu stood up as if nothing had happened. "That's fine! Big boys fall and rise in no time," Ballu said as he turned to check the dirt on his shorts.

"Big boys or fat boys?" Chetan asked, laughing at him. Riyaz who was sitting on a small stone couldn't control his laughter and fell. Everyone had a good laugh again. Each thought that the joke was on the other and laughed their hearts out. Just fifteen minutes in the friendly meeting, and they behaved like old friends who met after a long time.

They discussed about the 'Laughter Challenge' which was a popular programme. Two things were common between them. All admired Amitabh Bachchan, and as expected were crazy for Facebook and cricket. Ballu even tried to mimic his favourite actor, but failed miserably. The laughter show was a collection of jokes mimicked by the contestants. In addition, it was one of those very few innovative programmes originating from Asia and going westwards rather than the other way round. Dev and Chetan were room partners and were allotted the room number sixty-five in the opposite wing. Dev was popular with his DVD player and his huge collection of movies and songs.

Next day, the whole group geared up go to the infamous electronic market near the government medical college. Apart from songs and movies, Ballu managed to grab a couple of porn flicks to add to his already mammoth collection.

❖❖❖

again. This time around, the guava came down quickly and hit Dev. Dev's white coloured shirt bore scattered red marks on it. Everyone started laughing including Dev as if appreciating the spirit of the not-so-droll incident. Ballu apologised, but still confused, he enquired, "Why didn't the first guava come down?" "Where did the first guava go?" he put his question in a different way with a weird smile on his face.

"It hit Dev and you will have to wash his shirt now," Riyaz said as he tried to rub the marks on Dev's shirt. The marks were getting speckled due to the rubbing.

"The guava which hit Dev was the first guava," Aman justified his stance. Common sense is the most equally distributed commodity as everyone thinks he has enough.

"If this is the first guava, where did the second go?" Ballu asked, looking at the banyan tree while carefully examining the big trunk.

Chetan wanted to laugh but changed his plan seeing Ballu's face, which had turned red thinking about the fact that he would have to wash clothes and that too for someone else. Washing was not only the biggest headache for hostel students but also the source of most hostel fights.

"Thank god! Dev was not wearing his college shirt," Chetan said, checking the marks on the shirt. Ballu smiled and made a creepy face.

"Why would he wear his college shirt on a Saturday and that too at this time?" Ballu asked, looking at the shirt. Even Ballu checked Dev's shirt and advised him to wash the shirt with some lemon-filled solution.

"If it doesn't go, I will gift you a new shirt on your birthday. I could have given you my shirt but it won't fit you," Ballu said, managing a smile on his face.

Chetan reminded everyone about Dev's birthday on twenty-ninth February which only comes once in four years. "As this is a leap year, Ballu will have to wait for another four years to gift me a new shirt."

Aman was amazed on hearing his date of birth and month.

"This is the first time I have actually met someone who was born on twenty-ninth of February," he confessed and shook hands congratulating him for being born on such a special day. Chetan told them that his real name was Chakranarayan, but was called Chetan by everyone. As soon as Ballu heard the name, he laughed his heart out but apologised later, when he saw Chetan's flabbergasted look.

"Ballu is also not a very sweet name. It reminds me of the papa bear from jungle book," Chetan said showing a thumps down gesticulation.

"Ballu looks like a bear, but is not that sweet and lovable like the papa bear," Aman said, making an amusing face with his tongue.

The new friends laughed under the banyan tree as if they knew each other for years. Ballu still tried hard to scrub the dirt from Dev's shirt when the thought of washing his friend's shirt came to his mind. He then tried to use his ring, but pulled out when Dev felt embarrassed and asked him to stop. "I will give it for laundry," Dev said looking at the mark.

"Mr Richie-rich, dry clean and all. How much pocket money do you get?" Riyaz asked while dusting his pants. Dev came from a rich business class family, but was not comfortable telling everyone about this.

"Eight thousand is the maximum I get in a month," Dev whispered as if he didn't want them to hear the amount. He almost stopped when he told the amount.

"Oh my god... eight thousand... I can't believe it," Ballu said as he was busy swinging the branches of the big banyan tree. Seeing him, Chetan also took a big branch and tried his luck. "Chakri, keep it slow."

cover Ballu's mouth as he was about to speak. Aman stared as his eyes gave a 'shut up' kind of an expression. Ballu slipped behind to hear someone grumbling. A small pair of hands came from nowhere and pushed him. He was so scared that he couldn't even gather the courage to turn around and closing his eyes, stood motionless. Riyaz was happy that Ballu seemed hushed when they heard some people talking about the nuisance of the students, which was growing every year.

"Kids will be kids. Once the vacation starts, loneliness will creep in. The orchard is so big and beautiful that sometimes I feel it invites us to feel it," said the orchard owner checking the mess.

"At least they keep me fit and running," came a quick reply. The weather changed abruptly which was quite common on this side of the mountains. The skies grew darker and it looked as if it would rain anytime. Riyaz knew that they had to rush before the hostel gates were closed for the first year students. The gates were actually never closed, that was just a gimmick by the warden to warn the students. Aman peeped twice to confirm that everything was fine and whistled in excitement. Ballu adjusted his small turban and smiled at him.

He felt a sensation in his pockets. To be sure, he raised his hands to confirm that it was not any of his hands, which caused it. He thought for a while and ran outside shouting like crazy. Riyaz couldn't believe all this and remained in the small grubby hut. Now it seemed awful to see someone shouting like hell and disturbing the serene atmosphere in the orchard.

"What happened, you fool?" Riyaz came out and all the kids hiding in the hut followed. There were quite a few kids hiding in the pint-sized hut. Ballu stopped when he saw them. It was so damn embarrassing for Ballu that he threw the guavas, which he had guarded until now.

"I have some guavas with me. Do you want to have some?" Chetan asked, showing the guavas. Riyaz smiled and obliged. "I am sorry. I was talking to Dev," Chetan said as he handed his share of guavas to Dev. Ballu apologised for his so-called attention-grabbing shout and touched Dev to make sure he was not a ghost. Dev felt embarrassed, but still managed a babyish smile.

Other people who were hiding in the hut still tried their luck in the orchard as Chetan and Dev started counting their guavas. "You should have told me. I threw some guavas. It's just fun for me. I don't like guavas actually," Ballu said. Riyaz introduced himself and his friends to Dev and Chetan.

"We are in first year of engineering... what about you people?" Ballu asked offering a handshake. "I am doing electronic engineering and he is pursuing mechanical engineering," Chetan replied, pointing at Dev.

Aman was still not sure if their newfound friends were seniors or batch mates.

Ballu moved his eyes to scrutinise his new friends.

"Dev has a DVD player with all advanced features, if you want to join us you can come to his room around half past eight," Chetan exclaimed while eating something, which didn't look like a guava.

Guavas of the orchard were red inside, like the strawberries, which were a specialty here.

Dev offered some guavas to his friends who obliged and even thanked him for his benevolence. DVD players and laptops are considered luxury in hostels and students who had these luxurious items managed the minimum number of companions.

All four were enjoying guavas sitting near the banyan tree just outside the hostel premises. Out of excitement, Ballu threw a half-eaten guava in the air with all his might. Ballu took a deep breath and felt confused when everyone stared at him. The guava, which he threw never came down defying the laws of gravity. Ballu was amazed and in a fit of excitement, threw a full-grown guava in the air

"I want a housewife who will be at home full time."

"No way, I am not going to leave my job for anyone," she typed in.

"I mean at least after we have kids, as a homemaker wife would make a good mother," he repeated the words from his profile.

"Are you serious?" she asked.

"I mean, that's not a rule, but I just told you, my feelings."

It was more than five minutes and Priya didn't type anything. Anticipating the delay, he typed in his response. "Bye, I will call you later."

"No, I mean I will send a message if I am free," she typed in.

"That's fine, are you on Facebook?"

"I need to leave now. It was a pleasure chatting with you. Bye."

He was about to type when he received a message that, 'your chat mate is offline and cannot get your response.'

Meanwhile, he even started a conversation with one of his other responses who seemed more than eager to chat with him.

"Hey!"

"Aman this side, seeing you online," he typed checking his words carefully.

"This is Nisha. Thanks for your request."

"Same here. I work in the IT field and earn SIX LAKHS per annum."

"That's awesome. I have a boutique of my own."

Nisha was more than eager to give out her number.

"Can I call you now?" Aman closed his eyes in anticipation.

"Sure, you can call me anytime."

Aman locked his computer and ran to the breakout room. He was happy to see the empty breakout room apart from some people who were cleaning the coffee machine. "Hey, Aman this side," he sighed.

"Hey, I was just thinking about you."

"Are you from Delhi as well?" she asked even as the word 'Delhi' gifted a glitter in his eyes. "How do you know?" he asked spilling some water from the plastic glass.

"Honey, I read it in your profile."

"What qualities do you want from your man?" he asked switching off the lights in the room.

"He should be a man...." She stopped abruptly.

"What?" he literally shouted even as the people cleaning the machine were surprised.

As he turned around, some people entered the room.

"Give me a minute," he said, taking the phone from his left hand and using his right hand instead.

"The coffee machine is out of order," he said, as he gestured to one of his friends who tried pressing the buttons on the coffee machine.

"It's fine and running. Go ahead sir," said the worker who was handling the machine.

Nisha waited for some time and hung up as she wasn't getting any response.

He made his way out to the washroom, but the noise through the blower was annoying him even as he dialled Nisha's number and got an unexpected engaged tone. He waited for a minute and finally Nisha called him. They talked for some more time and Nisha asked him out. "Can we meet for a coffee?" she asked more as a formality even as she was sure of his response. "Sure. Let's meet at Churchgate and then decide," he shouted in a desperate bid to save his voice from being absorbed by the blower. "No, we will meet at Bank Stand," she insisted and he agreed. Aman was so happy that he was about to blow a kiss, but resisted his temptation. He went to his desk happily to have Raghu waiting for him. "This bastard will kill me one day," he whispered while coming to his desk.

"Aman, I wanted to talk to you. Please come to my cabin in the next five minutes," Raghu said playing with the keyboard.

"Sir, I have to rush to my sister's place," Aman said, checking the time on his wristwatch.

Raghu smiled while checking something on his mobile phone.

"Your choice, it was something important," he said as he passed his desk.

Releasing his gaffe, he rushed to Raghu's cabin.

"Are they both gay?" Ashok asked while sitting on Aman's chair.

"Who knows? They are not seen on the floor for a long time, not even in the cafeteria," Raghini pitched in to steal a thunderous applause, coupled with a series of giggles.

Raghu made himself busy checking something on his laptop when he saw Aman towards his cabin.

"May I come in, sir?" Aman asked even as he was already inside.

"Please take a seat," Raghu said, turning the laptop towards Aman's side.

"I wanted to discuss something important. I have a plan for your internal job posting." Aman could not believe his luck. "Today is my lucky day. I will marry Nisha most probably and would be a manager soon," he dreamt and even saw himself and Nisha dancing round the trees. Nisha had posted a revealing picture and Aman just couldn't get over it.

"See, once you clear the first round which I am sure you are capable enough to do so, I will take the second round in which I will make sure that apart from you, three other mediocre engineers will clash with you in the last round," he said as he showed an email from Mr Iyer. Aman managed to read the email and smiled.

"I don't want to read the email; I have absolute faith on you."

The smile on Raghu's face showed his happiness. "Don't worry about Ashok, I have given him a warning letter for regularly coming late to work which makes him ineligible and you just don't need to worry about Shilpa." Aman knew Shilpa was more experienced and had an edge over everyone.

"Sir, Shilpa is the barb in the flesh," Aman said as he tried reading some more information from the email.

"Shilpa is three months pregnant and I am sure the management will never make someone a manager if she will be out on maternity leave even for a quarter," he said even as Aman was stunned to hear the news and stood up in excitement.

"What are you telling? How do you know?" he asked even as he wanted to hear those words all over again.

"Don't you trust me?" Raghu asked, scribbling something on his notepad.

"I will be nervous if I have to compete against Chetan. He is a very good friend of mine," he said with a smile, but Raghu wasn't amused by this emotional approach and asked him to be more practical when it came to growth opportunities.

"I know Chetan's IQ level and he even had argued with Mr Iyer earlier, so even if he comes to the last round, I am sure Mr Iyer will kick him in his ass," Raghu screeched and gave a playful clap.

"So Mr Iyer will take the last round?"

"Yes, along with a senior human resource manager," Raghu said and stretched his arms in exhaustion.

"Chetan shares his last name with Mr Iyer so he stands a better chance," Aman said as he played with his sleeve button. Raghu laughed when he heard this and stretched his arms feeling exhausted playing table tennis all day.

"Caste doesn't work in office politics. Don't worry about caste and all in today's world," he reiterated while closing his laptop.

"Chetan is a good friend of mine and I feel he doesn't even want to grow," Aman said, and excused himself when his cell phone started ringing.

It was Nisha calling even as he failed to pick the phone on time. He took a taxi to reach in time, for he had a complete faith in taxi drivers of Mumbai who are capable enough to reach any destination in time using the shortest possible route, even if it required breaking some rules.

He managed to reach the restaurant just in time, and even apologised for the delay.

Nisha looked stunning in her black skirt and white sleeveless top.

They exchanged a few glances and after a decent conversation, hired a taxi.

"You are so beautiful, you remind me of Marilyn Monroe," he said as he took her hand in his hand.

In a moment of passion, they stared for some time and kissed even as the taxi driver adjusted his mirror to have a better view.

"Let's go to a five star hotel for a lunch and a night out," she said combing her hair.

Aman was in for a shock but agreed. "Night out! It might be a bit expensive," he said checking the metre, which was running swiftly.

"Three thousand for the room and you have to pay me another eight thousand for the night," she said looking in his eyes.

"What?" Aman's worst fears came true.

"Don't you want to continue our passion?" she asked candidly putting her hand over his shoulders.

"Stop," he said and the driver halted abruptly near the bakery.

"Get out. Get out of the cab, I say," he said, opening the door.

"You bastard, you seem to be a eunuch," she shouted even as a wide eyed Aman couldn't believe all this. Nisha threw a hundre drupee at him.

"Keep the change as a tip, you beggar," she said as she got out of the cab. Aman wore a stunned look, but the driver managed some giggles.

"Bitch," he shouted, gesturing the cab driver to start the cab.

"Good idea for not paying an escort," the driver said as he checked the mirror.

"Shut up!" Aman shouted as he buttoned up his shirt.

The excitement in him had finished, as he was motionless when he opened the door.

He made some coffee and sat on his favorite armchair.

He had Priya's number, but didn't have the guts or enthusiasm required to dial in. As he had kept his laptop in his office, he felt insanely handicapped without it.

"Escorts on a matrimonial website, I can't believe it," he said taking a sip of coffee.

He even tried watching television, but switched it off after some time.

A small beep signalled an incoming message. He read the message and a smile flashed on his face. "Call me, if you are free," read the message.

He went to the balcony even as darkness had taken over. He managed some courage and dialled in Priya's number.

"Hey!"

"Hi, it's good that you called. I was about to doze off in the next ten minutes. I am completely exhausted."

"That's fine. I will be a manager soon. I am sorry for my blurts earlier," he said leaning over the small stool kept there.

"Congratulations. Also, I speak the truth and like to hear the same."

"That's so nice and courageous," Aman complimented and tried to be as polite as possible.

After a couple of exchanges, the conversation diverted to ex-lovers.

"When I was doing my engineering in Panchgani, I dated Rhea. After we broke up, my romantic life remained stagnant mostly due to the work pressure," he said checking the noise at the ground floor from his balcony.

"Even my ex-boyfriend did his engineering in Panchgani. Which college?" she asked excitedly even as Aman felt happy to hear her breaths.

"Panchgani has only one engineering college which comes under Pune University. ZIT, to be precise."

"My boyfriend was a cheat. We met through Facebook and broke up through Facebook."

Aman smiled and asked the reason. "Meeting through Facebook is fine, but how did your breakup happen through Facebook? I mean you can share it if it's not personal."

"That's fine. He was a famous DJ and once he messaged my friend for a romantic slip," she said stressing on her words. Aman couldn't understand and asked for explanation.

"We had some romantic fun in Goa when we were together and he messaged my best friend asking her out for some wild fun and that bitch agreed. However, I caught her when I saw her reply. When I asked, he insisted that his profile was hacked and all, but I knew that bastard was fully capable for stooping so low," she said angrily and started crying.

"Fun in the sense... Are you a virgin?" he asked even as he used all his imagination to visualise her.

“What do you think?” she asked.

“I feel you are not, but I may be wrong,” he chipped in.

Priya wasn’t amused, but liked Aman’s candour.

“You are correct. How can you expect someone who was in a relationship and has been to Goa to still be a virgin?” showing her sarcasm, she reiterated.

“No, virginity is not a dignified thing, it’s just lack of opportunity for men. I am not a virgin for your information,” he tried his best to hide his virginity, which was an outdated concept in recent years, “You are a thinking beauty.”

“Thanks,” she thanked him for the compliment.

“You are also a nice guy, very calm and composed,” she said even as Aman was almost flying after the compliment.

They talked for an hour or so and then bade adieu for the night. During the conversation, she confessed about Hemant who was her ex-boyfriend.

Aman added her on Facebook as well and their talks continued with chatting in the day and long phone conversations in the nights.

When Aman insisted, they went for date that went very well, and he was pleased to know that Priya was more beautiful than her pictures. As expected, Aman proposed and she accepted after a week. That week was the longest in his life, even as he waited with bated breath. He was more than eager to have Priya’s name tattooed on his body, but after seeing Chetan’s fate, he changed his mind. Somehow, for a rich, handsome, qualified person, the impossible was accomplished by a matrimonial website.

Wherever you may be, love conquers all as it comes to you when you least expect it.

❖❖❖

12

29th February

From our birthday, until we die, is but the winking of an eye.

Chetan and Ballu managed to be at home in time for the cricket match. They rushed to the living room to check the match, but the power cut separated them from the cricket match. "That's horrible, the laptop also isn't charged properly," Chetan said, as he shut his laptop.

"Don't worry, I will check the score on Facebook through my mobile Internet," Ballu said even as the sluggish speed seemed determined to annoy him. Feeling frustrated, he tried his hand again at the Internet option, but it was taking ages to connect.

"I am ordering a vegetarian pizza. Do you want something?" Chetan asked keeping his hand on the receiver. Ballu could not understand the question and Chetan had to repeat.

"Order something in non-vegetarian for me," Ballu said, as he removed the battery from the mobile and put it back in.

"I will call you back," Chetan banged the phone.

"What happened?" Ballu asked keeping the mobile aside.

"How would I know non-vegetarian dishes?" Chetan yelled while resting on his sofa, stretching his legs and yawned.

"Chicken barbeque pizza and a bottle of coke for me."

Chetan started some stretching session and insisted, "You will call now."

Chetan seemed hooked to power yoga seeing the number of yoga related books neatly kept on the small bookshelf.

"It's the first number on the third page in the diary kept near the phone," Chetan said, turning his neck giving a pose similar to what Shilpa Shetty did in the inaugural volume of power yoga. Cursing the power cut, Ballu called in to have his favourite pizza ordered along with some vegetarian stuff for his friend.

While on the phone, the sudden movement in the blades of the fan indicated the arrival of power supply, which had Chetan rush towards the television in search of the remote.

"Also make the barbeque crisper and the vegetarian pizza with some garlic in it," Ballu continued. News was being telecast even as Chetan was just not able to change the channel without the remote. "Bring the card machine. We will pay with our debit cards. Listen..." Ballu hung up and ran towards his friend.

"Do you have sufficient cash? I have ordered two pizzas and some ice-cream along with the coke," Ballu said staring at the newsreader.

"What about me?" Chetan asked looking straight at him. "Didn't you order something for me as well?" Ballu smiled and said, "Yes, one garlic pizza for you. Also, do you have enough cash as I am running out of cash today," he said, trying to change the channel through the button on the television.

Ballu connected the laptop through the A/C adaptor and opened the Facebook to check the status of the match. Chetan was already logged on Facebook and this gave Ballu a brilliant opportunity to check Chetan's personal messages.

"Please stay away from my account and stop trying to call me," read a message with the name 'Tigress going berserk'. No rocket science was required to know the reason behind the message. Chetan was busy checking some combinations for changing the channel. He gave up and sat near the television waiting for the sports update. "I have always hated this bloody rain. It doesn't pour where required and only pours on cricket grounds instead," Ballu said, checking the latest update on cricket match between India and England.

"Absolutely true," Chetan replied, cursing the chaotic relation between cricket and rains and took the laptop. "It's raining and the pitch inspection will be done in an hour or so," Chetan said while giving the laptop back even as Ballu was trying to imitate his friends' yoga moves.

"Did you check my display picture?" Chetan asked playfully.

Ballu smiled and said, "No". The news was over and the match score was being displayed at the bottom of the screen on the news channel.

"England had won the toss and elected to bat. We can have our dinner until India bats then," Ballu said, confirming the news from a couple of sports websites.

The odds and evens on Facebook were in India's favour at 63:37 and Ballu added his rating to give a negligible raise to the ratings. "I am desperate to bet with someone," Ballu said sitting on the sofa with his wet trousers, which spoiled the comfort of the elegant sofa set.

"If India wins, you will pay the bill and I will do the same, if England does." Chetan thought for a while and agreed. "The first innings will take around three hours and the pizza delivery will be done in the next fifteen minutes, so anyways Chetan will pay the bill," he told himself and smiled back at him.

"I am going for a shower. Call me when the match starts." Chetan said while hopping to the other room. He displayed the thumbs up sign to confirm the betting.

"Where are you going?" Ballu asked as he put a finger in his right ear to unblock it.

"Where will a person go for a shower?" he asked throwing his wet jacket on the floor.

Ballu made an awkward face and continued surfing the Internet. He was known to go on a tour on Facebook as usual. His tour included checking display pictures of females in his friend list and then checking their friends and their friends before coming to his own account. He lifted the electric iron to find the remote neatly kept under it. "Thank god, I found it." He tried to change the channels, but either the remote or the television was just not responding. Somebody knocked at the door, which made him anxious, and he checked his wallet to confirm the amount. 'One-sixty five rupees' he shouted and instead of opening the door, he rushed to the washroom and knocked.

"What happened?" Chetan asked shutting the tap, which was making a lot of noise. "Somebody is knocking at the door," Ballu said putting his right ear to the washroom door.

Chetan was so irritated that he banged the door, poured some water on himself and said, "If someone is knocking, go and open the door." The knocking on the main door continued. "But, I don't have sufficient cash with me," Ballu said confirming the money.

"What has your money got to do with knocking on the door?" Chetan shouted again while opening the door and closing it abruptly.

"It might be the pizza delivery guy asking for the payment," Ballu said standing close to the door. "My wallet is on the shelf, but first check if he accepts cards." Ballu rushed to open the door to see the pizza delivery guy balancing some packets with his right hand, even as his left hand had some carry bags, which he managed to balance well. In spite of the pressure it generated, the smile on his face was still intact. Pizza delivery guys are always big hearted and somehow manage a smile even in the most intricate circumstances.

"Chetan Iyer!" he said, keeping the bags on the floor.

"Yes," Ballu replied even as the guy was confused to see a turbaned man with a South Indian surname.

"The order, pizza order," he said as he smiled and counted the number of packets.

The aroma filled the air making the angry young man Ballu look more like a hungry young man.

"Did you bring the card machine?" Ballu asked looking at the parcel when hunger took over.

"No sir. We accept cards only at the restaurants," he said keeping the bags on the chair. Ballu wasn't amused but his face displayed a different picture altogether.

"Okay, kindly wait for some time," Ballu said as he checked the shelf trying to find his friend's wallet. He finally found his wallet and was shocked to find only some coins in it.

Feeling embarrassed, he rushed towards the washroom but it was unoccupied, which made him restless. Chetan entered the scene with a towel wrapped around him.

"Hi," he said, rushing towards the shelf.

Ballu took his friend to the other room even as the delivery guy seemed enjoying the highlights of the previous match which were being telecast to substitute the live match held up due to the torrential rains in Chennai.

"Sir, please be fast," he said as he smiled. "Please."

"Just one minute," Chetan said as Ballu clutched him to the other room.

"What happened?" he asked shrugging off.

"I checked your wallet and all you have is nine rupees," Ballu said, placing the coins on the table next to them.

"What are you saying? Where are the three thousand rupee notes?" he asked as he checked the wallet. Ballu burst out laughing even as the delivery guy felt strange.

Chetan checked the wallet again and managed to bring out three notes from it.

"What?" Ballu asked, giving a stunned look.

Chetan asked him to hand over the money and he went to his bedroom.

Ballu who still bore a stunned look, checked the wallet to see if he could find some more money. He handed over the money after confirming the order and sat down to watch the highlights of the earlier match.

Chetan took his pizza and sat on the chair checking his messages on his phone. Dev's birthday was being flashed in the list of latest birthdays on the main page of Facebook.

"Twenty-nineth February is coming soon," he said taking a bite of his pizza.

"So what?" Ballu asked changing the channel.

"Where is the remote? I am searching for it since ages now," Chetan said taking some more bites of his favourite garlic pizza.

"It was under the electric iron right on the table," he said drifting towards the television.

"Who kept it there?"

"How would I know? You must have kept it and forgotten about it," Ballu said checking the news channel.

"So you don't know the significance of Twenty-nineth February..." he said, typing a message.

"Advance happy birthday wishes from ABCD," he typed in.

"It's a leap year which comes once in every four years," Ballu replied sleeping on the floor after the dinner. Chetan packed the bags and put them in the dustbin next to the door.

"Man, it's Dev's birthday. He will be twenty-eighth in a week," he said, even as Ballu stood up and rushed towards the laptop.

"Yes, I remember. He is coming to Mumbai on Friday, right?" he asked, managing a seat next to Chetan on the sofa. Ballu finally managed to remember Dev's birthday.

"Yes, we will call him directly at Prem's if he comes at night," he said drinking some coke. Ballu grabbed the laptop on the pretext of checking his Facebook account, but opened his favourite porn site instead. He had to close it, when he saw Chetan coming towards him. He opened Facebook and messaged Dev confirming the timings of his flight.

The match was abandoned after continuous rains slashed Chennai.

"That's crap, why do they keep matches in the rain-affected area?" Ballu asked, checking something in the local newspaper. Ballu was known for his dogmatism and normally no one dared argue with him, at least when it came to cricket.

"It rains everywhere in India," Chetan admonished scanning through the channels.

"Still, they should keep matches in Rajasthan or MP where it rains scantily, right?"

Chetan burst out laughing and made a mockery of his suggestion, "Send your suggestions to the cricket board." Chetan messaged his postal address via email, just in case Dev managed to land in Mumbai at odd hours. "I will keep a duplicate key under the carpet near the door," he messaged him again. "We will celebrate his birthday at Prem's," Ballu suggested while reading the newspaper.

"Prem's is lucky for us as well," Ballu said as he looked for the keys of his bike near the table. "I will make a move now, it's getting late."

Later, the messages continued until the D-day and as promised Dev landed at six in the evening directly at Chetan's place even as Aman was waiting for him at the airport. Chetan's apartment was locked and as per the instructions, Dev pulled the carpet to get the duplicate keys to Chetan's apartment. Twenty-nineth being a Saturday, gave ample reasons to be indolent for everyone.

Chetan returned to get the shock of his life. The door was opened and he could hear people laughing. Ballu and Dev were chatting on the sofa even as the TV was throwing loud music.

"I am so sorry, I almost forgot," Chetan apologised as he entered the room.

Chetan could not control his emotions and hugged his friend reminding Ballu of a scene from the worldwide hit, 'Brokeback Mountain'.

"Man, where were you? No contact, no messages, no Facebook," Chetan said checking his friend's trimmed beard.

"I almost forgot, happy birthday brother," Ballu said while completing a three way hug. Chetan excused himself later on and went towards the kitchen. "Call that fool, Dev is already in," Ballu said decreasing the volume of the television which was still displaying the same song.

"Shut it down," Chetan said gesturing with his hands.

"You have grown a nice, trendy beard like me," Ballu said, checking his friend's beard.

"What's the plan?" Dev asked sipping some juice.

"It's your birthday, you should tell us." Dev laughed and gulped the orange juice.

"Prem's! What else?" Ballu suggested while adjusting the pile of newspapers on the floor.

Chetan called Aman and asked him to come to his apartment.

"But what about Dev?" Aman asked. "He came to the apartment directly," Ballu shouted, taking the mobile from Chetan. Aman gnashed his teeth but the excitement of meeting Dev, calmed him.

Chetan brought some old albums reminding them of their old nostalgic moments of college and the hostel in particular. They were more emotionally attached to their hostel than their college, which was evident from their membership of countless hostel related communities on Facebook.

"I wish Riyaz would join us some day like Dev," Ballu said, checking the album cover, which had their group photo taken before the start of the marathon.

Chetan brought along a new album, which also included his wedding snaps. "I almost forgot, heartiest congratulations on your wedding," Dev stood up and hugged his friend who looked embarrassed.

"I will tell you something, before you hear from someone else. We have broken up and live separately now," Chetan said even as Dev was stunned and confirmed it with Ballu who nodded in anticipation. Chetan had always shared everything with Dev. Dev was desperate to talk to him, but decided to wait for the right moment.

"Also I have bought some gifts for you," Dev said, showing the small multi-coloured bag which he kept near the sofa. "No, not now." He shouted when Ballu jumped towards the bag. Aman entered the room to accelerate the celebrations.

One thing was common between them; they all jumped and hugged Dev when they saw him, reminding them of their college days.

"Let's go in my car," Aman said, showing them the keys of his new car. "Please."

Ballu posed and checked himself in the mirror nearby.

"Hot blooded men, guitars and rainy memories.... Where should we go?" Chetan asked putting his hand across Aman's shoulder.

"With a puff in my heart and a beer in my hand, it's raining again... my heart is paining again," Ballu sang making some imaginary guitar moves.

"Its not raining," Dev said, giving Chetan a playful clap.

"Three cheers for Prem's, long live Prem's!"

The general elections were scheduled for next week making twenty-nineth a dry day. "It's a dry day today. Didn't the manager inform you earlier?" Ballu asked confirming the news.

"I have two quarters of Vodka. We can arrange some snacks and sit in my balcony if that's fine with you all."

"Four men, two quarters of vodka, it's like an insult to our manhood. No rum, no party," Ballu added and took the car keys from Aman.

"Prem's is open on dry days even if the shutter is down. We could try talking with the manager." Exactly after fifteen minutes, they set out in Aman's car. He took a sharp turn and halted at the bakery. "I will be back in a minute," Aman said as he hopped out of his car.

"It's getting late, man," Chetan said hurriedly. Aman took a long time and returned only when he started getting calls.

"Sorry," he said hopping into his car. "Driver, please be fast."

They reached Prem's to see it closed, signalling the triumph of their anticipation.

Chetan and Aman had to convince and pay a hefty sum to get in.

"Thank you uncle," they shouted in unanimity.

Managing their favourite table wasn't that difficult as there were only two groups including them.

Tables were seen to be vacant even in the dim light at the bar and it was so different not to witness the noise and the crowd. Aman opened the small carry bag to have the chocolate cake popped up.

"Happy Birthday, Dev" were the words written with white chocolate on the cake.

"I know you like chocolate cakes," Aman said even as Dev was eager to share the gifts which he had brought.

The manager was surprised to hear their order. "Eight quarters of rum? Are you sure sir?" he confirmed while making a note of their order.

Dev was happy that in spite of some initial hiccups, everyone seemed settled in their life. Tears flooded their eyes when Dev cut the cake. "This is my best birthday, even better than our hostel adventures," he declared, giving the first piece of cake to Ballu who passed on the piece to Chetan who finally tasted it.

Ballu could not handle the excitement about the gifts. "Now tell us about the gifts you bought for us."

Dev smiled and opened the small bag, which he managed to guard, until now.

He carefully opened the bag even as Ballu was expecting something fragile to appear from the box. "What is this?" Ballu asked and Dev smiled in anticipation. "Oh my god! I can't believe this."

Dev had bought their old 'Magic Boxes' with him. Chetan took Ballu's magic box and opened it. "Did Ballu make a magic box?" Chetan asked as he checked the colour of the magic box. Ballu was embarrassed to admit the fact, "So what?"

Aman checked his magic box and felt so happy that he almost kissed Dev. "We love you, man." The bar manager was in splits even as the other group had finished their drinks and moved out. They were asked to leave from the other side of the bar to maintain the secrecy. He pulled out something, which looked more like a sheet of paper from the bag. "What's this now?" Ballu asked.

Chetan and Aman were busy checking their magic boxes when they shouted, "Oh my god!" Ballu could not control his happiness when the poster was rolled open.

Dev had brought the old Bryan Adams' picture, which he proudly flaunted in the hostel.

Ballu kissed the poster as he read the notes on it, even the poster looked old and had some ink marks on the sides.

"You are responsible for everything!" Chetan said to get some surprised looks and Ballu had just managed, not to spill his drink.

"What! Are you serious, dude?" Ballu asked as he patted his back.

"Now I know why our dreams never came true. Dev had our magic boxes, so how could we succeed?" he continued sipping some beer.

Dev agreed and smiled back in return to see his friends settle in their chairs again.

"What else? What were you doing all these years?" Ballu asked, stretching his hands, and slipped in some more rum.

After graduation, I worked for two years and then joined a motivational group in Bangalore. I have a friend named Ved in Bangalore police, who is working on a thesis for inspirational theories and we run a website called 'www.okiedoks.com," he said, taking a puff from Ballu's cigarette. "So you are a motivational speaker!"

The drinks continued for an hour and the repercussions started showing up.

They ventured into their old nostalgic college days and the party continued its drinking frenzy. After some time, Aman started to cry to get some stunned looks.

"What happened?" Ballu asked drifting his chair towards his friend.

"Nothing is going as per my will. I have a loan of fifteen lakhs, which kicks my ass all day. I am not as cool as I show off; I met my girlfriend through a matrimonial website. Life is shit," he said, wiping his tears.

"That's fine. You win some, you lose some. Don't take things so seriously," Dev consoled him while sipping a drink.

Ballu who managed to be quiet for a while, started to pour his drops of pessimism.

"Now, my story," Ballu insisted. Chetan gave a wide-eyed look even as Aman bit his lower lip in anger. "Shut up, you spoilt brat," yelled Aman banging his hand on the table, which triggered a mini earthquake as one of the drinks fell on the ground.

"I will pay for it," he said, when the manager came to the table.

"There is nothing in which I succeeded. It started when I got a second class in engineering," he said as he stood up and poured his drink on the ground, "My parents never wanted a child like me. Life is shit if you see from my eyes."

Chetan believed his life was screwed the most and started his story even as Ballu excused himself to go to the washroom.

"What about me? My wife caught me exchanging nude pictures and left me. My parents don't even know that their son got married and even divorced now."

Dev gave a confused look and sighed, "Divorced?"

"I mean separated," Chetan said, looking at the half-full, half-empty glass.

Ballu returned and continued his session of pouring pessimistic toxin.

"Give life a tough fight," Dev said and Ballu clapped for him. Ballu changed his gears to show some sarcasm. "Come into our shoes and you will understand the darkness of life from a batsman point of view," Ballu said filling his drink.

"But, you used to be a bowler, right?" Chetan chipped in.

"Okay, from a bowler's point of view," he replied and took a sip of his drink.

The next thirty minutes were filled with drunken discussions about life even as Dev felt frustrated and ordered something to eat.

"Let's play a game," he said and banged his hand on the table while looking around.

Hearing the word 'game', Ballu felt a bit uneasy.

"Life is playing against us and you still want to play your games. No more magic boxes please," Ballu said and stretched his legs on the adjacent chair.

"I don't believe in solving life's problem, I believe in living life," Dev said enthusiastically.

"Okay, shoot!"

He tore a piece of paper, made some chits and wrote something on it. He hurled the chits, which landed straight on the table. "Ballu, choose a chit," he said dispersing the chits.

Ballu wore a confused look and chose a chit to find his name written on it.

Dev kept the chit aside and asked Chetan to follow the same.

Chetan showed his frustration while choosing his chit, but finally managed to choose a chit and read out Aman's name. He even showed the chit as a proof.

He picked a new chit to have Chetan's name and the last chit had Dev's name.

He opened the magic box one by one, opening Ballu's magic box first.

"I want to be a rockstar," he read. Next, he opened Aman's box and read, "I want to be a manager of a big firm." Next he opened Chetan's magic box and read, "I want to marry Katrina." Ballu could not control his laughter and shouted, "Open your magic box now."

Aman checked the chits all over again. "I want to shock the world in a positive way," Dev read from his chit and put it in the box again.

"What's the game?" Aman asked checking Dev's magic box. Their curiosity was at their peak when Dev said, "Wait, let the order arrive."

The order took a long time to come even as it was half past twelve in the morning.

"Tell me..." Ballu asked eating a cucumber slice.

"Wait, let me come from the loo," Chetan insisted, and rushed to the washroom followed by Aman who tucked in.

After the order was served, and they were settled, Dev started his theory.

"The order of the day was Ballu, Aman, then Chetan and me. One will confirm his dream and the other three will make sure the dream will come true."

Everyone looked at each other, making some weird, confused faces.

"Like? I didn't understand," Aman interrupted as he ate his meal.

"I, Aman and Chetan will help Ballu to become a rockstar and vice-versa for others."

"But," adjusting his table, Chetan poked in, "Katrina has married her English boyfriend."

After a good laugh, Dev repeated his plan. "We will help you marry someone very special, even more special than Neha," Aman said giving a playful clap and smiled endlessly.

"She is special, no one can be like her," Chetan replied contradicting the statement.

"So, the fire is still there," Ballu interrupted even as he poured a drink again.

"Okay, we will help you marry anyone of your choice. Is that fine now?"

"Let's see how it goes."

"What about Dev?" Aman asked.

“You people have to make a plan for me to shock the world. It’s your problem from today,” Dev said while taking a bite of the vegetable cutlet.

“Done.”

“Absolutely,” Aman said as he drank some water.

“Cheers for our friendship,” Chetan yelled getting a thunderous applause. “Cheers!”

❖❖❖

13

The Game

Dreams have triggered greater things than the entire technology put together.

"What happened to the radio jockey interview?" Dev asked, taking a sip of coffee.

Even the sun was not able to disturb the serene atmosphere of a lovely evening at the coffee shop. Ballu who was sitting just next to him, dipped a toast in the cup of tea and smiled. "It was fun actually," he said, looking up.

Dev was sure that Ballu might not have cleared the interview gauging the cold response he received and even Ballu's eyes showed the frustration which he was trying to cover through his words.

"So, what are you plans now?" Dev asked, sipping some more coffee as he checked something on his laptop.

"I love the sedate ambience of this place."

"Me too," Dev sighed.

There is something exciting about these open-air restaurants – those which have a plastic decorative roof with no walls.

"I would look for a suitable job in April. I know an agent who will arrange for some fake experience for me to cover the time I wasted, just for ten thousand."

"What about our plan?" Dev enquired adjusting his chair. Ballu gave his trademark, vexing smile.

"I want to check something very important. Show me your laptop please."

"Okay," Dev pushed his laptop adjusting the teacups, which seemed to block the path. Ballu adjusted the crockery and kept the laptop on the table.

"It doesn't seem connected to the Internet," he said, checking the 'page not displayed' message on the Google homepage.

"Plug in the data card properly."

Adjusting the data card, he opened www.facebook.com to check his messages.

"He was going to message me. Let me call that bastard. Also I have the MTV Roadies auditions next Thursday."

"Who?" Dev asked looking at the upper side of the laptop.

"The agent."

Dev did not want to trouble his friend with his straightforward questions which can destroy the happiness of a nonchalant guy, and managed to divert the conversation to an entertaining one- a typical Ballu type of a dialogue.

"How is the new bike?

"It's great! Five hundred cc of raw power," Ballu said and after checking his Facebook account thoroughly with no tours today, he handed over the laptop.

"So you are a motivational speaker, right?" he asked, checking the hoarding displayed on the other side.

"Yeah!" Dev replied turning around in anticipation.

"I had practised thoroughly for the interview and even tried to get a reference, still the job eluded me and the guy who eventually got through, is one hell of a crap."

Dev smiled demonstrating calmness and said, "From a distance, everything seems to be pleasant."

Ballu could not take this as an answer and blurted, "That guy passes time all day at campaigns and is a part time model with a guttural voice. He is in my friend list on Facebook. His name is Rahul; I don't know his last name."

"Hmm. Tell me one thing. If someone scratches his ass, does he tell anyone about it?"

Ballu was surprised even as he managed a laugh after confirming their privacy.

"Are you taking a dig at my expense? Why would someone announce it?"

"Yeah, so how would you know about others' struggle?" Dev asked and wrote something on his notepad.

"Some things are easy to gauge," Ballu replied taking a deep breath, making his friend aware of his boredom at the argument.

"How many people have you caught scratching?"

"What are you up to?" Ballu asked

"Life takes everything from you... to give you everything," Dev replied after a very long pause.

Ballu liked the quote so much that he made a note of it on his mobile phone.

"Is that your quote?"

"No, that's my experience," Dev replied gulping some more water.

"Dev, you have matured so much. You have done so much for me," Ballu said as he hugged his friend.

They exchanged their seats as Ballu insisted on sitting on the other side to have a better view at a group of girls sitting at the corner of the restaurant, near the sideway.

"It's a great view from this side. I should have swapped the seats earlier," he said, as he ordered some more of his favorite coffee.

Ballu was known for not carrying his watch, and would either check the time on his mobile phone or ask others as he did this time around as well and got a shock of a lifetime.

When he enquired about the time, the girls changed their seats. Ballu had to swap his seat again to have a better view.

"I had told you about my friend in Bangalore, Ved. He is a police inspector cum motivational trainer and he has his theories which might work for you, I guess."

The word 'solution' can attract even the most pessimist person in the world and Ballu was no exception.

"I work so hard, still somebody else wins over me. I am talented and it's crap losing to average performers," Ballu justified giving a dumb look.

"Being talented puts a lot of pressure on a young mind."

Ballu smiled at the thought of being addressed as talented, and that too by a highly intellectual person like Dev.

"When you are young, the amount of frustration is proportional to the level of intelligence. The brighter you are, the more chances of getting frustrated arise."

Ballu came closer and made himself comfortable on the chair next to Dev.

“Some people are just plain lucky,” Ballu said, showing his pessimistic side.

“Luck is nothing. Success gives its own hints. When you get the feeling that people who don’t work as hard as you do, and still compete with you, that’s the hint success wants you to give. Success comes with its own price or else everyone would be successful, right?”

“These things are easier said than done,” Ballu justified, ordering some french-fries.

“What did Bryan Adams say?” Dev asked enthusiastically hoping for a blissful response.

“Choose easier options and live an ordinary life. Let’s see, how the auditions for the MTV Roadies go. I will keep you updated.”

“Success and failure are short lived so there is no need to take any of them seriously. Everything ends one day,” Dev continued as he checked the menu card.

“Absolutely true,” Ballu shouted, grabbing the attention of the people around him.

“Also, if you were trying for the position of a Radio Jockey, then practising hard on your guitar won’t work. Why will they take a guitarist for the position of a radio jockey?”

Ballu smiled as if he was waiting for this question.

“That’s true, but I play the instrument so well,” Ballu replied.

“True, but they have to run a business, right?” Dev justified. Ballu was never comfortable in arguing with Dev.

“Should I practise playing the guitar for the MTV auditions?” Ballu asked taking a sip again.

“Sure,” Dev smiled and patted his back.

“Dev Shetty, you’re an ideal man. A hero,” he said, giving a playful clap.

Failure tests the patience of a person and Ballu suffered from nervous breakdowns even as a teenager, so however hard Dev inspired, Ballu fell flat when it came to trying after a fresh failure. Working in your field isn't that hard and Ballu enjoyed practising for the Mumbai auditions. Trying was his only option but still on Dev's insistence, he made a plan and even studied clippings of the last year's auditions.

As per the plan, he managed to practise for fourteen hours on the first day. Second day started well, but yesterday's motivation did not carry over.

After a couple of drinks at Prem's, it was impossible for him to concentrate on anything.

Coming home, he tried his hand at his favourite song, "With a puff in my heart and a beer in my hand...."

He didn't practise much today and the frustration was building up, making him defensive. Getting defensive, a man can lose even from a winning position.

"Everything is crap. I will look for a job instead," he told himself as he threw his guitar on his bed.

He jumped on his bed and started crying slowly. Turning this side, he saw the Bryan Adams' poster and wiped his tears. It reminded him of Dev and his words, whenever he glanced at it.

The black and white picture was torn from the sides and was held by an army of tapes pasted sideways not to dislodge the beauty of the words written below it. "Choose easy options, get an ordinary life. Choose the toughest path, and get a life. It all bows down to how much you want something," were the words written below the poster. Before starting, and after his practice ended, he would touch the words to feel the value in it, but he was somewhat depressed today.

He opened his laptop to check if Dev was online, but it wasn't the case. He dialled in Dev's number to get a busy tone.

"Pick up, pick up please..."

"Hey, what's up?" Dev asked, even as Ballu smiled, hearing his mentor's words.

"I feel, I won't clear the MTV auditions."

"Be a man; give it your best shot."

"But," Ballu interrupted.

"Always remember, whatever happens in life, dress up and show up. Be a man! When you can see your goal clearly, you cannot lose your focus. Even in the toughest situations of life, if you can smile at life, life would definitely smile back at you," Dev continued with his voice breaking at times.

"I will give my best," Ballu promised, drinking some weird coloured fluid and kept the glass on the table.

Dev wished him luck for the auditions and asked him to practise continuously for the next six hours. He also promised him that he would be there at the auditions.

It was hard at the start, but Ballu practised the same tunes continuously until his fingers ached. He took a break, and it was almost two in the morning and Ballu was still practising at his place.

A day before the audition, Dev was at his place. The room was in a mess with clothes scattered all over and Ballu was talking on his mobile phone, when Dev entered the room.

"I will call you after some time," he said, disconnecting the call.

Getting up, he cleaned the bed to make it comfortable. "Hey! Thanks for being there man. I tried to practise for the last few days," Ballu said cleaning the bed sheet.

"That's great, I am happy for you. We will watch the clips and enact some role-play sessions, where I would act as a judge," Dev said, checking the laptop.

"Sure, I will be back in a moment," Ballu said as he rushed to the washroom.

Dev looked at the mess and found something interesting in their college album, which was lying beneath the layers of bed sheets.

Ballu removed his turban as he checked himself in the mirror near the table.

"How is my new look?" he asked, adjusting his hair with his hands.

"Cool! You should have tried this earlier, I feel." Ballu cackled and moved his hands through his hair.

"My dad will kill me if he sees me like this. I always wanted to cut my hair but... leave it. Let's prepare for the audition," Ballu said and sat on the bed next to Dev.

Dev took the laptop and after some tries managed to download some more clips of the last year auditions. "Roadies reminds me of our college days when we used to be ragged."

"Absolutely! So we must do what we did in college to avoid it, I feel," Ballu said, placing his mobile in the charging kit on the table.

"When you are going for the Roadies auditions, just be yourself. No preparations are needed," Dev added.

Ballu grabbed his guitar and played his favourite tune disturbing the strings.

Dev recorded as Ballu sang and played better than what he was capable of.

Squeezing a few breaks for smoking, they practised for a long time. Guitar was his passion and Ballu's world revolved around it.

"I will be at your place at seven in the morning, okay?" Ballu said, keeping his laptop on the table.

"At seven? So early?"

"We have to reach Andheri at least by ten; also I want to practise our favourite tune on the electric guitar instead of the normal one. All this may take a lot of time, right?"

Dev nodded in agreement. "Call me before coming and best of luck for the event," Dev said, wishing him luck.

Feeling exhausted, he felt sleepy, but the thought of checking his Facebook made him rush to his laptop. Chetan had not updated his status, but the display message showed his frustration at life.

'CHETAN - Fighting life's demons,' was his display message.

Chetan had made his side of story quite plain and simple.

"Do you think I can indulge in infidelity?" Chetan asked whenever the topic of his separation was raised.

Next morning, Ballu managed to land at Dev's place, but wasted time discussing their nostalgic college days. On Dev's insistence, they were at the Andheri Kurla Complex at half past nine.

"Oh my god!" Ballu shouted as he saw the crowd, which had gathered.

Sea of people thronged every corner, from the side of the restaurant facing it until the railway station, which was at least some twenty-five metres away from it.

"It's good that we came a bit earlier."

"Also, I see a lot of youngsters... college kids to be precise. I would look like a senior citizen compared to them. They have a better chance of making it to the finals, I feel," Ballu said, adjusting the buckles of his sack.

"Always remember the legendary Imran Khan's words when he was asked if they could win the world cup – chances are less, but they are."

"Yes, he was right, chances are less," Ballu said, touching his throat and complained about his throat. "Had it not been for this throat, I would have done it."

"Strength lies in a man, not in the circumstances," Dev said as he smiled and shot back.

After an hour, they were given their badges and asked to be ready for the group discussions round. "People who will clear the group discussions will be eligible for the main round," announced the video-jockey to get a thunderous applause.

"Just say what you feel. Don't contradict yourself. Have faith in yourself and in god," Dev said. Even the crowd was getting nasty with every passing minute.

Ballu hugged him and went to the group discussion room. What a sight!

He never expected to have more than a dozen competitors, but got a shock of his life.

He had to compete against forty-eight contestants.

"That's ridiculous," he yelled, seeing the number of people in the hall.

"Please be seated," the announcer shouted, seeing him argue with one of the guards.

Ballu had left his guitar with Dev and taken the sack along with him.

The topic was plain, but had a twist in it. "Should betting on cricket be made legal?" screamed the radio jockey even as the sound amplified through the mike.

Ballu decided to speak against the topic, but changed his mind at the last moment.

As soon as the bell rang signalling the start of the allotted time, people started to scream to make their presence felt.

"Betting will lead to match fixing," someone bellowed.

"No, betting is just fun and we all indulge in it, but won't accept the facts."

For the first twenty seconds, he was just not able to decide his take. The reverse countdown started signalling only one-twenty seconds were left.

"If betting is illegal, even promising something is illegal. Advertisements should also be banned as they promise anything and everything," Ballu said, standing up.

"Be seated," came a reply.

"Advertisements even allure us to drink a certain juice and get your dream girl."

Ballu was just off the track, and even his shouting at the top of his voice wasn't helping him. "Betting increases the interest for the game which is like religion for us."

The time finished and after a couple of more rounds with other people, the results of the group discussion round were to be announced.

Dev came along as they had some tea and snacks in the canteen near the auditorium.

"Let's see, chances are less, but there are chances," Ballu said, sipping his tea and offered a smile. Dev laughed on this and wished him luck. The atmosphere in the canteen tempted him to open the guitar and play something on it but the place wasn't good enough to showcase his talent.

"I have also applied for the Indian Idol auditions next week. I feel I have a greater chance there," Ballu said, checking his messages on his mobile.

After checking, he opened his favourite website using pocket Internet and found Facebook messages wishing him luck for the event. He replied to Chetan's message, thanking him for the wishes.

"Let's go!! The results will be announced any moment."

The number of people at the reception of the auditorium could be seen even from a mile.

"The results might have been pasted on the wall, I feel," Ballu said, running towards the reception.

The crowd near the centre wasn't even budging and he had to penetrate through it, making some weird noises. Within a minute, he was near the board and checked his number starting from the bottom.

"God is great!" Ballu shouted even as some unknown people hugged him.

"I can't believe it, I have cleared the first round," he said looking for Dev.

Dev was standing right next to him, but Ballu was not able to recognise him in the excitement, following the results. The crowd went berserk after the results were announced, and the board, which was used to display the results, crashed when the crowd moved.

"Please. Those who have cleared the first round should be at the audition in room number nine by half past three," the video jockey announced. "Let's celebrate," Ballu shouted in excitement. Dev knew that the battle wasn't over yet, but still agreed to be a part of the celebration.

Ballu took the guitar and played his favourite song, but the chaos absorbed the sound.

After some time, they were seen in the restaurant opposite the railway station near Kurla road, which was just some metres away from the venue.

"I just have to beat fifteen more people to become a rockstar," Ballu said, spreading his arms in excitement of the moment.

"Even if you win here, give the auditions for the Indian Idol event, next week," Dev insisted, as Ballu was always known for his complacency.

"Sure, it's a man's word," he promised and shook hands firmly.

"Raghu will screw me today. I will try to be as specific as possible," he said as he ate a piece of paneer.

"Just look into his eyes, he is a nice man who takes pride in being mean. I have a gut feeling that he might be a nice hearted gentleman," Dev said, drinking some water.

"As a child, I used to fear bald men, so even now I don't trust bald men," Ballu joked, but stopped abruptly when he saw a group of bald men enjoying their lunch nearby.

"What if he asks me to perform a physical task?"

"If he asks you to do sit-ups or something, just mention half your capacity."

"Why?" Ballu asked giving a puzzled expression.

"If you say twenty and do ten, it would be hell and everyone would enjoy your humiliation on national television," Dev said drinking some more water.

"Yes, I almost forgot. I have to inform everyone about my audition. It's the first time that I will come on the television. I hope they don't edit much of the audition," Ballu said, eating some more paneer.

"Just be yourself. No one can insult you without your permission."

Ballu couldn't understand and moved away to call someone through his mobile phone.

"Excuse me, please," Ballu waved and Dev smiled back at him.

He dialled his mother's number as he stood near the washroom, blocking the way.

"Talk in the aisle, son."

Ballu moved ahead and said, "Mumma, I have been selected for the final round of MTV roadies! You will see me on television soon."

His mother seemed confused but congratulated him on his victory and even switched on the television and scanned the channels to find MTV, which was airing some songs.

"I cannot see you on TV. Also you told you were going for your classes and went elsewhere," his mother said, switching off the TV.

"No, it's not 'live' but it will be telecast later, I think."

He called some more people and was ready for the second round. With Dev around, he felt secured, but still complacency crept in.

"I will be a rockstar soon. I have done it man," Ballu said, performing a dance step.

Dev wanted to keep his friend grounded, but just could not manage it.

Dev was asked to sit at the reception and Ballu along with other contestants were to wait in the waiting area. Dev gave a thumbs up gesture and Ballu smiled back signaling victory, while going inside.

The first person who went in came back crying sending a wave of terror through the contestants. It's really very disturbing to see a man crying his heart out and the act was in full flow at the auditions.

"What happened?" a fellow female contestant asked, showing her fake concern even as she checked to confirm if the camera was following the scene or not.

The contestant excused himself and ran towards the washroom as one of his friends followed him. The commotion was captured on camera without the contestants actually knowing it.

It was half past eight, and Ballu was the third last contestant to go in the interview room.

He said a small prayer and went in. Nevertheless, as soon he saw Raghu, the brand ambassador of the event, the energy gave way to nervousness.

"Good morning," he greeted the anchors with a smile.

"What?"

"I am sorry, good evening," he reverted after checking the time on the wall clock behind them.

"Is everything alright?" Raghu asked, checking his form.

"Yes sir," he showed some confidence with his loud voice.

"Why don't you carry a watch?" he was asked by Raghu's partner.

"Sir... that, I...," he just couldn't join the words and he started sweating when he realised that unlike what he believed, there were absolutely no retakes.

"Take it easy, man. Do you want some water?" Raghu said, ordering someone to bring some water.

"No sir, I am fine."

"So tell us something about yourself, something interesting."

Ballu swallowed his spit and started, but stopped abruptly.

"My name is Balwinder and I am a singer-cum-guitarist." He seemed happy after telling them about his favourite music instrument. He was expecting a question about guitar but life has a habit of making fun of our emotions and that too at the wrong time.

"We are waiting, be a sport, and be a man."

"Shall I play something on my guitar? Please...." He lost the plot in the first five minutes itself.

"Do you exercise?"

"Yes sir, I do."

"How many push ups can you do?" Raghu asked, taking a sip from the cold drink kept on the table near him.

He remembered what Dev had asked him, but still went with his heart.

"Twenty-five, I mean thirty."

Raghu threw the bottle of cold drink towards Ballu and he caught it at the second attempt.

"You will do thirty-five push ups."

Ballu was stunned as he moved his chair and taking god's name, managed to start. He had to stop after doing ten and took some deep breaths, even as Raghu asked him to continue or leave.

He tried his best but managed only eighteen push-ups and fell on the bright coloured flooring and just couldn't move.

"Check if he is dead?" Raghu yelled even as Ballu started breathing again, which sent a puff of dust in the air. The guards had to rush to help him but he declined.

Drinking some water, he requested to resume the interview but Raghu was adamant that he should finish the glucose-filled drink first. All this was off the camera, which thrilled him to the core.

Resuming the session, Raghu asked him some more personal questions.

"Tell me a single difference between you and a donkey."

"A donkey cannot be a guitarist," he responded with a smile.

"Good music?"

"Yes, sir."

Raghu finally asked him to play something for him.

In spite of being nervous and lethargic, he played the tune of his lifetime for more than five minutes.

Even the camera operator joined Raghu in appreciating the performance.

"That's awesome, good going," Raghu said and clapped for some more time.

"Thank you, sir."

"Would you like to try the remaining push ups?" Raghu asked and gave a cunning smile.

"Sure," he even stood up in enthusiasm.

"That's fine, take your seat," Raghu smiled as he banged his hand on the desk.

Ballu felt a bit relieved after the performance and smiled for the first time in the last hour or so bringing some humour in the process.

"Do you have a girlfriend?" Raghu asked as he stared at him.

"Yes, I mean no."

"Yes or no?" Raghu asked noting everything on the form itself.

"Yes..." Ballu said even as he looked nervous.

"What's her number?"

Getting a bit nervous, Ballu stood up and said, "How can I give my girlfriend's number on national television?"

"Okay, write the number on a piece of paper," Raghu said, as he passed on a notebook towards him, making him nervous again.

"Leave it. Tell me one thing. I will take you in the Roadies tour if you dump your girlfriend. What do you say about this offer?" Raghu asked writing something on his form.

Ballu was shocked and shivered, even as traces of sweat started to show again on his brow. He thought for a while and agreed to ditch his girlfriend.

"Damn it. You suck to the core. Get lost from here."

"Sir, but sir," he argued, but was thrown out by the guards.

Coming to the reception, the vidio jockey asked him something, but he ignored him and ran towards the waiting area, where Dev was desperately waiting for him.

Dev got up and ran towards his friend.

"Is everything all right?"

"Let's go from here. They kicked me out."

"But! Why? The results are still not out," pleaded Dev, even as Ballu packed his bags and was ready to make a move.

"Sir, you have to stay until the results are out or else you will be disqualified," said the guard, pointing towards the reception.

When Dev insisted, Ballu agreed to wait at the reception instead.

The last two contestants took a long time and even at half past ten, the results were pending.

One of the female contestants even argued with the guard who repeated his earlier statement. Food was served free, but no one was in a mood to have it.

Ballu was the most arrogant when it came to eating.

At around eleven, everyone was called for the results. Ballu knew he won't make it, but had gathered in the waiting area.

"Three people are selected from Mumbai this time. Manju, Kamesh and Rahul please move to the duty room," announced the radio jockey to a rather optimistic looking crowd.

The announcer told everyone the reasons about their exit and wished them luck for their future pursuits.

"Balwinder, you lost because you couldn't perform two tasks out of the three given," the VJ announced checking the results.

Ballu moved forward and argued. "What tasks?"

"You couldn't perform the push-ups and you agreed to ditch your girlfriend for the show, so you are out. Best of luck for your future."

Ballu was about to cry, but managed to smile as he hugged Dev and moved towards the main gate.

"Man, life is tough," he said, wiping his tears.

"Take it easy, life moves on. We will try for the Indian Idol instead."

"No, I will look for a job instead. I haven't eaten for the last eight hours, worked endlessly for the past week and what I get is a kick on my ass. I have lost faith in god."

Dev put his arms across his friend's shoulder and patted his back.

"You are on TV. What more do you want?"

"I want to be a rock star, I won't settle for ordinariness, after failing continuously," Ballu said, wiping his face with his hands.

"Success inspires, but failure teaches. Continue your hard work; we will make it to the Indian Idol for sure. I am with you. I will share some theories with you, if you don't mind."

"You won't listen. Tell me a sample theory," Ballu sighed pulling his hand out.

"Suppose you pin your hopes on something and you do not get it, still if by any chance you work hard, then something bigger than the earlier goal is destined for you."

"As in?" Ballu asked checking the time on mobile.

"Amitabh Bacchan wasn't selected when he applied for the post of a broadcaster for AIR, but he tried some more options and one day tried his luck in films and the rest is history."

"That's true. But it was him, he may be lucky."

"Luck is nothing. Everything is in our hands, patience is the key." Ballu wanted to have some drinks desperately. Ballu insisted and Dev had to agree for some drinks at Prem's. "Only a couple of drinks," he promised, parking his bike.

❖❖❖

14

Indian Idol

The impact of a TV show can be gauged from the fact that people can forget their love life.

Their favourite table was taken so they had to adjust nearby. Ballu even switched off his cell to avoid calls.

"I only drink when I am happy, so I won't drink today," Dev said as he lighted a cigarette.

"Shut up man," Ballu said, as he ordered a quarter of his favourite strong rum.

"It's good to have big dreams but it takes courage to go through the dark path it leads to. You are like me, and million others. We only feel like working hard when we see a light from the other side of the tunnel. If the light disappears, pessimism takes over," Dev said as he adjusted his chair. "Stay calm. Success is nothing but how we handle failure in our growing years. Frustration is a part and parcel of our life," he continued.

Ballu ordered some beer as well.

"Beer?"

"That leaves me with a beer in my hand," he sang his favourite song.

Dev tried his best but Ballu was in no mood to listen and after a couple of drinks, he had to take him to his place where he fell unconscious.

Later Aman and Chetan came at his place hearing about the MTV Roadies episode.

"Man, at least you were on TV. It's just the start. Remember our game, we have to help each other to fulfil our dreams," reiterated Chetan hugging his snivelling friend.

Ballu was just not ready to practise for the Indian Idol auditions even when Chetan and Aman requested. Their trip to Prem's increased, even as Ballu couldn't get over his frustration.

Ballu got the postal invite for the Indian Idol auditions, which were to be held at Mahim, this Friday. Ballu was to tear the invite but the Bryan Adams' picture somehow never allowed him to do so.

"Why does life inspire?" he asked as if Bryan Adams would answer his question. Theoretically, Byran Adams had answered his questions.

"Choose easy options, get an ordinary life," read the lines on the poster.

He called Dev to let him know about the postal invite and this brought him at Ballu's place with a newly injected enthusiasm.

Dev tried his hand at Ballu's guitar and failed miserably resulting in smiles spread across the room. "It's a difficult instrument for beginners, I have to admit," Dev said, keeping the guitar back in the bag.

"I am frustrated with life, guitar, my dad, my job and innumerable things. Also, I feel humiliated when compared to my cousins," Ballu said while typing a message.

"Life takes everything from you.... to give you everything," Dev reiterated even as Ballu turned his head to the other side. "Failure and humiliation are two different things. We take our failure as a way of naked humiliation. I know success inspires us to do more, but adversity teaches us the basics."

Ballu crawled on his bed adjusting the laptop kept on it.

As the auditions were to be held on a Friday, Chetan applied for a leave to be with his friend. As for Aman, it was a stark coincidence that whenever Ballu had his auditions, he had a date fixed through the matrimonial site.

"I had applied for a leave for the auditions, but my parents are coming with someone special," Aman said, when Dev told him about the auditions.

"Someone special! That's interesting," Chetan said, taking a sip of coffee.

"Someone from London is coming to see Neha."

"Neha?"

"I mean, my sister,"

"Oh, that's fine. We will keep you updated about the auditions. Also don't worry, I have a plan to bring him to the audition centre," Chetan said, wiping his hands using Dev's handkerchief. As decided, Dev was to directly come at the centre, while Chetan and Ballu would come there beforehand.

The auditions were to be held in the afternoon and Ballu was seen sleeping even at half past eleven.

"Your friend is waiting for you in the living room," his mother said, banging the cup of tea even as some drops fell on the table.

"Who is there? Dev?"

"Dev? Who is Dev? Chetan has come to see you," she said rushing towards the kitchen.

"You should have directly come to my room," he said, taking a sip of tea.

Reminding Chetan of hostel days, Ballu was ready in the next fifteen minutes and even managed to have a decent breakfast.

"You people put a lot of pressure on me. I know you are here to take me to the auditions, but I am really not comfortable with the idea of giving an audition, actually," he said, adjusting his spectacles to have a better view.

Ballu was always an insecure type of a person, but as Chetan was getting friendly with his parents, the submerged insecurity uprooted the tree of patience.

"Chetan likes coffee, bring some for him," he said as he literally had to push his mother into the kitchen.

Later, Ballu compelled him to take the flyover route and reached Prem's at around one in the afternoon.

"I can't believe it. It's just around a couple of hours for the audition and you are still taking it as a joke," Chetan said, locking the car door.

"Life is a joke. I am preparing myself for the frustration I will go through when the audition starts. Actually, I don't have any expectations now," he said as he walked past the counter.

"It's your life, fight or die."

Chetan had his favourite beer while Ballu who was more than eager to show his careless attitude, satiated on a quarter of rum. Chetan had to clutch him to his car even as he insisted that he is fully capable of handling the situation.

"It's so nice to have Dev back in our lives and..." he couldn't even complete the sentence and fell asleep with his hands in the upward position.

Reaching the venue, parking was the foremost issue as even before the auditions had started the parking was full leaving some places, which were reserved for the VIP area.

Dev had tried Ballu's number twice but Ballu did not even realise this.

Chetan called Dev at a small shrine near the venue. After some initial struggle, they managed to meet, in spite of the crowd on both sides of the road adjacent to the shrine.

"Why didn't you come at the venue directly?" Dev shouted in order to be audible in the noise created by the traffic jam.

"Parking was full so we had to park in the basement of the restaurant instead," he said, lighting a cigarette.

"Where is Ballu?"

"He is sleeping in my car."

"Sleeping? Is he crazy?" Dev asked as he followed Chetan to his car.

Even after repeated attempts, they were not able to wake him up and as expected poured a glass of water on him, which was more than sufficient.

"Hey, what's up?" he asked wiping his face.

"Are you drunk?" Dev asked, banging his hand on the car.

Dev and Chetan had to help Ballu until the audition center.

"Where is his guitar?" Dev said as he saw Ballu limping with his sack.

Chetan rushed to grab his guitar from the car. Ballu didn't even realise this and somehow reached the venue with cameras flashing all over.

Overall, the set and the crowd were almost similar to the MTV Rodies audition. People from all over were present at the auditions. "Don't worry, these are not the participants," Chetan said, as he saw Ballu's wide-eyed look.

"Four hundred twenty... I can't believe this," Ballu hollered, when the badge was handed over to him.

Chetan was sure Ballu wasn't as drunk as he was acting and clapped.

"What?"

"They have done justice to your personality by giving you this number," Chetan said as he burst out laughing.

"The number was different on the postal invite," Ballu persisted, but was asked to follow the orders at the reception. The funniest part was still to come. People were seen practising even at the entrance. Seeing many guitarists in the crowd, the half drunk, half-conscious Ballu was nervous again.

"You have the experience of participating in the roadies," Dev said, as he turned to check the number of people gathered at the mega event.

"It's bigger than the last years' edition," shouted someone from the crowd.

It was the same old story as most were with their friends or their family, creating a complete chaos with the noise. The venue had no canteen so people were seen enjoying their lunch near the hall itself. It might be breakfast for some, as people had turned up from all the parts of the country. They had to shell out a few thousands to be a part of the audience. The first participant came at around half past three with an extremely hopeless voice.

"The participants this year are horrible. Ballu stands a good chance," Chetan said, putting his hand over his shoulders. Ballu who had not practised for quite some time now, appeared more calm and composed than his friends.

After some more performances, they left to show some importance to their tummies. We could come by six and then join the crowd. Chetan thought Ballu might ignore them when the practice room was opened for the participants, but he was just not in the correct frame of mind and came along.

Even after the heavy dose of rum, he made sure he finished two full dishes of butter-chicken, even as his friends were mystified at his appetite.

The throat for a singer is what a bat is for a cricketer so they take full care of their prized possession, but Ballu had different plans. After finishing a smoke, Ballu bought a packet of cigarettes for himself.

"Are you crazy?" Dev asked watching his friend.

"What happened?" he reverted, taking a puff and blowing it high in the air.

After a few rounds of exchanging cigarettes and words, they were back to the auditorium when a guitarist came to display his talent.

"Ballu, one of your competitors," Dev said, clapping in response to a tune he played.

After the introduction part, he had promised something spectacular.

"I have bought an Old Persian Bible and I will imitate my Icelandic idols," he said, clearing his throat.

"Icelandic? What's that?" Ballu asked, making a weird face as he turned towards Dev.

"Icelandic is something from the Iceland."

"I know, I know, but where on earth is Iceland located?" he asked.

"It's way above England," Dev said, clapping when the crowd erupted.

The contestant tore the book in his hand and burned it on the stage itself, even as the audience clapped and some even stood up expecting a disaster waiting to happen.

"I had bought the Persian Bible on eBay by bidding thirty-five thousand rupees," he said when he was asked to explain the significance.

He prayed and sang one of the famous Beatles' songs to get a standing ovation from the crowd who were ecstatic after the performance and the ritual.

The burning of the book helped him create hysteria for himself and he was selected for the next round when the crowd supported him enthusiastically.

Chetan excused himself, talking on his mobile and went backstage without realising, and was stopped by the bodyguards who asked him to go elsewhere.

Just when he was going, some sheets of paper were flung at him. He caught one of the half-burnt pages and apologised to the guards with a smile.

He finished the call and started laughing his heart out. The guards couldn't understand and locked the door leaving him alone in the waiting area.

He ran to his friends and showed them the paper.

"What's this?" Ballu asked, checking something on his mobile.

"Do you remember the previous guy who burnt the rare Persian text?" Chetan asked as he managed to control his laughter.

Ballu stared at him and asked him to shut up.

"This is one of the pages he burnt. It's not a rare book or something, it's an English dictionary," he shouted, pointing towards the page and skillfully managed to grab others' attention.

Ballu, followed by Dev and many from the row started laughing even as they passed the page around. People just couldn't control their laughter when they came to know about the forgery of the pervious contestant.

"That bastard burnt an English dictionary claiming it to be a rare Persian text. I can't believe this," someone shouted, trying to grab the attention of the camera operator.

The camera operator and the anchors couldn't control their amusement even as Chetan was seen hugging his friends.

After an hour, Ballu was asked to report to the playing area as his turn was about to come.

Chetan wished him luck and he hugged Dev while going.

"Fight or die," he shouted as he turned towards the player's area.

After some more funny contestants, Ballu was called on the stage.

The anchor burst out laughing shouting Ballu's badge number.

"Sorry! Here comes Balwinder Walia from our very own Mumbai," he shouted as he took the name.

Dev and Chetan hugged each other and even managed to whistle around.

Ballu tried to find his friends, but was not able to do so amongst the audience. He just remembered Dev's words, "Life takes everything from you... to give you everything." Taking some deep breaths, he started playing his favourite song after his introduction round. "It's raining again, my heart is paining again," he started playing as well as singing in appropriate synchronisation.

"It's raining again, my heart is paining again...

Trying her plan, she deceived her man.

With a puff in my heart and a beer in my hand.

It's raining again, my heart is paining again.

That's leaves meeeeeeee with a beer in my hand."

He continued singing even as he stopped playing his guitar and concentrated only on the song, realising the public support he was getting. Dev and Chetan stood on their seats, dancing in anticipation.

A round of jubilant scenes followed the announcement of his entry to the main round.

Ballu grabbed the mike from the anchor and started crying to have a sudden inflow of clapping and cheering from the media hungry public.

"Sorry, I had to grab the mike to get an opportunity to speak," he said after apologising to the anchor who was all smiles even after the incident.

"I have to thank my friends Dev, Chetan and Aman for supporting me through my journey. God bless them," he said and handed over the mike to the anchor even as Chetan's eyes could not control his emotions and tiny droplets poured from his eyes. "Are you crying?" Dev asked as he clapped as hard as possible.

"No man! I never cry. Something went into my eyes," he replied, scratching his right eye.

Just after the announcement, Ballu ran towards the waiting area to greet his friends when someone from the crowd came to him with a pen and a paper.

"Autograph please!" a small kid not more than ten years of age was asking for his autograph. Ballu was surprised and could not understand the fuss.

"Sir, I am talking to you," the little boy said, giving the pen and the paper.

"Sardarji is a star now. Let's click some pictures with him before he moves to the big league," Chetan shouted, congratulating his friend on his instant fame. We never choose our destiny; destiny chooses us. The script was already written, it's just the drama that is pending.

After the show, he had to sign numerous documents and was asked to be present at their Worli office for the main round, which would be aired live. As expected, they headed straight to Prem's to celebrate the occasion.

"Prem's and rum are lucky for me. I didn't win in MTV roadies as I didn't have my daily dose of rum," he said, getting out of the car.

They managed their favourite table after requesting a group of college students to barter their seats, which they agreed after some persistence from Ballu's side.

Ballu opened his pocket internet to check his profile and was shocked.

"I can't believe this. It's not even an hour and I have received more than a dozen friend requests on Facebook. Either I am famous or Facebook is fast," he shouted, checking his profile.

Dev ordered some beer even as Ballu and Chetan ordered some rum.

"Let me check the number of girls in the request," he said, lighting a cigarette. Just as he was about to check, calls started coming which made Dev smile. "He is already a star."

"Let's celebrate in Goa," Ballu proposed sipping some rum.

Ballu offered the packet when someone asked for a cigarette.

"Take it. It's my day today," he said, sipping some more rum.

"We got to confirm about the trip with Aman first," Chetan said, adjusting his seat as Ballu blew the smoke directly on his face.

Chetan changed his seat to be more comfortable and stretched his legs on the chair next to him.

"I want some beer as well," Ballu said, keeping his mobile phone on the table.

"Beer! Are you sure?"

"Yes, that leaves me with a beer in my hand," he continued his performance, which wasn't appreciated at the bar, at least.

After some discussions and arguments, they agreed and chose Goa for their vacation.

Ballu dialled in Aman's number to get an engaged tone.

"What is he doing?" he said, keeping the cigarette in the ashtray.

Aman dialled Ballu's number checking his call.

"Goa?"

"Yes, everyone has agreed," Ballu said as he blinked his right eye.

Aman who was to go out for a new date via the matrimonial website had to cancel the date to be with his friends as he failed miserably to convince his friends.

❖❖❖

15

Managerial IJP

Corporate world has given a new meaning to the word 'FAKE'.

Management is the art of making problems so interesting that everyone wants to be a part of it and Raghu was good at this art. He knew people had named him 'TT Uncle' but some went a step further and mimicked him, when he was not around. He was fine with the TT part, but didn't like the uncle part. Apart from his shiny bald head and oversized belly, he thought he was quite charming. Everyone had their own reasons. Why on earth would someone take the Table-Tennis racket everywhere? He would never leave an opportunity to play Table Tennis. He could be seen with the TT racket even in the cafeteria. When asked, he would bluntly reply that the Table-Tennis court was just next to it. Some say that they had seen him with the TT bat even in the washroom.

After some discussions with the Administrative team from Bangalore, he forwarded an email to all his subordinates marking it as urgent. As soon as the email was sent, Raghu expected a buzz, as this would be the last IJP for this year. IJP is nothing but an acronym for 'Internal

Job Posting'. It was November and people were more than eager to complete their share of leaves by December, as the leaves would lapse at the year-end. Raghu kept his cell phone on 'silent mode' as he was expecting many calls. Even after an hour, there were neither phone calls nor any email queries, nothing as such even for the hottest menu of the hour.

Raghu had a gut feeling that someone might come to his cabin, so he arranged his glasses, laptop, his Table-Tennis racket and cleaned his cabin. Raghu was more passionate for Table Tennis than anything in this world. His cabin donned his poster size photograph while playing Table Tennis in a corporate level tournament.

Getting restless, he even peeped through the cabin to check if people were busy working or had slipped out for lunch. He had worked for eight years as an engineer before being promoted as an Operation Manager in this firm. He knew exactly what kept people busy in his office. Running towards his seat, he took the Table-Tennis racket and played an imaginary stroke followed by a weird sound using his tongue. Hastily, he opened the Facebook webpage, unlocking his laptop.

Zenith Corporation had a community on Facebook. Raghu who was also a part of community on the social networking site, uploaded the details of the email as a new post in the forum. Just as he was about to order something to eat, his phone rang. He had made up his mind to imitate Mr Iyer, but melted when he saw Shilpa's phone number being displayed on the phone. Without wasting any more time, he picked the phone and gave a tried and tested excuse even before greeting her. Talking to some people has its own share of irksome aftereffects but some people managed to calm our nervousness like ice spread on a worn-out body.

"Are you busy, sir?" she asked.

"Not really?" he replied, stretching his legs.

"I am going for my lunch, would you like to join?"

"Okay, come to my cabin while going," he said before disconnecting the call.

He got some email replies as well. He knew Facebook did the trick for him. He opened the Facebook post to see some replies as well as some questions.

"Why can't they call or email me instead of asking questions on the site?" he asked himself as he connected the laptop to the adaptor. Still, he was happy that he was in-sync with the new generation. These postings give ample number of reasons for managers to be happy as there is a new-fangled layer of shine added to their worth. They start getting gifts, compliments, smiles and everything they want. Aman had always been Raghu's favourite as he would meekly follow his instructions. According to Raghu, Aman's best quality was that he would never ask any questions, even when they were actually required. He was the one who took Aman's final round of interview. Even after an hour of the interview session, Aman had absolutely no queries.

Raghu emailed Mr Iyer who was the Director of the firm with some of his doubts regarding the IJP. Raghu was an Operation Manager and he felt scared, as the opening was also for the same post. Mr Iyer called him at around half past four to discuss about the posting and his queries.

As he had some time, he started reading his favourite book. *How to impress people* was a bestseller of its era and Raghu himself had read it ample number of times. Actually, it was quite popular with the corporate world, across all the continents ranging from Asia to Europe. In some time, Raghu was seen in Mr Iyer's cabin. Mr Iyer's cabin was double the size of Raghu's cabin and he would take pride in maintaining it.

"Good afternoon, sir," Raghu said softly settling in the chair.

"Good afternoon, Mr Rathnam."

Mr Iyer requested Raghu to be seated as he was busy checking his emails on his laptop. Suddenly the phone rang, but Mr Iyer was still immersed in checking his emails. Raghu made some noises to attract Mr Iyer's attention, but it seemed he was more interested in reading his emails.

"You are not required to pick every phone that comes in. You just can't be that accessible or else people start taking you for granted," Mr Iyer said, adjusting his spectacles.

Raghu smiled and enquired if Mr Iyer knew whose call it might be.

"You are repeating the same mistakes which I was known for as a youngster. If I tell you exactly who called me, it's fine... but if I don't, it would be hell for you. Men have fragile egos. Never challenge your boss or hurt his prestigious pride. There is a way of asking something and still maintain our pride and our boss's ego as well."

Raghu looked lost but now he knew why people respected Mr Iyer.

"I have a long way to go, I feel."

"Don't try to impress me, be yourself," Mr Iyer said, pointing to a poster displayed on the wall. Raghu turned around to see a big Abraham Lincoln poster on the wall.

"Be yourself. Work hard, respect everyone around and have patience," read the lines on the poster.

Mr Iyer asked Raghu to check if Raghini from the Human Resource department had called. Raghu who was dumbstruck did not realise this. "Check the number getting displayed on the phone next to you," Mr Iyer shouted.

Raghu stood up, but was requested to be seated. Raghu checked the 'received call list' and it was Raghini's call. "Yes sir, Raghini Madam had called."

"What Raghini Madam, she is ten years younger to you. You should call her Raghini," he said, taking a sip of coffee. Raghu made a dumb face combined with a plastic smile, which made him look like an earthen pot that tries its best to avoid attention.

"There are three types of people, one who are important at that moment, one who are always important and some who are never important, yet call just to maintain relations. When you are busy, you should only pick up calls from people who are important for us that moment as people who are always important like your parents, easily understand that you are busy."

Raghu felt so inspired that he wanted to write all this down, but decided to memorise it instead.

"True, but I didn't understand. How can someone be important only for that moment," Raghu asked drinking some water. Raghu was nervous and this showed on his face.

He was happy that Mr Iyer always insulted people by calling them in his cabin instead of shouting on the floor. Most managers take pride in calling a spade, a spade. It's just that the spades in the question are their juniors, as they like to show their superiority.

"People who deliver important couriers, your investment broker and some people like them are important only for that moment," Mr Iyer said, keeping his laptop aside.

"You had some doubts about the email that I had sent, right?"

Raghu nodded in agreement.

"As you handle more than seventy engineers, so I felt we should have two operation managers to make your work easy. You know how much I care for you people," said Mr Iyer, smiling at Raghu who was dumbstruck at the explanation.

"Sir, I feel I am quite capable to handle these people."

"I know that, but as you work so hard for the company, the management thought of decreasing your work. I feel they might promote you to my level, if I get promoted to the next level," Mr Iyer stressed on the word 'if' and was still seen smiling.

Raghu got his answers, but was happy that in spite of all this, he was still the operation manager.

"Let me know if you want to go for a long leave or something. If you have any questions you can call me when I am not busy or when I am not sleeping," Mr Iyer said as he opened the laptop once again.

"How will I know if you are busy or not?"

"That's your problem, and you are talented enough to figure it out yourself."

"Yes, sir," Raghu replied.

"Also, I heard that whichever company you leave, gets closed," Mr Iyer asked managing a spark of humour in the managerial discussion.

Raghu felt embarrassed and fondled his overcoat.

"I mean the ICC Corporation has shut down and even Pagmarsis is closed. Raghu Rathnam, you are the man. Let me know when you leave our company and why don't you work with Microsoft?" Mr Iyer moved his chair and smiled.

Raghu tried to be polite and reminded his boss about the upward movement of the stock market.

"I have a request for you, sir," he said, smiling at him.

Mr Iyer gave a concerned look and murmured, "What?"

"I had sent you an email, kindly go through it."

Mr Iyer scanned his emails to check the latest email and found the same email with the exactly same subject line, sent earlier as well.

"So you think I don't have any work, right?"

"No sir, I don't even have the guts to think something like this."

Mr Iyer closed his laptop, stood up and started drawing something on the whiteboard.

He drew a watch and started to explain, gifting a worried look on Raghu's face.

"Have you seen a watch?"

"Yes," he said, scratching his head.

There are three types of hands in a watch, the second hand, the hour hand and the minute hand. Do you know which hand works the most?"

"The second hand," Raghu thought for a while and said.

"That's the difference between a manager and a director. No one can see the hour hand work, but it works the most. It may move very slowly or even at negligible speed, but it has given an identity to the second and the minute hand. The hour hand is the most important hand and everything revolves around it."

"Oh!! Absolutely correct, sir."

Mr Iyer handed the bundle of paper kept near the table to Raghu and asked him to make a presentation of it in a month. The small bundle may have more than two hundred pages and Iyer's supervisor had given him the bundle for a review and had ordered a presentation concerning the paperwork.

"What's this, sir?" he enquired, taking the bundle.

"You should tell me. I have gone through it, but I need a report from you in a month."

Raghu looked confused but managed a smile.

"You were leaving right?" Mr Iyer said, as he made himself busy checking something on his laptop.

Taking the bundle, Raghu smiled again and left the cabin. One thing was common whenever Raghu and Mr Iyer met, it was Raghu who smiled and Mr Iyer handled the frowning part.

As soon as he entered his small cabin, he noted down the tricks he had learnt from the meeting. His mind unintentionally started comparing his cabin with Iyer's. The two cabins were very different, even in terms of size and the furniture flaunted in it.

Raghu's cabin was designed and utilised miserly, even as he had managed to squeeze in more accessories than the pint-sized glass cabin could handle. He had even kicked some chairs out of the cabin to make way for some fashion accessories related to abstract art bought at the company's expense. Looking at the bundle, he called his team and handed over the pages from the bundle, distributing them equally.

"What's this?" Ashok asked counting the number of pages given to him.

He was sure of Raghu's modus operandi and as expected, Raghu repeated the same instructions given to him by Mr Iyer.

"You will answer this question. I have gone through it, but I need a report with presentations from you all in two weeks," he said keeping the first set of papers with him. Outsourcing embossed inside outsourcing, was at its display best.

❖❖❖

16

Finding the Secret Well-wisher

Never try to find a secret well-wisher, the wishes might vanish.

Raghu started winning his Table-Tennis matches and this proved that people were taking the IJP seriously. Raghu was surprised to see an email from an outside domain in his mailbox. Scared that it might be a virus-loaded email, he deleted the mail. Checking the subject line, which read, "Kind attention - Mr. Ratnam..." he opened the deleted items and checked the email, opening it.

"Respected sir,

Subject:– Regarding the IJP for the post of Asst. Ops Manager.

I have known Chetan for a long time and I can assure you that he is the right candidate for the post. He is hardworking and is capable of taking even the toughest of decisions with ease. Apart from his qualifications, he is known for his sincerity.

Kindly make the right choice. God is great.

Yours sincerely,

Your company's well-wisher"

Raghu was hundred percent sure that Chetan had sent the email. "secret_welwisher@gmail.com" ringed a bell. "These boys will try the same old tricks, poor Chetan," he told himself. He saved the email, just in case; the countdown boils down to Chetan versus Aman. "This email would be kind of a hit wicket for Chetan. Hahaha."

He dialled Aman's number and called him urgently to his cabin.

"Please come to my cabin as soon as possible," he sent an SOS.

Aman was not interested in playing any more Table Tennis matches with his boss and took his own sweet time to get back. Raghu came running to his desk but couldn't find Aman. "Where is Aman?" he asked but no one seemed interested. Fuelled with anger, he shot back.

"I am asking you," he shouted, tapping the unattended computer with his TT racket.

"I think he might be at the cafeteria," Ashok said, giving a look of being immersed in his work.

"Ask him to see me urgently," Raghu said as he turned towards the next row to greet Raghini.

"How is it going?" he asked, planting a life-size, facade smile on his lop-sided, poker face.

"I was just thinking about you. Actually, I was going to call you right now," she said, showing her mobile log.

"Really? I am honoured."

"Yes sir. I wanted to discuss some things about the rolled out IJP," she said, checking for the detailed email on her laptop.

"I will call you in an hour," he said, checking the time on his wristwatch.

"Sir, I need to go early today. Can we discuss this a bit earlier?" she asked, flashing her thousand-watt smile, which melted him.

"Okay, you can come whenever you want. Just let me know," he said while going.

She could see Raghu entering his cabin and taking a deep breath, erupted in splits of laughter. Ashok joined the fun. "TT uncle tried to play a match with you, but I liked the smash you gave him," he joked, giving a playful clap.

"That bastard called me last weekend to discuss official matters," she said, unlocking her laptop. "Did you see his TT racket? He just doesn't leave it. I can't believe it."

Everything about Raghu was a gag appetiser.

"Also, the company must charge him extra for utilising the sports room all day," Ashok said, scratching his head.

She opened her Facebook account and replied to some messages and even commented on Raghu's new look on Facebook. "You are looking awesome," she typed, as a response to his display picture.

Aman drank two cups of coffee, one after the other in nervousness and made an awkward face when Ashok gave the marching orders. "Your friend was looking for," he said standing near the desk.

"Friend? Chetan?"

"Your best friend, TT uncle," he said and rushed back to his seat.

"Raghu sir, I had told him about my break," he said, typing his password to unlock his laptop.

He was in no mood for Table Tennis and added some notes to his presentation, managing Facebook and his work simultaneously hand in hand.

He walked towards Raghu's cabin even as he saw Aman coming and made himself busy checking something on his laptop.

"I was in the washroom," he said, as he was halfway through the cabin door.

"That's fine, take a seat."

"Thank you. You called me for something important," he said, making himself comfortable in the chair.

"Chetan is sending me emails from an unknown email address," he said, turning the laptop screen to show him the email.

"Secret well-wisher, that's interesting," Aman said, checking the email.

He read the email and managed to read some more emails, even as Raghu was drawing something on the whiteboard behind his chair.

"I know Chetan for a long time. He won't stoop so low. It's someone else. He is a man of honour, sir," Aman said and turned the screen of the laptop to its original stance.

"What!" Raghu gave a confused look.

"Call me at this number and we will discuss about the offer," he replied and even added his mobile number at the end of the message.

"Let's see," Raghu said while giving a big smile.

Aman thought that he was the only one who knew about Chetan's separation, but that was not the case. Somehow, everyone knows everyone else's secrets in the corporate world, as Raghu asked him about it.

"How is Chetan's married life going on?" he asked, making himself busy with his work.

"It's going good."

"Are you sure?" Raghu asked again giving his trademark cunning smile, which exploded astuteness all over.

"Why?" Aman asked, keeping his eyes firmly on the poster behind Raghu.

"I heard they have separated. He has even updated this on Facebook, right?" Raghu asked, opening his Facebook account.

"No sir, I meet them at weekends. They are fine. I can assure you," he said.

"Calm down, I am sorry if it hurt you," Raghu said and gestured him to be seated.

"That's fine sir. It's his life," Aman said and managed a smile on his usually obstinate face.

Aman excused himself and thanked his boss for all his help.

"That's fine, son. Best of luck!" he said, waving at him.

Due to the separation, Chetan was mentally quite disturbed and even finished his quota of leaves. As he was Aman's friend, Raghu even helped him to take more leaves than what was allotted to an employee making his leave balance slip into a negative count. Raghu was trying his best to help Aman, and even recommended his name to higher authorities. Raghu's plan had almost succeeded.

The first round of the IJP was tough, damn tough. Nine people cleared it and only four of them cleared the second round to be eligible for the final round.

The final round was to be held on a Saturday and somehow Chetan had pepped Armaan to be in the final round. Chetan was surprised by his own performance, but he was not in the right frame of mind, when it came to his office life. Raghu had managed to alter Chetan's score to reduce competition for Aman and succeeded with the help of some HR employees.

Chetan congratulated Aman and wished him luck.

"Same to you, my friend. Even if you become the Manager, I will be delighted," Aman said, as he hugged his friend.

"I feel, Shilpa also stands a chance," Chetan said, pointing at her.

Shilpa was sitting right next to Raghini at the other side of the floor and was very popular amongst everyone.

"Shilpa doesn't stand a chance," he said as he sat on Chetan's chair.

"Why is that so?"

"Come here. Don't let the secret out. She is three months pregnant," he whispered in Chetan's ears. The wide-eyed Chetan managed a smile, even as his mind started scrutinising Shilpa's body.

"You know as if you are responsible for it."

"I wish I was," Aman said, giving a playful clap.

"She doesn't look pregnant. At times, it turns out to be gas, which is responsible for the bulge," Chetan said as he kept looking at her.

"It's hundred percent true. Raghu told me," Aman said while checking his cell phone.

"Hmm, if Raghu had confirmed it, then it must be true," Chetan said and maintained his gaze at her.

She felt embarrassed at the attention she was getting, but managed a smile on her face.

"What about Ashok? He is more experienced than us," he said, sitting on the desk nearby.

"It's either you or me," Aman said confidently, patting his back.

"Let's see what happens. I will be happy even if you become our manager," Chetan said and shook hands.

"Amen," he said and walked away, but came back abruptly.

"What happened?" Chetan asked worriedly.

"Someone has sent an email asking Raghu to nominate you as the manager."

"What? Who sent the email and for what?" getting near, Chetan asked.

"Secret_welwisher@gmail.com, this is the email id through which the email came."

"How do you know?" Chetan asked, getting up from the chair.

Aman asked him to follow him towards his desk. Aman had managed to persuade Raghu to have the email forwarded.

Chetan sat on Aman's chair and read the email thoroughly.

"I can't believe this. Who would have done this?"

"You! I mean Raghu feels that you have sent this email," Aman said as he smiled at him.

"Is he crazy? If I wanted to ask for a favour, I would directly ask for it. Sending emails and that too without names is not my game," Chetan said, forwarding the email to himself.

Aman thought for a while and said, "Neha?"

"She doesn't know Raghu's email id and she would never do such a thing. She hates me like hell."

"How are you so confident?" Aman asked, sitting on the chair next to him.

Chetan took his mobile phone from his pocket and showed the last message he received.

'Go to hell. Please don't call me again,' read the message.

Aman read the message and laughed his heart out. Chetan looked angrily and he stopped abruptly while returning his mobile. "I am sorry."

Chetan who was known for his no-nonsense nature was shocked to find a well-wisher.

"Is Aman doing this?" he asked himself.

By Friday afternoon, Ashok's nomination was disqualified when the issue of warning letters came to the attention of a senior human resource manager.

Raghu had reminded him about this and made a detailed report of his leave pattern and his office login and logout timings. That left him with three contenders for the coveted position. Aman went to

Raghu's cabin when he was called. "Let's try a table tennis game, what do you say?" Raghu asked locking his laptop.

"Sure sir. I got the good news some time ago."

"As in?"

"Ashok has been disqualified. We received an email from Raghini about that."

Aman smiled and put Raghu's laptop in its sack and searched for his TT racket.

"I did all this for you, my son. I want you to be the next manager. God bless you."

Aman was so touched by the words that he touched Raghu's feet and asked for blessings.

"I am always there for you."

"Sir, I am grateful to you. I am so happy to get a manager like you. You are one in a million," he said, while taking blessings.

"Let's go for a match, then."

"Sure sir. Can I play with your TT racket today?" Aman asked.

Raghu never shared his TT racket with anyone, but he could do anything for Aman.

"Sure, let's go."

They rushed to the new sports center, even as people alienated Aman from their group chats.

"I am hundred percent sure, Aman is gay," Ashok said, when asked about his disqualification.

The new sports centre was vacant with the TT racket lined up on the table itself.

“Sir, Mr Iyer was born and brought up in America. There is a chance that he might go with Shilpa. Also she is quite attractive,” he said as he served at the table.

“Iyer might be American in his thinking, but he is a sexist at heart. He would never allow a woman to be a manager,” Raghu said while smashing the ball.

Aman managed to play badly and lost the first set by a huge margin.

“Would you prefer a female manager at a young age of thirty?”

“Never, I mean anyone but Shilpa. I am not against women, but I hate that bitch,” he said, playing a shot, which eluded Raghu.

“Nice shot,” Raghu said and ran to collect the ball.

“Don’t worry. Mr Menon, our human resource director will be with Iyer at the final stage. I have talked with him about your candidature,” he said as the conversation proved more important than the game. Aman lost in straight sets, but won his manager’s trust.

Saturday arrived quickly in terms of the things that happened on the preceding Friday. Dev who was staying at Chetan’s house finally managed to have a word with his former roommate. He was busy watching TV when Chetan came to the living room with their breakfast.

“Good morning,” Dev said as he turned the trolley.

“Very good morning.”

“So, are you ready for the interview?”

“Yes, I went through some management notes as well,” Chetan said, serving some tea.

“Don’t get me wrong but why did you guys split?”

Chetan was not very comfortable discussing his personal life, but when Dev insisted, he agreed to tell his side of his story.

"She caught me while chatting with someone else," he said, taking a few more sips.

"Chatting with someone else?" Dev looked astonished.

"Actually she made a fake email id, and then chatted with me when I was in office and we became friends."

"Then what happened?" Dev asked, as he seemed more eager to listen.

"She asked a picture of me and I sent it."

"Then?"

"She didn't like this and screwed my happiness," Chetan said, taking a bite of his favourite corn sandwich.

"Sharing pictures – is that a crime?"

"Not my face picture..."

"Then?" Dev pinched in some more.

"My nude picture," Chetan said feeling embarrassed.

Dev burst out laughing, as he just could not control himself.

"That's the reason, I don't share this with anyone," Chetan said, keeping the cup of tea angrily.

"I can't believe that you shared your nude picture with someone," Dev said and started laughing again.

"Shut up!"

"I would have understood if Ballu would have done it, but you...."

They finished their breakfast and then were busy watching the news channel.

"Do you love Neha?" Dev asked, decreasing the volume of the television.

"No," Chetan said, taking a sip of carrot juice poured in the cup kept on the table.

"Are you sure?"

"Hundred percent, but why are you asking?"

Dev drifted to the other side of the sofa and Dev followed him.

"If you don't love her, why don't you remove the tattoo of her name from your hand?" he asked, pointing to the tattoo on Chetan's hand.

"I never got the chance, actually."

"Really? I saw you kissing the tattoo last night," Dev said, eating his sandwich. "See man; don't make a fool out of yourself. You love her and if you did not, you would have removed the tattoo. It takes only a small operation to do so."

Chetan blushed and smiled at him.

"Shall I ask you one thing?"

"Ask ten things man," Chetan said and sat on the marble floor.

"What is more important to you, success or love?"

"Of course success," Chetan replied without even thinking for a while.

Dev sat next to him. "There are two types of people in this world and for both - love is the most important thing," Dev said as he smiled at him again.

"So," Chetan asked candidly.

"You still love her and cannot live without her. Even if you apologise, that fine."

The moistness in Chetan's eyes was visible even as Dev was sure of Chetan's love towards his wife.

"Love can make up for many great things missing from your life. The heart suffers a lot not by the violence of others, but by the silence of the loved ones."

Chetan wanted to cry but controlled his emotions when he heard the thought. He was speechless. "Be vocal to express your love, body language is not always useful."

Dev was just not allowing Chetan to speak. "If you decide whom to live with, life would be simpler, but less magical. Love isn't a decision, it's a feeling inside, so let your heart have a say. Don't you understand? Your heart beats for her."

"Nevertheless, what about the interview?" Chetan asked, switching off the television.

He checked the time on his wristwatch and confirmed it with the time on his mobile.

"If you get little in love, you want more, when you get more, you desire even more, and one day when you loose it, you realise little was enough."

Chetan managed to change the conversation and told him about the secret well-wisher.

"Do you have the email address? I will ask Ved to provide more information about it."

"Yes. Secret_welwisher@gmail.com." Dev typed the email address and sent a message.

"Within an hour, I will let you know the sender. My friend Ved is an expert in this field," Dev assured. Romance does not knock the doors; it shatters its way through.

"I want her back. Come with me, we will get her back. Let the IJP go to hell," Chetan said and hugged his friend.

Love is a victory of imagination over intelligence, a victory of dreams over reality.

"What if she doesn't agree to come with me? Should I go there or not?"

"In the arithmetic of love, one plus one is everything, and two minus one is nothing," Dev continued.

Chetan got his answer and rushed towards the washbasin to wipe his tears.

He locked himself in the bathroom and cried for some time.

After some time, Dev came into the kitchen as Chetan was preparing something.

Most women are complex to analyse. Women are not to be understood; they are to be loved.

Chetan lifted his hands and sat on the kitchen table.

"Women are very emotional. If you give love to a man, he will ask for money, after that, he might ask for success, then fame and the list goes on. However, if you give love to a woman, she will love you back. That's the difference between a man and a woman," Dev said tasting the curry kept near the table.

"You are amazing, I can't believe that you are still single," Chetan said and had to repeat his words when the frying created an irritating noise which absorbed the buzz.

"Not everyone is lucky to have true love thrown at them," Dev said, looking at his friend.

"I will be back in a moment," Chetan said as he went towards the bathroom smiling incessantly. After bathing, while getting ready, Dev was ready with a bouncer.

Chetan made himself comfortable on the sofa when Dev came in.

"Is your wife's name Neha Deshpande?" he asked.

Dev was shocked to hear the name. "Yes, why?" Dev smiled calmly even as Chetan stood up.

"She was sending emails for your promotion. I just confirmed this through Ved," Dev said, disconnecting the call, which was still running.

It was a big day for him, not because of the IJP but for the fact that he had decided to listen to his heart and rushed to Neha's apartment along with Dev.

For a change, they were silent while driving. He stopped his car near her apartment, but felt scared at the thought of meeting her. "Stay with me when I talk to her," he said, as he locked his car.

Neha's mother just couldn't control her emotions when she saw Chetan. She rushed to inform Neha's father.

"Oh my god!" Dev said, as he checked the reaction.

"Don't make me nervous," he said while entering the house.

Neha was taking a bath and that gave an ample opportunity for them to talk with her parents. They chatted for some time before the tea and snacks were served.

"Good that you came. You make such a beautiful couple. She loves you a lot and cries all day," her mother said while serving tea.

Chetan was happy to hear this and smiled when Dev blinked at him.

Meanwhile, Mr Iyer and the human resource team waited for an hour for Chetan even as he had switched off his mobile.

The office looked empty and the noise of the blowers running at full flow disturbed the stillness.

"We will wait for some more time and the last round would start with the candidates available," Mr Menon said while distributing some forms.

"We have filled these forms," Shilpa said, checking the header on the form.

"You need to fill in twice," he said in a hoarse voice and turned towards his cabin.

Raghu was happy and did not even try Chetan's number when he found his 'switched off' status.

"Some people are just not worth the opportunity," Mr Iyer said even as Aman managed a smile.

Aman was getting restless and requested Mr Menon to wait for some more time, but he was not ready to listen.

"No, you should go ahead with the procedure," Mr Iyer said, as he frowned at Aman.

At last, after some discussions, Mr Menon announced the disqualification of Chetan on disciplinary grounds. They went ahead with Shilpa and Aman, even when the latter insisted on waiting for some more time.

Aman was surprised when Chetan was not even receiving calls on his other number.

At half past eleven, the final round started.

It was the toughest round of exams that he had ever given. Many management scenarios were hurled at both of them. Even after the recommendations, Aman was finding it difficult to answer the questions. Each had been given four scenarios and had some secondary IQ tests. Raghu went to his cabin after waiting for sometime at the waiting area near the training room.

"The results would be out in an hour, after a round of meetings," Mr Menon said, collecting their answer sheets, which were not required at all, as they had a 'one on one' session. Aman tried calling his friend again who was still not picking the phone, even as his first number was switched-off.

Neha's father apologised on his daughter's behalf, which made Chetan embarrassed.

Neha was furious when she came to know about his arrival.

"I am not going to talk to him," she said when her mother tried to persuade her.

Chetan typed a message filled with apologies and sent it to her even as she was in the adjacent room. Neha was happy to see the message and finally agreed to talk to him when her father requested her.

Neha walked towards the balcony and Chetan followed her.

It was strange to see both blushing at each other when he came to the balcony.

"What?" she asked, directly looking at him.

"Nothing! I wanted to apologise for what I did. It would never happen again," he said, as he just didn't let her speak.

"I know."

"There is one crazy man for every woman, and I am that crazy man for you," he said, moving to the farthest part of the balcony.

She blushed and smiled at him as he kept the cell phone, which he was carrying, on the edge of the small balcony wall.

They talked for some more time and hugged each other when Chetan proposed her again.

"I love you," she said, as she kissed his cheeks.

"I never knew I would do this. Staying away from you made me realise how much I love you. Success stands second best, you are my world! I can trade anything to be with you," he said even as Neha just could not stop blushing.

They came into the living room where Dev was seen chatting with Neha's parents.

"He has sacrificed his IJP to come here," Dev said, keeping his mobile on the sofa.

"IJP?" her mother could not understand.

"Internal Job Posting. He was to try his luck at becoming a manager, but he came here instead," Dev said with a smile on his face as he drank some water.

"She is my life, my everything. I will become a manager when I have to," he declared, looking straight at her.

Neha was blushing as usual even as Chetan thanked his friend for the help.

Chetan and his wife even went for a round of shopping along with Dev. Dev tried his best to allow privacy to them, but Neha was adamant.

At last, he called Aman who was ecstatic about his success.

"It's the biggest day of my life," he declared, looking at Mr Iyer who was seen consoling Shilpa.

"What a day!" Chetan said, looking at Dev while having their lunch at a restaurant, next to the shopping mall.

❖❖❖

17

Where is D?

Survivors don't know that the Captain of the ship was the first to die.

Dev had shifted to a hotel near Bandra, when Neha joined Chetan at his apartment.

Ballu had some time before his Indian Idol schedule and somehow the group managed to squeeze in a mini vacation to Goa. Against the popular verdict, they went in pairs in two separate cars when Chetan and Aman tried to bring in their 'better halves', but they did not turn up.

Completely exhausted with the journey, they decided to rest in Aman's room at the hotel. Aman who was eager to introduce his love, started his story even when Ballu was busy making other plans and seemed to be pissed off.

"Goa reminds me of Facebook!" Aman said even as Chetan and Dev seemed perplexed. "I got my love because of Facebook," Aman said, taking a sip of cold drink.

"What? Is he in your friend list?" Chetan asked.

"He? What are you guys up to?" Aman asked, making a weird expression.

"I am sorry, she?" Chetan apologised, adjusting himself on the beanbag.

"You will be shocked to know that Priya's ex-boyfriend was from our college."

"What? Who?" came a combined question.

"She was dating Hemant."

"DJ, he was an asshole. Bastard made me eat the spit filled food one day," Ballu said, taking a puff. The laughter continued for the next five minutes.

"DJ claims someone had hacked his Facebook account and sent a romantic message asking someone to rekindle the Goa romance," Aman said, taking a puff.

Ballu was busy smoking when he realised something. "What?" he shouted spilling his drink.

"Somebody hacked that bastard's account. Now I know what had happened."

"Now what?" Aman asked, wiping the drops of beer, which fell on him.

Dev moved the curtains to have a better view of the beach nearby. "That looks so beautiful from here. I can't even imagine how beautiful it would look from near."

Chetan moved in to have a better view as well.

"Once when I went to check my Facebook profile in the college library, I found someone had not logged off from his account. I did not recognise the account, but DJ were the words mentioned on the profile. I checked and deleted some pictures, wherein he was posing with models in Goa, and replied to a message with the exact same words, 'Let's rekindle the Goa romance.'

“What! Are you serious?” asked a bamboozled Aman, and kept his drink on the floor.

“Trust me, I had typed the message,” Ballu insisted, coming near, dragging his beanbag.

“I can’t believe this. You made my love story. Thank you, man,” he said as he got up and hugged Ballu. “Cheers for Aman and Priya,” Chetan said taking a sip.

“Also for Chetan and Neha,” Aman followed. “For ABCD.”

They had managed to click more than a hundred pictures in the last fortnight. Chetan had maintained an album of the pictures.

“Let’s go to the beach,” Ballu suggested adjusting the curtains. “Let me take a bath first and then we could move wherever you want.”

They were seen on the beach which was not as crowded as it should have been, maybe because of the sunset which eluded natural light to the beach.

They were enjoying their drinks under their makeshift hut on the beach when someone approached them.

“What do you want?” Ballu asked as he adjusted his table.

“That’s my punch line,” the stranger said, entering the hut. “What?”

“Yes, what do you want?” the stranger asked again, smiling at them.

Aman turned around even as Ballu stood up.

“Do you people want to enjoy?” the stranger asked, taking a seat.

“We are enjoying already.” The stranger smiled as he drifted towards them.

“I mean, if you want to increase the level of your pleasure, I can provide the dose and the pose.”

“What?” Chetan asked, keeping his drink on the table.

“If you want any kind of drugs or women, I am the right man,” the stranger said and even showed his card.

The card read as real estate agent Ahmed.

"Mr Ahmed, we don't want to settle in Goa, so kindly leave us alone," Aman said, stretching his legs showing his exhaustion.

Ballu seemed happy to hear the words and asked the agent to come with him.

"Come outside, we will talk there," Ballu said, blinking his left eye.

The agent happily obliged even as Aman and Chetan seemed to be pissed off.

"He will never change," Chetan said, taking a puff as he changed his seat and slept on Ballu's bed.

Ballu took him to a distance and after confirming their privacy; he smiled and asked for more information. "Do you have any album?"

"No sir, I don't have any album, but you can tell me your demand and I will make sure that it gets fulfilled, even if it's related to cocaine," he said, showing his card again.

"I don't want drugs. What is the age of women available?" Ballu asked, taking a puff of a local brand of cigarette.

After the sunset, the beach seemed almost unoccupied.

"Teenagers are the best," Ahmed said, smiling at him as he dug his feet in the sand.

"Can you arrange foreigners?" Ballu asked, throwing his cigarette.

"It's difficult, but I will try. It might take some time," he said, checking his phone list.

Ahmed dialled a number as Chetan arrived at the scene. He gestured him to return to the hut. "I am still single, let me enjoy the place," Ballu said, tapping his feet.

"Why don't you understand? It's risky," Chetan said, pulling his T-shirt.

Chetan threatened the agent and he escaped through the small bar.

"Take life seriously. You will compete for the Indian Idol show. What if the police come to know?" Chetan said, checking the time on his wristwatch as darkness had almost crept in.

Ballu was not amused by the fact that Chetan kicked the agent away.

"What happened?" Aman asked, throwing his pillow at him.

Boiling with anger, Ballu took his T-shirt off, kept it on the table nearby, and slept on the bed next to it. He interrupted when Chetan was to tell his side of the tale.

"The agent was trying to fool me. I kicked him away," Ballu said, taking a cigarette from Chetan. "You can ask Chetan. He intervened or else I would have killed that bastard. You know how much I respect women."

"Yes I know, now keep silence," Aman said, lighting a new cigarette.

Ballu seemed angry, removed his pyjamas as well, and changed to his favourite khaki shorts.

"How can you do this to me? I was responsible for Priya's break up with Hemant. You should appreciate my effort," he said as he sat on the small bed.

"Facebook made my life. You just added some twist," Aman said, turning to the other side, even as the smoke filled the hut.

Dev had gone to the hotel for some urgent work and they were still waiting for him.

"This is not done. I will tell Priya about this. Then let her decide."

Aman burst out laughing and with a breaking voice said, "Go and tell." Ballu smiled when Chetan asked him to be silent.

"Okay, Facebook made your love story, now Facebook will break your love story," Ballu said, checking the empty matchbox looking for a matchstick.

Dev came rushing and hurriedly collected all his clothes, which were dispersed all over. "What happened?" asked Chetan staring at him. Dev confirmed the time and changed his shoes sitting near the bed.

"One of my friends has met with an accident near Thane, I have to rush. I will try to catch the next available flight from Panjim airport," he said even as Chetan and Aman helped him.

"Should we come with you?" Chetan asked dialling Neha's number.

"You carry on. It's nothing serious. He is out of the ICU now. We will meet in two days before Ballu's show starts."

They hugged Dev as he took a taxi to the airport. "Thank you, mates!"

While the dinner was being served, they were more than eager to make plans for Dev's dream. "The game sounded childish, but within a month, we managed to win three matches in a row," Chetan said, taking a bite of a sandwich. Ballu filled the empty glass for himself and ordered some more chicken salad. "The chicken salad is delicious."

Ballu ordered some seafood as well even as Chetan managed his vegetarian fare.

"Yes, we are almost done. Dev came like an angle of god in our lives. It's all because of him," Aman said, squeezing some lemon pieces.

After the dinner, they made some rough plans for Dev to maximise his dream of shocking everyone in a positive way.

They had some more drinks and Ballu seemed to hit the groove.

"I never understand Chetan. He is a vegetarian Brahmin, but he drinks and smokes. How come?" Ballu asked, gulping his drink and asked for more.

"That's my personal life," Chetan said, increasing the volume.

They danced for some time and slept in same room even as they had booked two separate AC, deluxe rooms.

Ballu who was sleeping on the big king-size bed, was seen sleeping on the floor, the next morning.

"How come he is sleeping here?" Chetan asked, even as Aman did not have any answer.

Aman folded the bed-sheet and ordered breakfast for them.

"I don't know, he might have fallen from the bed or you might have kicked him."

"Who? Me?" Chetan asked and smiled.

They tried to wake him up but his siesta just did not seem over yet.

"We had two rooms booked and we haven't even checked the other room properly," Chetan said, checking the keys of the other room.

Ballu was disturbed and moved the blanket to check and fell asleep again.

"What's the time?"

"It's half past ten. Did you call Dev?" Chetan asked, checking a message on his cell phone.

Aman took aim and kicked Ballu, but he seemed more concerned with his slumber.

"I had called Dev in the morning but his mobile seemed out of the coverage area."

They went to the main lobby, gave their clothes for laundry, and went ahead discussing their plans. Ballu managed to wake up after an hour to find the room locked from outside. He called the reception to get the room unlocked through a duplicate key.

Aman and Chetan were having their breakfast at the hotel's restaurant when Ballu came into the scene.

"What?"

"How come you people locked the room when I was sleeping," he asked, banging the table.

Aman was just not interested and ordered some more sandwiches.

"We tried to wake you up, but you just didn't entertain us."

Ballu sat on the chair next to them, ordered some breezers, and shared some pieces of cutlets from Chetan's plate.

"Also, how come I was sleeping on the floor?" he asked.

"How would we know?" Aman said, keeping his mobile on the table. They discussed their lives, Dev and the upcoming cricket tours for the next one hour.

The beaches, lavish dinners, parties were on their menu for the next two days and they returned to Mumbai completely pooped but in high spirits.

Chetan and Aman went to Hotel Sunshine near Bandra to meet their friend, even as Ballu was preparing for his show. He was surprised at number of friend requests he received on Facebook. "I am famous now." He even uploaded his pictures of MTV Roadies and Indian Idol auditions on Facebook and started getting responses.

"He might be at the hospital with his friend, I feel," Aman said, locking his car.

Chetan was busy on his phone and disconnected the call when Aman shouted.

"I am sorry, what did you say?" he asked, checking his mobile phone.

"What's his room number?" Aman asked, dialling Dev's number.

"I don't know, actually. We will have to check with the reception."

They enquired with the guard who directed them to the reception. Aman removed his glasses and smiled even as Chetan was waiting for his turn to talk to the person at the reception.

"Yes sir, how may I help you?" a soft spoken, smiling face invited a dialogue.

Aman pushed Chetan and asked about Dev. "Our friend has been staying in this hotel since last week. We want to meet him," he said, smiling at the receptionist.

Chetan received a call and moved away from the reception.

The noise, which resulted from the shifting of equipments made it hard for the people to converse. Aman had to repeat his question again. "I want to meet my friend."

The receptionist received a call on the phone next to her. She excused herself and picked the phone smiling at Aman. Aman waited for some more time and reiterated.

"I am so sorry sir. What's the name of your friend?" she asked, writing something on her handbook. "Dev," Aman said.

"What's the last name?" she asked, checking the logbook.

Aman wasn't sure of Dev's last name and looked for Chetan in the crowd. He dialled Chetan's number to find an engaged tone. "Chetan," he shouted as the receptionist smiled and made herself busy checking the log.

Chetan appeared from nowhere. "What happened?"

"What's Dev's last name?" Aman asked feeling a bit irritated.

"Dev Kumar Shetty," Chetan said, checking a travel card from his wallet.

Chetan and Aman stood there silently until the receptionist finished searching.

"Dev Kumar Shetty," said Aman, confirming with his friend again.

The receptionist checked for the name in the logbook and even in the computer records and just could not find any matching records.

"I am sorry sir; there is no one with the name Dev or Dev Kumar Shetty staying in the hotel today."

"Has he left?" Aman asked as he disconnected an incoming call on his mobile phone.

"I am hundred percent sure, there is no one with the name Dev Kumar Shetty."

"Can I check the log book if you don't mind?"

"Sure," she said and handed over the logbook. "That's fine."

They checked it thoroughly but could not find their friend's name.

"There is a gentleman named Shanker Shetty in room number three hundred twenty six. How old is your friend?" She asked, checking the computer records.

"He is twenty-eight year old, may be twenty-nine," Aman said after confirming it with Chetan.

The receptionist checked the records again. "Shanker Shetty is sixty-eight years old, so he might not be the person you are looking for. You can call your friend and find out yourself," she said, picking up the phone, which buzzed again.

Aman and Chetan took turns in dialling Dev's number, but could not succeed in going through. "The number you have dialled doesn't exist," beeped the message when they tried dialing his number.

"That's ridiculous," Chetan said checking the number again. "I had even helped him shift his belongings. This is strange and mysterious."

They called the call centre who confirmed that the number does not exist and no one was allotted the number in the last six months.

Not only shocked, they were staggered to the core. Ballu called them to show his concern and was taken aback. "Come to my house. We will see what can be done," Ballu said, taking a sip of coffee. They rushed towards Ballu's house still trying Dev's number.

"I used to talk with him for hours together on this number. How is it possible that this number wasn't allotted to anyone?" asked Aman, entering the house.

Ballu's mother prepared buttermilk for them. "Aunty, Ballu is a star now."

His mother was happy to see the sudden change and thanked his friends for it. "How did this happen?" she asked, serving the chilled buttermilk.

"Dev did it," Aman said, taking the glass.

Ballu's mother was confused when she heard the name.

"Who is Dev?" she asked, sitting on the chair near the sofa. Ballu joined them, but refused the glass of buttermilk offered to him.

"Mumma, he is the guy who used to come at our place when I used to practise for my auditions. Do you remember him?" he asked, even as Ballu's mother could not recognise him.

"Chetan used to come with you, right?" she asked.

"Okay, apart from Chetan, who used to come?" Ballu asked, stretching his arms.

Ballu's mother seemed to be utterly baffled. "No one," she said in a rather confident manner.

"No problem, I will show his pictures to you in a moment," he said, asking his friends to follow him to his room.

Ballu tried dialling Dev's number but never got any response.

He had uploaded more than fifty pictures of their group on Facebook under the album title, 'ABCD' and was ecstatic about it. He opened his album even as Chetan was busy checking some magazines kept on the table.

Ballu checked the pictures of their arrival in Goa to find some pictures with Chetan and Aman. He checked every picture and even searched his hard drive for more pictures but could not find any of Dev's pictures. "I can't believe this. How is this possible?" Chetan shouted, and kept the laptop on the bed. Chetan and Aman surrounded him on the bed.

"The pictures are great." Feeling frustrated, he banged his right hand on the table.

"Shut up!!" he hollered. Ballu laughed but stopped hastily seeing a red-faced Aman.

"I don't know what is going on, but there are no pictures of Dev with me," Chetan said while rechecking his album. Chetan also checked his mobile phone thoroughly but could not find any pictures of Dev.

"Is he playing with us?" Aman asked, checking Ballu's album on Facebook. "I am really scared." Ballu rushed to check his sack and said, "I have some tickets and some passes with me. The passes have our names printed, right?" Aman nodded in agreement.

"Yes, let me check his number again."

Ballu checked the ticket, passes and everything associated with the trip, but was stunned at not finding anything which could prove Dev's existence.

"I only have three passes. Where is the fourth pass?" Ballu said, confirming the names on the passes. Aman felt anxious and checked Dev's Facebook account.

As he checked his Facebook account, he was shocked to the core. He just could not speak anything and gave a wide-eyed look.

"What happened?" Chetan asked as he checked the magazine, which had a sexy Kareena Kapoor picture on the cover page.

Ballu rushed and checked the account and photocopied Aman's expressions.

"What is wrong with you guys?" Chetan asked. "Are you alright?"

"Come here," Aman said, turning the laptop screen for his friend to check.

Chetan checked the account and said, "What's wrong with you guys? He has just changed his name on Facebook." 'The game has ended,' read the name on Facebook.

"Check the wall," Ballu said as he still could not control his emotions. Chetan checked the messages and gave the same wide-eyed expression.

"How is life in heaven?" was one the latest messages on his wall. He checked some more messages and was stunned. "I still can't believe that you have left us," said a message.

They checked the account thoroughly and just could not speak.

"The strange messages started six months ago on ninth September. He died before ninth September, I am sure," Aman's mobile slipped from his hand and landed on the bed.

"The messages suggest that he died last year. How is it possible... he was with us for the last month. We even celebrated his birthday last month," Chetan said with tears in his eyes. Dev was his room partner and was more close to him than his friends. Ballu took the laptop along with him to the study table. "I have my Indian Idol clip; he was there with us at the audition, right?"

The atmosphere looked as if they were mourning something. He checked the clip, but Chetan and Dev were just not there in the clip. They even checked the messages sent by him but could not find the messages. "This is a good joke," Ballu said and threw his pillow at Chetan. "I can prove that Dev was there with us," Chetan said, checking his mobile call list. He called Neha and told her about Dev. She could not understand anything. "Come home and we will see," she said.

They rushed to Chetan's house taking the shortest possible route using the flyover near Bandra. Even while driving, Aman and Chetan were discussing about Dev and his sudden disappearance.

They reached Chetan's apartment to receive a warm welcome from Neha. "You were asking about someone, I could not understand as your voice wasn't clear enough," she said, switching off the TV. She served some snacks and tea.

"It's nice to see you. You look stunning in a black sari," Ballu said, taking a sip.

Neha smiled and acknowledged the comment. "Thank you."

Chetan who brought his laptop, sat on the chair in the living room. He opened Facebook to confirm the status again. Turning towards Neha, he said, "Dev has disappeared."

"Who has disappeared?" she asked, playing with some spoons.

"Dev, who was with me when I came to take you last week."

Neha seemed puzzled and thought of it as a joke. "Who had come with you?" she asked again.

"Dev, my friend."

"You came alone to take me," she said as she sat next to him.

"How is that possible?" Chetan asked, dialling Dev's number to get the same message.

Neha was hundred percent sure that Chetan was alone when he came at her apartment.

"How will I gather courage to come alone? Dev inspired me. Also I spoke his words," he said, locking his laptop. Aman was the only one who was sure that Dev had disappeared suddenly like he had entered their life.

"He is god's man, he can do anything. Where are our Magic Boxes?" Aman inquired, smiling at him. Chetan rushed to his room to look for the magic boxes, but just could not find them.

"Let's call the hotel in Goa," Ballu suggested, drinking some water directly from the jug. Aman had saved the number in his mobile and dialled the number to get an engaged tone. He dialled again and found the reception who confirmed the names of the people on those dates.

Neha also congratulated Aman for his promotion. "Thank you," he replied, firmly shaking hands.

"Yes sir, Chetan Iyer, Aman Gupta and Balwinder Walia stayed in the room number eighteen and nineteen on those dates. I have reconfirmed it," the receptionist said, and Aman disconnected the phone. Neha who could not understand anything from the conversation, excused herself and went towards the kitchen.

"Neha, you sent an email to Raghu to get Chetan promoted, right?" Aman asked while typing a message on his mobile.

"What! What are you people up to? Who is Raghu and what email are you talking about?" she bombarded her questions making a disdain of Aman's allegation.

"You sent an email to my manager, right?" Chetan pitched in.

Neha was not sure about the episode but got a clue of the concern.

"I would have loved to do that, but how will I know your manager's email address?"

Aman and Chetan looked more confused than the rest. "I can't believe this. You did not send the email, then who sent it?" Chetan asked, keeping his mobile on the table. Ballu was sure that it was Dev, who might have done this to bring back Chetan and Neha.

"It's possible," Aman reiterated, replying to a message on his mobile phone.

They smiled in anticipation missing their friend dearly.

"Life takes everything from you... to give you everything."

❖❖❖